Sixteen Songs About Regret

J.S. COOK

Dreamspinner Press

Published by
Dreamspinner Press
5032 Capital Circle SW
Ste 2, PMB# 279
Tallahassee, FL 32305-7886
USA
http://www.dreamspinnerpress.com/

Sixteen Songs About Regret

Cover Art by Reese Dante
http://www.reesedante.com

ISBN: 978-1-62380-492-3
Digital ISBN: 978-1-62380-493-0

Printed in the United States of America
First Edition
May 2013

For Paul, just like always.

Glasgow, 1960

WHEN the landlord called a fifteen-minute break, Simon escaped into the lavs to take a piss. His dad's friend Gus was in there, standing in front of a urinal like someone straddling a pig. Simon hated taking a piss in front of anyone, but he'd been nipping beer behind Roger's back all night. He tried for nonchalance, nodding at Gus as he unzipped his fly, pretending he was home. If he squinted he could just imagine the frosted window in his mother's bathroom, right above the toilet, and the fuzzy cover on the tissue box and the crocheted dog covering the extra bog roll.

"Eah, watch out for the splash, now." Gus's grin showed a row of stained and yellowing teeth. There were black hairs in his nostrils and he'd been careless with his shaving, judging by the various tiny cuts decorating his chin and cheeks. He smelled like armpits and dirty underpants and the locker room at the rec center.

Simon was nonplussed, uncomfortable. "Splash?"

"When you get your dick out—it'll be a big one." Gus's laughter sounded like someone scraping out a metal pot. "Watch the splash, by the way!"

Simon struggled to ignore him, wishing Gus would finish up and go away. But Gus, sensitive to an acquired target, wasn't going anywhere; in that way he was like the bullies at school, the older boys who held Simon down and rubbed his face in the dirt of the schoolyard every dinnertime. Gus tripped the flush handle of the urinal and stood against the wall, arms folded. "I bet you've got all kinds of girlfriends, don't you? Young lad your age."

"I haven't actually." Simon did this at least half a dozen times every bloody day, and yet he couldn't manage to piss now for love nor money. Whatever possessed him to come here? He'd be better off at home, alone, or in Majorca with his mother and Maureen. He decided then to forget about it, to cross his bloody legs and hold it, if that was what it took. Fuck Gus anyway.

"Where are you going?" Gus grabbed his arm, spinning him around. "Not leaving, are you?"

"Fuck off out of it!" Simon tried to wrench his arm away, but Gus was strong. To his mature adult strength, Simon was nothing. "I'll tell me dad!"

"Tell your dad, will you?" Gus slammed him into the bathroom wall, and Simon was crying, begging to be left alone; Simon was pleading for his life. He thought—even then—that Gus only intended to kill him. Gus gathered a handful of Simon's navy jumper and swung him around, throwing him to the floor. "Tell your dad? I'll tell your fucking dad something, I will."

He never felt such horrible pain. He had never been violated in this manner. His cheek was pressed into the filthy bathroom floor and he could taste the sticky afterlife of spilled lager, the spent acidity of old cigarettes. His spectacles, unequal to the force exerted by the man on top, shattered, crushed against his nose, the shards of broken glass cutting into him. His neck was bent so that he could see the tip of his own shoe, the dark sock incongruous against his pale flesh. His trousers had gone, somewhere. His underpants had gotten caught around his knees, binding him in place. Outside, in the pub, he could hear the landlord shouting at the punters over the microphone, telling them to shut the fuck up, that the band was coming back. Gus, then, on top of him and around him and somehow in him, and the weight of Gus driving all the air from his lungs. Gus was doing it in utter silence, but Simon could hear his own breath rasping in his throat. Gus pushed into him and there was a flood of sticky moisture, then the dank air painted horror against his naked back. He lay very still for a long time. He couldn't allow himself to move. He didn't hear Gus leave, and yet he must certainly be alone here in this filthy loo.

Gus had done something to his insides. His belly hurt like he'd been punched. He could hear the music starting and he knew Roger would be looking for him, but he couldn't face his father. He pulled himself upright and peered into the mirror: his spectacles, destroyed, were dangling from one earpiece, and there were bits of glass embedded in the skin of his face. His mouth was bleeding and he had a black eye, rapidly swelling shut. He looked like someone who'd done a turn inside a meat grinder. He looked like he'd been run down by a lorry. He stood looking awhile, wondering at the stranger in the mirror, and it seemed to him that the face regarded him with suspicion and disgust. He found his trousers balled up near the urinal, opposite, and shoved his legs into them. He fled the pub by the side door, running down the gravel drive that led out to the street, holding his trousers up with one hand, peering into the darkness with weak, night-blinded eyes.

Back at Roger's house, he calmly packed his suitcase and called a taxi to take him to the station. All the way down to London, he counted objects outside the window: telegraph poles, nuclear reactors, pigs in a field, and finally, a flock of wild swans lifting from the surface of a mill pond. When the train pulled into Euston Station, he was wide awake and trembling with the residue of countless cups of railway coffee. He went straight into the bathroom of his mother's house and ran the bath as hot as he could stand it. He could never tell, he knew this, and so he went about the place locking all the doors and windows, shutting himself inside. He was hardly aware of his own weeping; it seemed like he'd been crying all the way from Glasgow. He got into the bath and scrubbed himself, trying to rub Gus away. The hot water crept into the savaged places of his body, hurting him, making him clench his teeth against the pain. What Gus had done made a furtive itch inside him; he was filled with Gus and everyone would know. Everyone would know the thing that Gus had done.

There was a full tin of aspirin tablets in his mother's medicine chest and a bottle of sleeping pills that his mother got from the doctor after she and Roger first separated. Simon held very still to read the label on the sleeping pills. He read it over carefully, sounding out the phrases of it in his mind. It reminded him of lurid old stories, like Marilyn Monroe taking too many pills and drinking too much booze, or Dickie Pride, dead at twenty-seven of an overdose, at the height of his career. So much for dragging himself up out of the anonymity of bloody Luton.

He rolled the little pills in his palm, counting them. He could take one and then another and another until… but Simon wasn't brave like that. He knew he'd never have the guts to do it and he was afraid of making a halfhearted attempt, of failing to do the job completely and ending up a vegetable. He put the bottle back into the medicine cabinet and deliberately shut the door.

For several days he stayed exactly where he was, locked inside the house, watching telly all day and all night, dressed in his pajamas. He watched documentaries and rubbishy programs about unwed mothers and young fellows on the dole. The telephone rang and rang, taunting him, but he wouldn't answer it, he wouldn't give in to it. He knew it was his father calling and he didn't want to talk to him, so he ate instead, that sad old story, like those *True Confessions* magazines his mum liked, girls dying of thwarted love, girls taking pills and drinking vodka to wash away the pain. He ate everything in the fridge and then he went into the pantry and ate the esoteric things Nina had set aside for baking: raisins and bitter chocolate and dates formed into bricks, confectioners' sugar and self-rising flour. His own nausea was a revelation, even as he was facedown in the toilet, but that just reminded him too much of the men's at that awful pub in Glasgow. He went into his mother's bill envelope in the cupboard and took the money that he found there, and he ordered all sorts of different things—Chinese takeaway and fish and chips, Indian curries and hot pot.

Roger wasn't entirely to blame—his father didn't *make* it happen, but Roger let it happen. There was really very little difference in the end. Simon understood this; he was thirteen years old. He was thirteen years old and he understood that a friend of his father had raped him in the filthy bathroom of a questionable Glasgow nightclub—raped him for no good reason other than the fact that he felt like it and Simon was there and maybe he knew that Simon was no match for him, couldn't possibly defend himself. Simon understood this and he blamed his father.

"Why aren't you at your father's place?" Nina, arriving home from Majorca slim and tanned and sporting a new pearl bracelet, seemed surprised to see him there. "You're supposed to stay with your dad." She moved through the house, ripping open the curtains, clearing away the curry boxes and the chip-smelling papers, tossing away Simon's considerable (by now) collection of fizzy drink bottles. "Have you done nothing but sit here and watch telly?"

Simon shrugged at her. "I might have done."

"What happened to your face? What have you done with your specs, eh?"

"I got into a fight with some blokes at school." As soon as it was out of his mouth, he knew he'd fucked it up good and proper. He backed himself up, rewinding his own thoughts. "No, there were some young blokes up at Dad's, and they were making fun of me—"

"For Christ's sake, Simon!" Nina sounded utterly disgusted. "Go put some clothes on. And get the hoover out. This place looks like a proper rubbish tip!"

While Simon was in the bedroom changing, he heard Nina on the phone, probably calling Glasgow. Simon strained his ears to hear, but could only catch the ends of certain phrases.

He says some boys were making fun of him. He says he ran away. He says you took him to a pub one night and one of your mates took advantage of him in the bathroom. Oh, yes—he says he's the man in the moon.

Simon stole the other bottle from the medicine cabinet, just in case. Late at night, when he couldn't sleep, he sat up in the moonlight, counting the little pills.

1: *Elemental Blues*

London, 1972

THERE were always people waiting, afterward—after the concert was over, after Simon (lately "Abelard") had toweled himself off, after Stephen Abednego and Jacky Stride and whichever record company bigwigs were waiting in the limo for the past twenty minutes had taken themselves away and were busily insufflating copious amounts of cocaine and quaffing ice-cold bottles of champagne—there was always someone there. It was to be expected: Simon Duckworth was famous, and not just a little bit famous but hugely famous, especially in America after his appearance at the Picador Club. "Stepney Simon" was a household name and his manager, Jacky Stride, was scrambling to sift through the bulk of invitations that came pouring in from clubs all over America. Every single one of them wanted to book Abelard, wanted Abelard to come and play, wanted to replicate the resounding box office success that had been Simon's American debut.

The week before, when they played a flurry of smaller clubs in Boston, one particular girl was always waiting at the stage door. "She says her name is Angela." One of the roadies shouted this at Stephen, but Stephen merely shrugged. It had nothing to do with him, nothing at all. All of that was Simon's business; Stephen merely wrote the lyrics and quaffed a lot of cheap American beer and went along on tours because he had nothing better to do. He wasn't interested in any of the groupies who habitually clustered round Simon, and Simon himself couldn't be bothered, but that had more to do with his arrangement with Jacky. In every way that mattered, Simon and Jacky lived together, were a couple, and shared everything, including Simon's inventory of illicit drugs, which had lately grown to include speed and downers as well as the usual cocaine. Every night the girl was there in Boston, and every night she chased Simon's limo round the corner—chased Simon 'til he disappeared into the night. "Let me go home with you!" she screamed. "Let me be with you! You can save me!" Simon was very often party to the dubious overtures that fanatics accord the newly famous: underpants and bowler hats, choccy and fur boas; all of it was tossed onstage as he hurled himself around, bawling Stephen's words into the microphone. The fans here were all daft, these Americans, but they adored him.

Stephen was drinking American beer underneath the awning that had been erected over the vast outdoor stage. The temperature was hovering close to one hundred degrees and Simon was already sweating underneath his velvet frock coat. The lace on his shirt collar was sticking to one side of his face, and his wire-rimmed specs were slightly askew, lending him a comical aspect. The makeup girls hadn't managed to make his hair lie down, and some disparate strands of it were rising from the back of his head like long-forgotten ghosts. His costumes, in keeping with his stage name, were very romantic, almost Byronic; the clothes were Jacky Stride's idea. Watching from the side of the stage, the dark, narrow-shouldered Scot had the facial expression of a rapacious meadow vole and his gaze never left Simon. It was almost as if he were willing Simon to behave accordingly.

"I can't wear these fucking boots. This fucking shirt is fucking killing me. Where the fuck is my water?" Simon's tirade, now so practiced that it might as well be scripted, had become an expected diversion every night of the tour; Stephen, watching wearily from underneath his awning, lifted one corner of his mouth in something that might have been mirth. All of it was affectation, a posture: Simon the rock star acting the way he thought rock stars ought to act. Simon the rock star driven half out of his mind by speed and coke and disco biscuits, was complaining bitterly about the velvet coat, cut to hide his slight potbelly, and the over-the-knee boots with their complicated set of buckles and laces. Jacky had seen the boots in the window of a shop in SoHo and ordered fifteen pairs in every color of the rainbow. The boots had built-in lifts to add an inch or two to Simon's modest height.

"All of it, my friends, is artifice." Jacky was fond of saying this to anyone; he said it now, catching Stephen's eye and nodding at him, pretending that they liked each other even as Stephen turned away to pop the tab on another can of Schlitz. The piano tuners—there were two of them—scurried about with oscilloscopes and tuning forks, winking at one another in the midst of Simon's tirade. Stephen sensed something dangerous throbbing in the air between Simon and Jacky. Perhaps the bloom had even now gone off the proverbial rose. "Don't be such a goddamned child." Jacky moved close to Simon, so that he was right in Simon's face. The lifts in Simon's boots forced Jacky to look up at him. "You're acting like a five-year-old." Jacky palmed a small, smooth vial into Simon's pocket, said, "Go in the back and get yourself sorted," and Stephen knew where this would end. He hoped someone would remember to brush the blow off Simon's velvet jacket before he came back out to face his adoring fans.

The outdoor auditorium was packed so full of bodies that Stephen could see nothing in front of him but a writhing, heaving tide of humanity, shouting out for Abelard with their arms in the air, like the faithful come to their messiah. Stephen left his awning to negotiate the complicated tangle of wires and cables running behind the stage; the bass player was crouched behind the battery of amps, sucking on the largest party joint Stephen had ever seen, and Stephen had by now seen plenty. In the confused jumble of people and instruments, it was hard to find Simon, but Stephen's unerring instinct led him back into the darkest places where Simon always liked to hide. The lenses of Simon's spectacles flashed at him as Simon lifted his head.

Stephen crouched down beside him. "He's a cunt."

"I know." Simon's voice was small, with a chemical edge, and Stephen wondered how much coke had already vanished up Simon's nostrils. "He wants firing. I should fire him, shouldn't I? Do you think I should? What should I say to him?" But mere firing wasn't good enough for Jacky Stride, and they both knew it. Stephen reached down to help Simon to his feet; he tottered for a moment, the lifts putting him off-balance. The first chords were already pounding through the atmosphere, and somewhere out in front the bass player had abandoned his party joint. "Remember that girl in Boston?" Simon had to shout this into Stephen's ear as he turned the corner to take the stage. "Remember what she said?"

"They all say something." Stephen reached over and pulled Simon into a bone-crushing hug. He held on to Simon for a long time, bodies so tightly clasped that he could feel the hammering of Simon's heart through skin and flesh and clothing. "Give the people what they paid for. Give 'em hell."

Simon stepped away, hesitating for just a moment, on the verge of becoming Abelard. *What do you want to call him that for?* Stephen had been contemptuous of the pseudonym from the beginning. *You know they cut his balls off, right? You do know that Abelard ended with his balls cut off.*

Simon swiped at Stephen, clutching his hand, squeezing the fingers together, grabbing at the poet like a lifeline, and then he was gone, a phantom in a costume, a body drawn inexorably to the stage. Stephen waited, listening like he always did as Simon's voice swelled to a bombastic wall of sound, filling the auditorium.

SIMON DUCKWORTH'S father had once upon a time been the sax player in a swing band, long before swing was hip. Their band was called The Dosh Monkeys, and they had enjoyed something of a following in Stepney and the other Tower Boroughs, and there had been some talk of them cutting a record, but nothing ever came of it. Roger had fancied himself a ladies' man back in the day, so when he'd first clapped eyes on Nina Harris—petite, dark-haired, an excellent dancer—he told his bandmates, "That's the girl I'm going to marry, see." Nine months later, with the grudging acceptance of Nina's mother, Betty, they were married; a month after that, Nina had become pregnant and secretly hoped for a girl. She'd always wanted a girl so she could call her Chantal Marie and do her hair up in bubbly curls like Shirley Temple. The pregnancy had been a bit of an inconvenience, because Roger thought he'd continue his musical career for just a wee bit longer. The band was scheduled to do a run of dates up through Manchester and Liverpool, maybe even branch out into the Continent. "Can't you get rid of it?" Roger had asked her. "You can have another kiddy, later on." Nina went home to her mother and had refused to see or speak to Roger for a week or more. At last Roger turned up with a frilly bassinet that he'd bought at an oddments shop in Islington. Nina's brother Roy had laughed when Roger brought the thing inside the house. "What if the baby's a boy?" he'd asked. "You can't put him in that—you'll make a poof out of him!"

Roger found a job working at the gas company, and he and Nina bought the maisonette in Essian Street and brought Simon there to live once he was born. Roger was playing a gig at a bingo hall in Brixton, dutifully delivering the big band and swing numbers his peers remembered from the war, when Nina went into labor. Someone dispatched a taxi to fetch him, and he'd left the band in the middle of "Sweet Lorraine," arriving at the hospital in time to see his infant son's squashed red face peering up at him from Nina's arms. "Bit small, isn't he?"

Nina had suffered an extraordinarily long postpartum depression, and her sister Sheila came to stay with them to help care for little Simon and pick up around the house. For the first three months of Simon's life, Nina did nothing except listen to the wireless, smoke cigarettes, and cry. She'd cried at *The Archers* and *The Goon Show* and she'd cried at *Much-Binding-in-the-Marsh*, and the adverts for washing powder. For the remainder of her marriage to Roger, she'd been subject to sudden fits of wailing, of covert sobbing in the kitchen. She despised swing music with a passion and screamed at Roger to stop reminiscing about the war.

Long after Simon should have been in bed, he'd sit on the pantry stairs (the configuration of the narrow downstairs passage amplified any sounds coming from the front room) and listen to his parents fighting. Usually they'd fight about Roger's job, or the state of the house, or the things that Nina cooked for tea; sometimes they'd fight about Simon. Roger didn't think that Simon needed the expensive piano lessons that Nina insisted on; Nina thought that Simon had the makings of a musical genius. "It's not fair, making him give up his music. You'll break his heart."

"What about me?" Roger had shouted. "What about my music? Oh no, I'd to get a job up at the bloody gas company!"

The day before Simon's thirteenth birthday, he'd come home from school to find Roger gone and Nina sitting at the kitchen table, smoking a cigarette. When Simon had asked where his dad had gone, Nina told him they were getting a divorce, and his father would be moving up to Glasgow that weekend.

"It'll just be the two of us from now on," Nina said. "Just you and me. Think you can manage to look out for your old mum?" She'd seemed inordinately cheerful, as though she'd been relieved of a great anguish.

"I don't want to stay with you—I'm going with me dad." Simon packed a few things in his valise, followed his father to the train station, and clung to him. "I'll be a good boy this time," he said. "You'll see, you won't have to leave and Mum won't get angry any more. If I'm good, will you stay with us?" There was no time for explanations: the whistle blew and Roger had to get on the train.

"You can come and visit Daddy at the weekends, and on school holidays. You can even come for Christmas if you like." Roger gave him twenty pounds, told him to spend it on some record albums. "Get some of that music that you like."

"I want you to stay." Simon had planted himself on the platform and refused to move.

"Simon, I have to go." Roger had untangled Simon's fingers from his sleeve. "Honestly—now there's the whistle. I've got to get on the train." He'd pulled Simon into his arms and hugged him. "Come and see me soon, there's a good lad."

He sat in a forward-facing compartment, and had steeled himself not to look behind. He couldn't bear the sight of it. He couldn't bear the sight of Simon's tear-stained face, or the forlorn slump of his shoulders as he stood on the platform. He held the image of Simon in his mind as the train pulled out: a fat thirteen-year-old boy with thick specs, standing with twenty quid clutched in his pudgy fist. *He'll never amount to anything*, Roger thought. *He can't possibly amount to anything.* He wondered what would become of Simon, left to Nina's devices. He ought to have some say in how his son was being brought up. He ought to have some influence, after all.

"I didn't mean it." Nina had called him as soon as she'd got home from her holiday, which wasn't like her. Usually she'd write him, if there was something she needed to say, and save the pence a long-distance call would have cost her. Roger had held the phone pressed against his face and listened to Nina hissing down the line at him. "I told him not to wander where I couldn't see him." He'd said this in his own defense. "I told him not to."

He wanted to ask her what had happened, but he didn't have the guts.

2: **Say Goodbye to Sunday**

STEPHEN had come down to London from his father's house in Orkney, traveling the 700 miles and then some all because some bloke working at a music shop in Denmark Street had asked him to. What sort of person did that? What sort of madman packed his life into a cheap old cardboard suitcase to travel some 700 miles to meet up with a stranger about a job? "Are you sure?" his mother had asked him. "You don't know this Simon Duckworth. There might be nothing in it at all." There'd been a tiny little advert, hardly visible, in the back of *New Music Weekly* (Nude Music Weekly, the lads at home called it, on account of the Page Three girls in there, showing off their tits). The advert said, *On the Front Stoop, London musical publisher—songwriters and poets, do you desire a change?* There had been some fine print about being responsible for one's own traveling expenses, but Stephen had already seen enough. He pelted over a thousand yards of Orkney's rocky soil to find his father, mending a sheep fence down by the water. "Dad, can I?" Stephen held the roll of razor wire so his dad could nail it into place; the cold wind tore across his face, making his eyes water.

"Are you sure?"

But Stephen was, and he wanted this, and by teatime the next day, he was at the pier, waiting for the ferry with his parents and his little sister. And then he was standing on the deck, waving to them as St. Margaret's Hope and the island of South Ronaldsay pulled slowly backward and away from him. *I'll be back by the weekend,* he told himself, then amended it to Christmas. The distance between was too great for him to journey lightly. He wasn't really leaving, just going down to London for a while to see about the job. He expected he'd feel more sorrow if St. Margaret's Hope truly was his home, but Stephen and his family moved from Grimsby when Stephen was twelve and his sister just a babe in arms. Lincolnshire had gotten too touristy, his father said, and Grimsby had become too lit up at night. He wanted to look out across the land and see nothing but the close and holy darkness settled in around him like a Dylan Thomas poem. So Stephen's father minded the sheep, and Stephen's mother carded and combed and spun the wool, and Stephen's sister complained about the cold and the way the wind was forever moaning round the corners of the house. When Stephen slept at night, he dreamed of elevators and the giant Ferris wheel he'd ridden in Grimsby the summer before they left. There was a Ferris wheel in London, almost certainly. There were a lot of things in London.

WHEN Stephen's train pulled into Paddington Station, he was sound asleep, and he woke only reluctantly, hauling himself up out of the sticky morass of his dreams with profound regret. It was either very late at night or very early in the morning, and the line of taxis outside in the street looked faintly surreal: a row of giant, glistening beetles, like something out of Kafka. He stood on the platform for a long time, watching the trains shuttle in and out, mesmerized by the chuff and click of their steel wheels against the filthy railway tracks.

"Are you the lyricist?" A voice behind him, steady even at this late hour. Stephen turned to see a young man about his own age with wire spectacles and a gap between his front teeth. His soft brown eyes reminded Stephen of a sad cow, an illustration from a children's book he'd had, once upon a time.

"I'm Stephen Abednego—" as though this were sufficient explanation. Simon gripped Stephen's outstretched hand with surprising power; his nondescript denim jacket and his bland, spectacled face belied the ripple of brute animal strength that chased up his forearm.

Simon had a car, an old black Mini with the lock gone on the driver's side door. There was a metal bar with a tiny padlock and an even smaller key. Stephen thought there was something frighteningly fastidious about it: all the horrid stories that he'd ever heard about hatchet murders and dismembered hikers rose up collectively and pressed themselves against the space behind his eyes. "I didn't think you'd want a hotel," Simon said. The Mini started up with a roar, rattling like a flatulent battleship. "You can stay at mine."

Stephen risked a glance across the car, gauging Simon's strength. He decided to keep his fingers on the handle of the door, just in case.

"Will it bother you, staying at mine?" Simon shouted to be heard over the roar of the Mini. Luckily, there was scant traffic at this hour, so his constant looking over at Stephen was unlikely to put them in mortal danger. "Mum said it was okay, just so long as we don't wake her and Gerald—"

It occurred to Stephen that Simon lived with his mother. In a gust of relief, all the air went out of him. The stories he'd heard about lunatics in London were just that—only stories. No one was going to abduct him off the train, murder him, and chop him into tiny pieces. It was going to be all right. He told himself that everything was all right as Simon's tiny car negotiated one-way streets and roundabouts and cluttered little lanes full of hooting partiers on their way home from late-closing pubs and dance parlors. When they finally stopped on Essian Street, Stephen felt he'd landed on a strange, uncertain planet.

"Gerald's the light sleeper—me mum could sleep through a thunderstorm." Simon pushed Stephen ahead of him through the darkened house, a long, narrow maisonette that flared slightly toward the back. He laid down Stephen's cardboard suitcase as though it contained the Hope diamond. "'Fraid you'll have to kip in with me for now—we can nip out and get ourselves a set of bunk beds in the morning. Bathroom's that way." And Simon turned his back, shucked everything except his boxer shorts, and fell into the bed.

Stephen groped his way to the bathroom, resisting the urge to break down and cry. He peered at himself in the mirror over the sink. The desire to simply turn and flee was overpowering; could he find his way back to get the train? He tried to recall the route they'd taken through the labyrinth but everything melted together in his mind: streets and roundabouts and narrow little passages, groups of girls in spangled dresses and big hoop earrings and boys in platform shoes and satin shirts, and Simon's small, strong hands on the steering wheel, and then the gasworks and Essian Street. Which way was home? If he tried to find it now, he'd never get there.

"Stephen…?" Simon's head peered round the door. "Are you all right?" His voice was gentle; without his specs, his face was open and curiously defenseless, the face of a blind baby animal.

"I think I should go home," Stephen said. He could feel his face pulling in on itself, his features readying themselves to cry. Barely seventeen, for Christ's sake, and 700 miles away from everything he knew, everything familiar. "I might have to go home."

"Fuck me," Simon muttered, and Stephen was momentarily stunned until he realized it was just an expression. "I've been a proper twat and all. Are you hungry? You want a cuppa? Bite to eat?" He wrapped his arms around his naked torso and squinted at Stephen. "It'll be okay. Mr. Stoop's an arse, but he's all right. And I've got a couple good ideas for some songs."

"I don't know if I should stay… I don't know if I can even write songs."

"How old are you?"

Stephen blinked. "I just turned seventeen last month."

"Seventeen." Simon squinted at him. "You're only seventeen and you've come all the way down here on your own?"

Hearing Simon say it made the entire thing seem like a horrifying ruse. The skin of Stephen's face was tight; in a minute he'd be crying. Maybe he was crying now, and didn't know it.

"Here, it's all right." Simon wrapped an arm around him, briefly. "Come on to bed. It'll all look different in the morning." He grinned. "It always does."

IT WASN'T Stephen's overwhelming physical beauty that got to Simon, not at first. He scarcely even noticed it, taken up as he was with the astonishing fact that here, in the person of this Orkney farmer's son, here was someone who at last understood. Here was the cliché: the kindred spirit, the soul mate, the ideal beloved. If he imagined Stephen to be his savior, he couldn't really be blamed for it. He was wired that way, made to fall in love with anyone who showed the slightest interest in him or who liked the same sorts of things that he liked. Let some stranger appear and smile at him, and murmur favorably over his record albums, ask about his mother, and Simon would cave in like a wet Battenberg cake. "You're too soft," his father used to say, when his father lived at home, when his parents were still miserably married. "You want toughening up. You want to show the other lads who's boss." Simon wasn't the boss, and couldn't be. He wouldn't know how, so naturally he ended up in situations where he was under someone else's boot, forced to obey someone else's whims.

It wasn't Stephen's extreme natural diffidence that got him either, or even the fact that Stephen came from somewhere as far away as Orkney (at least by way of Lincolnshire). Stephen *believed*—in something—and this made him special, and it lifted Simon's life out of the commonplace as well. On the rare occasions that Stephen made the long trip home to see his parents, Simon would sink into a lingering depression that didn't lift until Stephen's train pulled into the station. Simon was always there, waiting, when Stephen stepped down from the train, and Stephen invariably walked into Simon, was crushed in his embrace as though he were a soldier just returned from a long and costly war. Stephen wouldn't think to call it love, but in the privacy of his own imagination, Simon did. Almost from the very beginning, almost from the very first moment, he knew. It took a handful of days, a scattering of weeks, or perhaps it happened the moment Stephen stepped down from the train platform, or late at night while they huddled together at Simon's upright piano, working out a song. It happened. The knowledge of it grew in him until he couldn't suppress it any longer: one morning, while Stephen was in the shower, he confessed.

"Where is he?" Nina, as usual, was smoking and drinking tea. She wouldn't actually eat anything until she got to work, and then only a piece of toast with jam, made in the insurance company's kitchen. *Cheatham and Tyrell: Your Friendly Insurance* is where Nina worked—Cheatham and Steal, Stephen called it, or Coppin' a Feel. He was forever trying to stay on Nina's good side, perhaps because he recognized his own strange status in their household. Nina liked this little joke so much that she adopted it, announcing it to them every morning. "I'm off to cop a feel, then." Simon would get embarrassed but Gerald and Stephen found it enormously funny. Nina had been at Cheatham and Tyrell since Simon was first at school; between herself and Gerald, they managed to pay the mortgage on the miniscule maisonette where they all lived and purchase a few cans of lager for the weekend. If Simon was a bit short of cash, he could always play a set or two at Harry Butcher's boozer, like he used to do before the job at Stoop's. But nowadays he rarely did, because he and Stephen were too busy hatching plans for their own futures and imagining the many ways in which they might become celebrities.

"He's having a shower." Simon lingered round the kitchen counter, wanting to say something. He grabbed his mother round the waist and lifted her off the floor, squeezing until she shrieked. Simon often made these kinds of overtures when he had something significant to say. "Can I tell you something?"

"It's him, isn't it?" Nina ran the tap over her spent cigarette, put it in the bin. "I can kick him out, you know—send him back to Scotland, if that's what you want." She fixed him with her basilisk stare, and Simon felt his innards turn to stone. *She knows*, he thought, shriveling under that gaze. He was never good at disobedience; it was something Simon never learned. Until Gerald came along, and even before that, he understood the mysterious dyad of mother and son, and he instinctively knew he was to mind his mother and behave himself. "Has he been pestering you? Cheeky little—"

"I love him." Simon blurted it out between breaths and waited for her to lift her hand and belt him a good one, right in the face. He forced himself to stumble on, say the rest of it. "Oh God, Mum, you've no idea how much I love him. He's—"

Nina's face hardened, her mouth a thin line of dark lipstick. She turned away and lit another cigarette, blowing the smoke out through her nose. "He's the best friend you ever had," she said. Her voice was high and tight, held together with some dark anguish. "Isn't that right?"

"Yes." Of course Simon understood this; she was his mother, after all. "That's what I meant, yeah."

"Your Uncle Ralph tried that sort of thing, you know—after he came home from the war." Nina's hands moved jerkily among the dirty breakfast things, rinsing dishes in the sink, stacking teacups in a wobbly pile. Down the hall, the sound of the shower hesitated and then cut off completely, and Simon heard the bathroom door open. "Did I ever tell you about him? He blew his brains out, oh yes, indeed he did."

His stomach clenched itself into a tight knot. "Mum, you don't need to worry, I'm not—"

She turned on him, her eyes fixing him in place like an insect on a pin. "Of course you're not." She smiled thinly. "Now run along to work."

In the evening, when Simon got home from work, Gerald was waiting for him, emptying the ash cans in the back. "There you are," he said. "I thought the fairies had got you." The entendre was lost on Gerald, a gentle soul who couldn't make a deliberate joke if his life depended on it. He handed Simon a rubbish bin. "Hold that steady 'til I get this right." The household rubbish cascaded into the bag, smelling of wet tea leaves and orange peels, and Nina's cigarettes. "Your mum had a little talk with me this morning, after you'd gone to work." Gerald took the bag from Simon, sealing it up with a deft twist of his large hands. Gerald was so unlike Simon's father, Roger: quiet where Roger was loud, gentle where Roger was harsh. Simon often pretended that Gerald really was his father, introducing him to others as "my dad." The only time that Simon ever heard from Roger was at Christmas and on his birthday, when a card always arrived with a fiver in it, all the way from Glasgow. Roger had married again, and had a second family, a group of three or four children whom Simon knew only as a row of blurry faces in a yearly photograph. He never gave a toss what their names were. He only knew his father loved them better. That was the only thing that really mattered, and even though it was childish for a man of twenty to still hold such grudges, Simon treasured this one and kept it hidden deep inside of him. It justified his lingering anger against Roger, and the burning resentment he felt whenever Roger's name was even casually mentioned, coupled with a painful yearning.

Simon blinked at Gerald through his glasses, a delaying tactic he often used to good advantage. "What did she say?"

Gerald patted Simon on the shoulder and led him over to the stone bench by the wall. "Come and have a sit down. I'm not as young as you." The air was cold out here but not unpleasantly so, and the smoke from various other chimneys drifted upward without the interference of the wind. Their house had no garden as such, just a square of ashy paving stones fenced about with a brick wall, roughly six feet high. A door in the back of the wall let onto an alley, which led in turn to the school, the old gasworks, Harry Butcher's pub, and the small canal where Simon kissed a French girl one Saturday afternoon.

Simon was fifteen, and the girl's name was Solange, an exchange student from Provence. When Simon tried to put his tongue in her mouth, she slapped him and called him bad names, and that night her sponsor family called Nina and complained that Simon had taken undue liberties. For weeks afterward, Simon waited in an agony of suspense, certain that French gendarmes would turn up on his mother's doorstep at any minute and demand he be taken away in chains. That had been another occasion for one of Gerald's talks, like the time before that when Simon had been caught wanking in the closet. Gerald had been characteristically gentle and polite with him. *It's the sort of thing a chap does in private, Simon. Best keep it to your bedroom, eh?*

"What did Mum say?" Simon was on the defensive at once. "She said something, didn't she?" Blind panic began to claw its way up into his throat. "She's going to send Stephen away—that's it, isn't it?"

"Sit *down*." Gerald tugged on Simon's arm until he did. "We can have a talk, can't we? You and me? We always could before."

"If he goes away, I'm going with him."

"No one is going anywhere." Gerald patted him. "Your mum is just worried, that's all. You and Stephen spend a lot of time together—you work together, you go about with him on the weekends. She's thinking that perhaps you should have other friends, besides Stephen."

"She thinks I'm a poof."

Gerald sighed.

"She does, Gerald! She said as much to me in the kitchen. She told me about Uncle Ralph."

Gerald nodded. "Uncle Ralph." He gazed at Simon for a long moment. "Are you?"

"Bloody hell, Gerald—"

"Because it doesn't matter to me one bit, and I want you to know that."

The declaration filled him with tender filial love. "I'm not."

Gerald smiled, and rose to go back into the house. "Well, fine. But it's just as fine if you are."

"I'm *not*!"

"Fine."

The conversation bothered him, and when next he found himself alone, he stripped, examining himself in the full-length bathroom mirror, wondering about his body. What was normal, exactly? When Simon was nine, his mother had taken him to the family physician for a checkup; the doctor had weighed and measured him, declared him too heavy for his height, and asked Nina if she'd noticed the scratches on his thighs.

What scratches? I've not seen any scratches. The wounds were six to eight inches long, of significant depth, running parallel to each other, dark and livid. Later, in the car on the way home, Nina quizzed Simon about them. *Where'd you get the scratches? Did you do that to yourself?*

At first he wouldn't answer her. Fear of his mother rendered him mute. But Nina kept at him, all through that evening and into the next morning. She interrogated him mercilessly as he sat eating his breakfast at the kitchen table. *Did you do it? What for? Tell me right now or else. I mean it, Simon.*

I wanted it to go down. He spooned porridge into his mouth. *It kept coming up and I wanted to make it go down.*

Nina stared at him, her dark eyes snapping dangerously. *What the bleeding hell are you talking about? Do you want me to belt you?*

You know, Mum. He was distressed, near tears, his open mouth half full of cereal. *When you wash me, you make my thing come up. I wanted it to go down. It wouldn't go down.*

Remembering it now, he wanted earnestly to forget. Recalling it would benefit him nothing. He wondered if his mother might have something to do with how he felt about himself, about Stephen. His uncle Roy came round every Christmas and enjoyed telling the bassinet story: *Don't put him in that, you'll make a poof out of him.* Standing in front of the mirror, he examined himself carefully. Did he seem odd to other people? He thought about television shows like *Morecambe and Wise*, men in wigs and dresses; he understood the names the lads at school used to have for boys like Randolph Wheeler, who was thin, effete, and blond long before David Bowie made it fashionable. Was that how people thought of him? What made them think it?

At twenty, Simon wasn't particularly tall but he had since lost the baby fat that made him appear too pudgy in his clothes; with his hairy chest and muscular arms and legs, he was a fully formed adult male, devoid of flamboyance or camp. If anything he tended toward a bit of outrage in his accoutrements and clothes—Mickey Mouse T-shirts in violent hues, denim dungarees spangled with badges bought from a Woolworth's vending machine, a fun fur coat in royal purple. He looked like every other young man living in London at the time. There was nothing to suggest that he was any different.

"I WANT to talk to you."

Stephen's hands were elbow-deep in the supper dishes when Simon came into the kitchen. Nina and Gerald had gone down to the pub for a pint before bed; Simon had been watching some old rerun on the telly. The smell of sausages and mushy peas still lingered in the kitchen, overlaid with Nina's cigarette smoke and the knickers drying on the line up near the ceiling. It was the same all over in the houses of the working class; in Stepney everybody smelled alike.

"What's the matter?" Stephen was beautiful at seventeen, with his green eyes and his loose-limbed, lanky body and his ready smile. Of course he was lovely; of course Simon could see nothing past him.

"Nothing… I just need… the sooner I can get it over with…."

Stephen withdrew his hands from the dishwater and wiped them on his jeans. "Just tell me, then."

So Simon did.

Stephen started to laugh. He laughed and laughed until tears rolled unobstructed down his cheeks. He laughed until his stomach muscles started to cramp from the strain. When he found breath enough to speak, he told Simon he was daft.

Simon says, like the game the kiddies played: *Simon says laugh until you cry.*

Simon was crying then, crying and trying not to show it. He bolted blindly from the kitchen, struggling with his specs, wanting to make a hasty exit before Stephen saw such evidence. It wasn't safe to trust someone with proof like this; it could be used against you. What on earth did Simon tell him that made him laugh like that? What did Simon say? *Simon says, Simon says…*

Simon says, "I love you."

Not as a brother or a friend.

You do know what I mean, don't you?

I want us to be together.

Simon said, "I love you."

And Stephen laughed.

Simon fled, fumbling his way down the long hallway of his mother's narrow house. At the end of the corridor there was a laundry cupboard, installed when the house still retained its original configuration—that of a Victorian manse—before being split into modest maisonettes. This had been a favorite hiding place for Simon, and as a small boy, he would seek solace here, away from Nina and from his father's sudden and inexplicable rages. The cupboard was empty—Nina maintained it was too dark and inaccessible to be of any practical use—and just large enough to contain a frightened boy. It still contained Simon, if he clasped his arms round his bended knees and ducked his head. He sat there in the dark, burning with humiliation, hating himself and listening to various noises from the rest of the house: the television, a tap being turned on, Stephen's footsteps walking out of one room and into another. He could still see Stephen's incredulous face, that moment of shock before he dissolved into helpless laughter.

I love you.

Simon! Don't be daft.

"Simon?" Stephen's voice sounded close to his head and Simon jumped. "What are you doing in there?" He rapped his knuckles on the door. "Simon? Look, I've been a right twat. Can't you come out? I want to talk to you."

Simon hugged his knees and stayed very still, not trusting himself to move or speak or even breathe but waiting 'til Stephen got sick of listening to silence and went away.

3: *We Sometimes Fall*

"I'VE been here since half seven this morning." Stephen wouldn't look Simon in the eye. "I wrote something." He shoved a crumpled slip of paper at Simon and left: a sheet torn from one of Morris Stoop's postal ledgers, a song lyric initially written in pencil and then laboriously erased and copied out again in pen. There were smudges on it, dirty fingerprints, the ring from the bottom of a teacup. Stephen had inked the title of it boldly across the top: WE SOMETIMES FALL.

Simon's heart slammed into his ribs as he unfolded the sheet. He couldn't bear to look at it; the letters hurt his eyes. It wasn't merely an apology. It was so much more than that. He wasn't sure what Stephen was trying to tell him, and he didn't have the courage to ask, not after last night's awkward scene in the kitchen.

He shoved the sheet into his trouser pocket and went through to Morris Stoop's office where the music publisher was entertaining a girl singer and her manager, a vicious-looking dark-haired Scot from Glasgow. It was Simon's job to pour the tea and hand the biscuits round, which he did with a certain alacrity. The girl singer wasn't pretty—her face was too long and she had a lantern jaw—but there was something sad and soulful in her eyes that attracted Simon. She was wearing a pink baby-doll dress with a huge purple bow under her bust, and too much dark eye makeup and her blonde hair had been teased and sprayed into an improbable beehive. Simon recognized her as "Jukebox" Ginger Thyme, the voice behind the fleeting top 40 single, "His Daddy Always Comes," but the Scot was a mystery. He caught and held Simon's gaze and their hands touched when Simon handed him his teacup and something hissed and burned behind his eyes. "Are you a singer, yourself?" His accent was pure Glasgow—The Gorbals, but Simon couldn't have known that. "Or do you just hand the tea round?"

"Simon is a bit of a composer," Morris Stoop put in, hurriedly. "I've been bringing him along."

"Bringing him along to what?" the Scot asked.

Morris Stoop smiled thinly. "That will be all, Simon. Shut the door behind you."

The Scot said something else, something that Simon didn't catch, but Jukebox Ginger smiled at him as he closed the door. He went through to the packing room, where young men like he and Stephen sorted, picked, and packed up parcels of sheet music to send through the post. Stephen was nowhere to be seen. Simon laid the empty tea tray in the little kitchenette just off the packing room and took a flight of narrow, dark stairs down to the loading dock where Morris Stoop's fleet of two broken-down lorries sat waiting for their mother lode of printed music, but Stephen wasn't there, either. "He's gone to the post," Charley said when Simon asked him. Charley was Mr. Stoop's neurasthenic eldest son. He spent his days hanging about the premises and pretending to work in exchange for twenty pounds a week and all the cigarettes that he could smoke. Most of the lads called him Charley Chimney on account of his prodigious tobacco consumption. "Been gone awhile." Charley took a long, deep drag on his cigarette, squinting against the smoke. "Might have got run over by a bus or something."

The image bloomed in Simon's imagination: florid, horrible; he saw Stephen lying crushed and broken in the road and he didn't think that he could stand it. He jumped down off the loading dock and ran out into Denmark Street and stood there staring at the traffic passing by. "Stephen?" He leaned out as far as he dared and bellowed Stephen's name. "Stephen? Where are you?" Two young girls, dressed in Carnaby Street's best, giggled as they passed him. *Lost your boyfriend?* "Stephen? For God's sake, at least give me a chance to read it." He took a breath, nerved himself, looked both ways up and down the street, and plunged into the swirling maelstrom of passing cars. Immediately his ears were assaulted by the blare of horns and people were shouting; a man in a yellow Fiat strayed so close that Simon felt the heat from the vehicle's exhaust against the legs of his trousers. He took another tentative step, squinting into the bright midday sun. "Stephen? It's not funny anymore. Come on!"

A London bus, lumbering its way toward Covent Garden, accelerated, the driver catching sight of a green signal ahead. Simon, squeezing past a cab and nimbly avoiding a man on a bike, stopped just in time. The bus thundered past him and he leaned back, his fists clenching involuntarily, his face frozen in an improbable rictus of horror. He gained the pavement on the opposite side of the street and fell hard against a parking meter, his legs unable to hold him.

"Simon." A pair of familiar hands caught him under the arms and pulled him upright and he was looking into Stephen's face. "What the hell are you doing? You could have been killed." He shook Simon none too gently. "Are you trying to top yourself? Is that it?"

"I was looking for you." Simon pushed his glasses up on his face. "Charley said you'd not been seen. I was afraid you'd got hit by a lorry or something... no, a bus. He said a bus." This last bit seemed important but Simon wasn't sure why.

Stephen held up a packet of envelopes. "Had to run to the stationer's 'round the corner. Stoop wanted this special kind, the long ones. We were all out." He regarded Simon with a wary gaze. "You're completely mental—you know that?"

"But you are all right... you didn't get hit by anything?" Simon was violently relieved, wanted to embrace Stephen but feared rejection. Ever since the scene in the kitchen, he couldn't decide how to act around Stephen, whether he should continue as though nothing had happened or take courage in both hands and address the matter.

"Of course not," Stephen scoffed. "You've got to calm down, mate. You're strung too tight. One of these days, you're gonna snap, you mark my words."

AT FIVE o'clock Simon found Stephen in the cloakroom, putting on his coat. "I was going to get the train," Stephen said. "I didn't know if you'd want me in your car after everything."

"Don't be an arse." Simon pushed him through the door out to where the car was parked.

"I wanted to tell you I was sorry." Stephen waited as Simon unlocked the passenger door for him. "About laughing at you. That's why I wrote the lyric. It sort of says what I wanted to tell you, only it rhymes, of course."

Simon's face burned and he mumbled something faintly apologetic.

"I've been reading this book, you know. This chap Aristotle, some old Greek he was. He said that love shows us the way to beauty." Stephen dug the book out of his pocket. "If you want to experience beauty, then you have to learn the art of love."

"The art of love." Simon frowned. "What does it mean?" He turned the key and the Mini sputtered, hesitated, and finally caught.

"I think it's like knowing what to say to someone." Stephen's lean fingers tightened on the book. "So you don't make an arse of yourself."

Simon's mouth quirked at one corner. "Like you did?" He regretted it as soon as he'd said it. "Sorry."

Stephen grinned. "I think we should go home." He watched Simon put the Mini into gear, watched Simon's hands on the wheel. "Did you read it?"

But Simon wasn't giving anything away, not while last night's hurt lingered in his memory. "I might have done." *You love me? You love me? It's like a girly novel, isn't it? It's like those love comics that Debbie Powell reads at dinnertime.*

"Cunt." Stephen probably knew Simon had read it, because Simon had no patience at all. "You did. I know you did, you twat."

"Fancy going to the pub tonight for a bit?" Simon glanced sidelong at Stephen. The idea of being alone in the house with Stephen made him acutely uneasy. Something difficult had been breached; he understood this. Something else had been erected in its place.

"I'm skint." Stephen sighed theatrically. "I've no money 'til I get paid from Stoop."

Simon took the roundabout, negotiating it with ease, and they were on their way, headed back toward Stepney, back toward home. "Mum and Gerald are going down to our Maureen's to play cards." Maureen was Simon's aunt, close enough to him in age to be addressed familiarly. "Maybe we can get a takeaway and a few cans and have a night in?"

"I told you, I'm skint—"

"Oh, bloody hell, Stephen! I'll buy it then." Simon had been at Stoop's longer than Stephen and, therefore, earned a higher wage; he was also much more careful of his funds.

"So do you think you can work it up a bit? Maybe after supper?"

Simon considered. He had some ideas about the music, how it needed to go. He was certain the song would be slow, meditative, with a subtle rhythm reminiscent of two people making love… no, that image was too muted… two people having sex… clinical… two people fucking. It would have a rhythm like two people fucking, like a long slow fuck outdoors on a hot summer afternoon; or maybe a cold winter's afternoon, in the grey hours between dinnertime and night, with snow falling outside the window, upholstering the white silence. It seemed as though it might be that sort of song, like a slow fandango, like bodies meeting in the space of a tender, taken breath.

Stephen watched Simon's hands on the wheel of the Mini.

THEIR bodies collided in space, and the darkness in the bedroom was full of noises: sighs and whispers, subvocal exclamations that could mean anything, or nothing.

"Quiet," Simon murmured in the darkness. His mother and Gerald were sleeping just the other side of the wall and he couldn't imagine explaining it to them, or to anyone. "We've got to be quiet."

"Here," Stephen whispered, "I want you here. Right here." The world had shrunk to the size of the room; the universe was just him and Simon. Simon's face was close to his, close enough to kiss that gentle mouth, and the feeling of it went through him, a palpable thrill. He knew what this was called. He knew what the Orkney lads back home would call this, and he wondered if he ought to worry. Kissing Simon felt like kissing anybody, like kissing Judy Garson back home, except Simon was really good at it, knew how to do things with his lips and tongue that Judy had never, ever done. Kissing Simon was sweet and hot, and made Stephen's cock rise, hard and pulsing. "I wish you'd touch me." It didn't even sound like him, whispering in the dark. It didn't sound at all like Stephen. Still semiclothed in jeans, his shirt unbuttoned, he rolled onto his back, took Simon's hand, and pressed it against the bulge of his erection. "I don't know what to do."

Simon laughed. "Neither do I." He bent low and pressed his open mouth against the peak of Stephen's nipple, amazed when Stephen's body bowed into a rictus, rising off the bed. "Like that?"

"Just like that." It couldn't be his voice, trembling, eager, shuddering on the edge of some revelation he would never make in daylight. It couldn't possibly be him.

He watched Simon's hands on his body.

"Yes." Stephen's pleasure peaked and spread, obliterating him. "Oh God, yes. Yes."

"YOUR mum said you should come home with me for a visit." Stephen hovered near him, not quite touching him, his body held carefully aloof. They were in a record store off Tin Pan Alley and Simon was paging carefully through a bin of foreign imports with his usual deliberation. Simon was wearing a bright orange T-shirt with the words DIG IT printed on the front, a faded denim jacket, and jeans that used to be too small. He'd been nicking Nina's diet pills, tiny orange ones for which her doctor was all too willing to write numerous prescriptions; the pills made Simon agitated, nervous, often morose, and paranoid. Sometimes he would take too many and stay up half the night, watching the cracks in the ceiling above his head and listening to the thunderous murmur of his heart. Simon had always been the nervous sort, starting at subtle noises, imagining ghosts in the dark. As a small child, he was prey to screaming nightmares and he would wake in a lather of sweat, inconsolable. Nina would try to bring him into her bed but Simon only screamed harder, clinging to Roger's arm with a grip that left livid bruises. In desperation, Nina took him to their family doctor, but the man told her nothing except that young children sometimes have nightmares and that Simon would eventually grow out of it.

Three days ago he and Stephen did things in Simon's bed that Simon would have never thought possible, but Stephen, never the most loquacious of young men, was silent on the subject. Simon couldn't quite figure out what was going on in Stephen's head. If he was angry, then his anger was a gentle sort, without demands behind it. If what Stephen felt was closer to regret, that too was muted, since he appeared to Simon's critical eye as more or less himself. Worst of all—Simon didn't dare consider it—was that Stephen felt absolutely nothing, that what happened between them amounted to precisely nothing, that there had been others and being with Simon was ultimately no big deal.

Simon thought to buy something for Stephen but couldn't make up his mind. He'd been through the contents of the record bin at least half a dozen times, choosing and discarding Stevie Wonder's *A Place in the Sun* and the Troggs' *Give it to Me* and a single by some obscure band named Blind Ham. Stephen, standing behind him, watched this without comment.

"Mum said I should go to Orkney?" Nina would have started the housework by now, hoovering and polishing while Gerald puttered around outside. In the course of her housekeeping, she would turn out Simon's bedroom, mop and dust and sweep, hoover, pick up his dirty socks, and strip his bed. (Ever since Simon turned thirteen she had never looked too closely at his bedsheets.) Nina would do all this with a cigarette hanging out her mouth; Simon was terrified that smoking would kill her in the end.

"Yes. We can go up in the train. Well, 'til the boat, anyway."

"I was going to buy you something." Simon put the albums back into the bin. "I wanted to buy you something." He wondered if he might be sick on the train, or if he might be compelled to drink endless cups of treacle-thick railway coffee. Ever since that time up North, ever since the pub and what happened—Simon had never, not even in his own mind, called it rape—he'd rather take the bus.

"It's an overnight," Nina said this to him later, handing Simon his ticket at the platform. "You both can sleep practically the whole way." She packed his case; Simon had no idea what was in it. "It'll be nice for you to get away." *What if Stephen's family doesn't like me?* They would share a sleeper compartment, him and Stephen, with a little pull-out bed and curtains at the windows. "Ring me when you get there," Nina said, and then the train jerked suddenly into motion and the whistle blew three sharp blasts. "Have a lovely holiday!" Gerald was smiling broadly, waving at them, but Nina just seemed relieved.

"Have you ever been to Scotland?" Stephen asked.

"I've never been anywhere," Simon said.

They sat up talking as the train was pulled relentlessly north; around eleven Simon went to the buffet car and fetched them some tea. Stephen was unusually animated, talking about his mother's flowers and his father's sheep, gesturing broadly with his hands, laughing in a breathless way, as if all of this were just a little beyond him. The Stephen that Simon knew was quiet: a slender, restrained figure in faded denims and a cotton shirt carelessly unbuttoned, silver rings on his slim fingers, a pen in his hand.

"About the other night—" Simon started to say something but was interrupted by the conductor asking for their tickets. The man lingered for a while, chatting amiably, asking about the weather down in London, wondering what their jobs were. "We write songs," Simon said. "On Denmark Street. You'll hear about us one day." He wondered if this was cheeky; the man was at least Gerald's age, probably older. Perhaps he shouldn't have said anything. Perhaps saying something would somehow jinx it, make it not come true. If they failed, it would be all his fault.

Somehow during all of it, Stephen managed to get ready for bed and wanted the light off so he could sleep. The bed was narrow, barely big enough for both of them, even with Simon's newly svelte physique. Did Nina think of this when she booked their tickets? Simon, unaware of ticket prices for a trip like this, didn't want to ask. Nina always took care of things for him; Simon didn't bother doing much of anything for himself. His mother always understood the sorts of things he liked, his tastes in food and drink, the sorts of clothes he'd wear. He had always been safe with Nina. Yes, that was right, wasn't it? He was always safe with his mum. He was safe.

The only illumination in the tiny chamber was a reading light set into the wall above their heads; when Simon switched it off, they were plunged into a tomblike darkness, a smothering confinement made more sinister by the small compartment. Simon's heart began to beat harder in his chest and a bubble of anxiety formed beneath his breastbone. He forced himself to breathe and to recognize the contours of their compartment and Stephen's solid shape lying beside him.

"Aren't you going to get undressed?" Stephen asked; Simon had crawled under the covers fully clothed and the starched railway sheets pinned him to the bed with the efficacy of a straitjacket. "You won't get any sleep dressed up like that." Simon was grateful for the darkness and the curtains at the window. He never liked undressing in front of anyone and he couldn't let Stephen see him because that wound was still too raw.

Put your hand on me... touch me like this. It wasn't like Gus had been; it wasn't anything like Gus, and after a little bit, Stephen had leaned down and put it in his mouth. Simon had come as hard as he'd ever come in his life, and had shivered and cried, and had held Stephen to him, their naked skins pasted together with his body's subtle fluids. *I love you.* He hadn't been able to stop saying it; the words had just tumbled out of his mouth, unbidden. *I love you, I love you, I love you.* He'd waited until Stephen had drifted into sleep, then had gotten up and put his pajamas on. He hadn't minded being naked in the dark but in daylight was different, and anyway, there'd been a chance Nina would stick her head in the door first thing in the morning and Simon could imagine her reaction if she'd seen him and Stephen lying nude together, their bodies slick with sweat and come.

It doesn't matter to me one bit. Gerald would be different; Gerald would understand. Nina would claw Simon's eyes out if she saw him. She wouldn't allow anybody else to touch him.

He remembered shopping for clothes with Nina when he was fourteen—*fourteen*—barely pubescent and terribly shy, as well as plump and awkward. He remembered sweating in the dressing room, trying to force his unwilling flesh into the jeans his mum had found. *You're just like a fat little pig,* Nina had said. *You can't fit into anything.* In the end, they ended up getting a pair of "big and tall" jeans ("They're a fair bit larger in the thighs and seat," the shop assistant said, trying not to smile). Nina watched every bite that went into Simon's mouth after that, and on the weekends, when she and Gerald would treat themselves to Chinese takeaway, Simon would get a salad or some vegetable sticks, with a tiny dab of salad cream and a cup of tepid skimmed milk.

"I can't wait 'til we get there." Stephen's voice was close and hushed, and holy in the darkness. Stephen was much too close to him, too close; his proximity made Simon remember the kisses they had shared, their hands on each other's bodies, but Simon couldn't ask him to move because there wasn't any room. He wondered what Stephen would do if he leaned over and kissed him or laid a hand on his bare shoulder. Would Stephen pull away? Would he pretend not to understand? There were so many things Simon wanted to say, so many words he knew he would never utter. Whatever courage he'd once possessed had utterly evaporated.

"You should go to sleep." Simon took his glasses off; it was hard to talk over the lump in his throat. "It's a long way." He turned onto his side away from Stephen, afraid that some stray shaft of moonlight might pick out the moisture gleaming on his lashes. He shivered as Stephen's arm slid around his waist.

"You're my best friend." Stephen's breath was warm against the side of Simon's face, and there was silence. "My best friend."

Simon's first view of St. Margaret's Hope came as he was standing on the deck of the ferry. Their crossing from the mainland had been rough; Stephen vomited twice over the side before subsiding into a miserable heap on one of the many benches lining the deck. Simon stood beside him, rubbing his back and making soothing noises, grateful that the vomit went cleanly into the water—he had never been very good with bodily functions, and the sight of snot or shit or some other physical effluent could put him off his feed 'til teatime. But the landscape—beautiful, gloriously stark—enticed him. As the boat approached the quay, he could see the gleam of window glass from the houses on the shore and the knots of people waiting with their cars.

"There's Mum—" Stephen started forward, straining to see her, blind and deaf and senseless in that moment. Simon, watching Stephen's parents surge toward him, felt the unmistakable sting of jealousy and hated himself for it.

THE air here was so much purer than the concentrated smog and fog of London, and the light so direct that Simon wore his sunglasses almost all the time. Stephen had forgotten the curative qualities of the air or how the wind would tug and push at him; he had also forgotten the silence, and the village lying at the edge of a huge expanse of green with the sea beyond, murmuring drowsily in the distance. There was ample time for everything, and endless sunny days for Simon to lie flat on his back on the grass, his ears filled with the sound of the sea, the warm air tugging at his tousled hair and the hem of his shirt. "I think my sister fancies you," Stephen said. (Right now they were hiding from her.) "She kept looking at you all through breakfast."

Simon didn't reply to this particularly, knowing that Stephen was trying to get a rise out of him. Stephen persisted in pairing Simon (at least metaphorically) with his young sister; the topic was the subject of endless jibes about how Simon would marry Stephen's sister and they would live in the back of a tour bus while Simon traveled round the globe, playing the piano. Simon wanted to ask him: does it mean nothing to you, what we did? Are you going to pretend it didn't even happen? Instead, he asked Stephen if they would always be friends, because it was impossible for Simon to imagine a future without Stephen in it, even as he was driven to make jokes of his own. "You'll run off some day." Simon poked him viciously in the ribs. "You'll marry some girl and leave me all alone in Stepney with my mother and Gerald." He wanted a particular response, but instead, Stephen found the notion hilarious.

"And the knickers on the clothesline in the kitchen."

"And the knickers… in the kitchen." What had he hoped for—expected? A declaration, a promise of undying fealty. A response to the things he'd said that night in bed: *I love you, I love you.* A single white gull circled them slowly with its wings spread wide. The sight moved Simon almost to tears and he reached out, wanting to draw Stephen into his embrace, but Stephen, insensible to the moment, was up and away over the fields, whistling with his coat slung over one shoulder.

Simon watched him go, shielding his eyes with one hand, the other thrown above his head in what he hoped was a carefree gesture. It was enough, he told himself, just to be near Stephen. It was a measure of how much Stephen loved him that he'd invited Simon up north, that he wanted Simon to come and meet his family. The rest would occur in its own time, when things were right, when Stephen understood that he belonged with Simon, and with no one else but Simon. It would happen. There was plenty of time.

"STEPHEN says you've both made great inroads with your music. This Mr. Stoop—" Stephen's mother, Vera, dumped the remainder of the shepherd's pie onto Simon's plate. "—is he nice to you?" The Abednegos had electricity but Stephen's dad preferred not to use it, in the interests of economy. The light, nearly endless in the summer time, meant that the oil lamps wouldn't be lit until at least eleven-thirty, if at all, and everyone would be in bed by then. Unlike Stepney at night, there were no noises, no lights on the bedroom wall from passing cars, no sirens in the dark. If Simon happened to wake, all he would hear was Stephen's quiet breathing and the murmur of the ocean in the distance. Sometimes he imagined that he'd slept when actually he'd just drifted for a while in a twilight state, unaware of time. He never realized how the city seemed to press on him, how the tiny house in Stepney was confining, claustrophobic, full of the smell of Nina's endless cigarettes, and Gerald's laconic voice, and the quotidian clatter of the milkman in the mornings. But the sweep of the sky and the vast emptiness of the land was sometimes a bit much for Simon and he would find himself suddenly close to tears without knowing why.

"What about your parents?" Vera handed the teapot round the table counterclockwise like a ritual. Stephen's sister, Jane, couldn't stop staring at Simon, at his hands and his soft brown eyes with their luxurious lashes. *You've got lovely eyelashes,* she told him. She was very shy and very young and as beautiful as Stephen. *You're a very pretty boy.* "I expect Stephen's underneath your mum's feet?"

"Oh, no, not at all, he's… my mum likes him…."

"He'd best be helping out around the house and all, if he knows what's good for him." Stephen's dad's name was Robert, and where Stephen was tall and slender, Robert was short and thick, with a peculiar Northern brusqueness. "He's a lazy bugger sometimes."

"Oh, no, he's—" *Wonderful.* "He helps out."

"Your dad must be very proud of you," Vera said. It occurred to Simon that this was the sort of thing Vera would say, that she seemed to be a kind person who wanted to make others feel at ease and so she would say this, even if it wasn't necessarily true, even if she suspected otherwise.

"My parents are divorced." The food stuck in his throat, was impossible to swallow; he felt like they were all looking at him. "I never see my dad." A confession of sorts, but he didn't feel any better for all that. What made him say such a thing?

"Tea, anybody?" Vera's voice, cheerful and determined to break a silence as oppressive as the grave.

STEPHEN'S bedroom was located at the top of his parents' sprawling white house and to the rear of the property, backing onto the sea. In every respect it was a typical young man's bedroom, except the walls were lined with bookcases and every one of these was full.

"You read a lot, don't you?" Simon ran a hand over the spines. "And they're arranged in alphabetical order." He pulled out a copy of Walter Scott's *Marmion*, handsomely bound in dark red leather. "Good Christ, Stephen. Who does that?"

Stephen reached over and took the book out of his hand, placed it back on the shelf. "You do," he scoffed, "with your record albums. I've seen you. It's a bit mental." He sat down on the bed, which was carved out of oak and big enough for four people. "Do you know what tonight is?"

Simon shook his head. "Saturday?"

"It's Midsummer." Stephen tilted his head. "Don't you know anything?"

"Yeah, I read about it once. Local types—savages, really—used to get themselves all kitted out in blue woad and run about the hills screaming bloody murder." Simon raised one eyebrow. "That suit you?"

Stephen ignored him. "It used to be the biggest pagan festival in Britain, long before the Christians got hold of everything. People would imbibe hallucinogenic substances, really amazing stuff that made them think they could fly. Sometimes it was put into your skin through all these little cuts, belladonna mixed with goose grease."

"Goose grease?" Privately, Simon thought Stephen read too many books.

"And they would couple in the ploughed fields."

"What do you mean, 'couple'?" It suddenly occurred to Simon what he meant. "They'd fuck? Out in public?" The notion outraged him. "In the dark?"

"It'll be light 'til midnight tonight," Stephen said. "And it's only ten-thirty now. Want to go outdoors?"

"Are there going to be bugs?" The idea made him itch. "I don't fancy bugs." What he really wanted to ask hit closer to the truth of what they'd shared back home in London: *Do you want to couple with me in a field? Is that what you want?* He knew he would never have the courage to ask.

They slipped out into the summer night together, shoes in hand, wary of waking Stephen's parents or his sister, Jane. The night sky was lit in a wide band from the horizon to the zenith and stretching as far as Simon could see. In London, the blackness of the night was punctuated with artificial light, with street lamps and neon signs, shops and vehicles and the transitory brightness of its great pedestrian hordes. Up here, at the fringes of the world, the sky went on literally forever.

They fell into an easy step, walking side by side in silence, following the old School Road out into the fields. On any ordinary night it would have been dark but now, with the summer light at its apogee, it was nearly as bright as day. They passed an isolated farm, its tractor lying unattended by the cow shed and the farmhouse itself dark and quiet. Now and then Simon's hand, swinging naturally as he walked, would brush the back of Stephen's, and he wanted more than anything to take hold of it, to grasp and claim it, but he was afraid. Since their arrival a week ago, they had slept peaceably together every night in Stephen's bed—peaceably and chastely. Sometimes Simon lay awake, watching the play of moonlight over his friend's still face, meditating on the curve of Stephen's lips, the dimple in his chin. Stephen slept soundly and unlike Simon—who thrashed his way from one side of the bed to the other—didn't move during the night.

They found an empty field, open and unploughed: a pasture for the local sheep and horses and the occasional hairy-coated Highland cow. Simon followed Stephen down the gentle curve of the land until their progress was interrupted by a low rock wall. Stephen hopped up on this and patted the stones beside him. "Come on."

The sky was darker above the wide band of light that lit the horizon, and a sprinkling of stars showed themselves faintly against a wisp of cloud. "It's really beautiful," Simon said. "It's ever so beautiful. It's like nothing I've ever seen." The night was warm, and a slight breeze, smelling of salt and stones, found its way to them from the sea. "It might not even be real, that's what it's like."

Stephen turned to him, smiling, and laid his finger on Simon's lips. "Shh." Simon, chastened, fell silent, but then Stephen pulled something out of his pocket: a small, flat bottle. "Nicked this from my dad. He'll kill me if he finds out." He yanked the cork out with his teeth and spat it into the grass and then handed the bottle to Simon. It tasted of cream and apples and something else he couldn't put his finger on. "Mum makes it. She always has. Isn't it good?"

Simon took another pull, enjoying the pool of warmth the liquor made in his stomach. "Fantastic." He cleared his throat. "Are we ever going to talk about it?"

"Simon, look, I never—" Stephen ducked his head.

"Right." The refusal to discuss it, to even engage, stabbed him through and through. Simon hopped down off the wall and began walking quickly back the way they'd come.

"I'm going down to the beach," Stephen called, but Simon wouldn't answer. Simon watched him until he was merely a scribble on the far horizon, a dim figure haloed by the gathering sky.

Once he was out of sight, Simon turned around and followed Stephen, walking slowly with his hands jammed in his trouser pockets, his myopic eyes straining to keep Stephen's slender figure in sight. He followed the curve of the field as it swept down to the sea and Stephen as well, until both came to a decisive halt on a deserted shingle beach. He stood gazing over the water, seemingly lost in some private reverie; when Simon touched his shoulder, he started, turning round. "You came."

The supposition that he wouldn't made a painful knot in Simon's gut. "Yeah, I suppose I did." He stood gazing over the water, watching the play of lights across Gills Bay. He reached to touch Stephen's shoulder again, and this time he let his hand rest there, feeling bones and tendons shifting under the sunburned skin.

"Here." Stephen sat on the sand and indicated Simon should as well. The night was clear and warm and very beautiful, and something about the beauty of it made Simon sad. "No, move closer." Stephen reached out and tugged Simon near. "If we'd any matches—or any wood—we could have a fire. It's what they do." He nodded toward the far shore, where several brightly burning fires dotted the beach opposite. "Tonight is when the wee Orkney lasses—" He feigned a Highland accent. "—will place tied straws into the fire to see who they'll marry."

Simon tried to laugh and couldn't. "Who are you going to marry?" he whispered. He dug a hand into the fine pebbles, digging deeper and deeper, relishing the pain as the tiny stones grated against his fingers. The air smelled of salt, of sand and blooming clover; it reminded him of a song his grandmother used to sing, long ago, when he was barely out of short pants:

> *Will ye go, lassie, go,*
> *And we'll all go together*
> *To pick wild mountain thyme*
> *All around the blooming heather,*
> *Will ye go, lassie, go.*

"It's easier," Stephen murmured, not looking at him. "Isn't it? To sing instead of talking." He shifted his body so he was facing Simon. The action started a small cascade of pebbles, a tiny landslide slipping into the space between them. Simon made to speak, but Stephen laid his fingers across Simon's mouth. He turned his hand, cupping Simon's jaw, rubbing Simon's lower lip with the ball of his thumb. The kiss was slow, deliberate, keen and sensual as rain, and when Stephen pulled away, Simon pursued him, capturing his mouth and returning the kiss. They lay side by side and close together, gazing at each other, silent. Simon reached out and pulled Stephen's leg around his waist, slid his own leg between Stephen's so that their bodies were meshed together. He drew a finger down Stephen's chest, popping open the buttons of his shirt. He bent his head, his tongue drawing a hot trail on Stephen's skin, hesitating for a moment at the button of his jeans, and then—

And then.

Stephen's cock was hard, blood-warm, and throbbing, and he cried out when Simon took him in, swallowing him whole. His hands clasped the back of Simon's head, cradling his skull, holding him and guiding him and it was good, so good. Simon didn't care what other people called it. He didn't care what anyone would say. This was what he told himself as his own pleasure built along with Stephen's, driving relentlessly forward. He fumbled with his zipper and delved inside, taking himself in hand, gladly stroking the smooth column of taut flesh. The long muscles of his thighs shuddered as his completion neared, then he was there, the sky above him fracturing into brilliant starbursts washed with pallid summer night. Simon didn't make a sound, just turned his head to the side and panted through it.

The earth wheeled silently through space, and when Stephen opened his eyes, the stars had moved. "We fell asleep," he said. Simon's tousled head was lying against his shoulder, and Simon's glasses were clasped in his out-flung hand. He looked peaceful and beautiful, and in the quiet of Midsummer night, Stephen almost loved him.

4: *Bite My Hand*

JACKY STRIDE wasn't the sort of man to linger over sentimental nonsense, and as far as Simon Duckworth went, he admitted nothing apart from the usual worries. Simon was easier than most, not prey to fits of pique or expensive tastes, not interested in groupies or weird sex, or any sex at all, for that matter. The only downside that Jacky could see was Simon's unfortunate tendency to drag that Lincolnshire lout around with him wherever he went—but surmounting problems like Stephen Abednego was all in a day's work for men like Jacky. He'd see to it that Abednego was pensioned off somewhere, given a little cottage in the wilds and enough cash to keep him in paper and pens for the rest of his ridiculous life.

Jacky was as concerned with Simon's weight as Nina, and kept Simon supplied with as much high-grade cocaine as Simon needed to get him through a show. The drug effectively banished Simon's appetite and lent him an effervescent energy that music journalists were beginning to notice. Jacky was careful about who spoke to Simon and made it his business to shepherd Simon from the car to the stage and back again; if some member of the press attempted an impertinent question, Jacky's sidemen (two enormous Glaswegian footballers) simply removed the obstacle. It was a good arrangement and it suited both of them, and if certain other people thought that Jacky exerted a bit too much influence over Simon, too bad. Simon Duckworth had become a very hot property, one that was getting hotter by the minute, and Jacky intended to be there to see the apotheosis of his nascent superstar.

It wouldn't be easy—he knew this when he signed on—because Simon's lengthy tenure under Nina's thumb had made him weak, needy, and almost ridiculously helpless. Jacky worked hard to make Simon Duckworth what he was, or rather, he made him into *Abelard*, and it was Abelard who sold the records—not Stepney Simon, fucking about in Essian Street and asking his mother for pocket money. He'd be nothing without Jacky Stride to back him up, and it was in Simon's interest to remember where he came from. "All is artifice," Jacky was fond of saying. "I brought you out of Stepney and I can send you back again." No one ever doubted that Jacky meant it. Jacky meant every word he said.

Jacky came from a part of Glasgow that no one ever talked about, a narrow defile of filthy streets and boarded-up shop fronts where the very pavement seemed to exude despair and isolation. Old women scuttled quickly to and from their morning's business, and young men in scuffed Doc Martens stood watch on street corners, spoiling for a fight. It was a horrible, grim place with an overhanging stench of industry and a particular redolence of spent chip grease—a cold place with nothing to redeem its unstinting, eternal ugliness; a place that felt like the end of the world.

Jacky's father worked on the docks and spent his fourteen-hour workdays welding bits of metal together with a blowtorch. The one thing Jacky remembered about him was his hands: huge and grotesquely padded, a pair of lethal mittens. His father always seemed to be squeezing something—the handle of a cricket bat that he kept behind the kitchen door in case of burglars; the steering wheel of their old Morris, habitually broken down on cold winter mornings. His father was an enormous red-haired man with pale blue eyes; he could down a can of lager in two swallows and still have time to belch. He terrified Jacky's pale blonde mother and left her weeping at the breakfast table while Jacky got ready to go to school. Jacky didn't resemble either of them, with his small frame and his narrow, pointed face. Someone in his remote ancestry (most likely on his mother's side) had been a breeder of horses in Spain in the 15th century, but Jacky could find no evidence of this, and as for himself, horses frightened him.

As a child he imagined he'd been left by fairies or he was the son of some vanquished Highland laird, and by the time he was fourteen, he tended toward impromptu trips over to Edinburgh to see if he could find his rightful antecedents in the ancient stones of Edinburgh Castle. If he missed too much school, the truant officer would come round to their house, but only after his da had gone to work and only when his mother was there alone. The truant officer explained to Mrs. Stride how young Jacky's presence was requested and required, in the manner of old navy commissions, and hadn't he best come along to school? But Jacky was already far away, speeding toward Edinburgh on the train, and his mother had no way of reaching him, no way of making him come back. Absolutely no one, including the truant officer, wanted to travel down to Clydeside to find Everett Stride. It wasn't worth the aggro.

Jacky's mother died of breast cancer when he was seventeen and his father had a fatal stroke a year later, leaving Jacky free and orphaned. It occurred to him that he was now the sole owner of the family's entire wealth, except his father had mortgaged the house so many times that it and the land it stood on belonged to the bank. His father was scarcely in the ground before the bank officer arrived to change the locks. He found Jacky standing in the backyard and asked, "What do you want us to do with the furniture? I'm sure it's of great sentimental value, everything you have left of your parents." The bank officer was himself not a bad man, but instead a man with no imagination; he could not fathom anyone having so little filial feeling as to simply abandon the remnants of the family seat.

"I don't give a toss," Jacky replied. "Keep it yourselves or give it to the Poor Relief." What possible use could he have for the contents of this sad house? And what was in it anyway? A few broken down chairs, some cracked and pitted crockery belonging to his paternal grandmother, his father's shortwave radio.

Jacky met Simon Duckworth at a concert in Belfast after a mate of his told him about some new piano player who was making the rounds. Jacky caught the train to Stranraer and then the ferry across the Irish Sea, and when Simon appeared, Jacky was positioned as near to the front as he could possibly get without actually sitting on the stage. His initial impression of Simon was something less than ecstasy: a little fat fellow with spectacles and tiny, darting hands—a shy misanthrope who couldn't even make eye contact with his audience and who played his entire concert with his gaze firmly fixed on his piano keys. "He's a bit of a joke, isn't he?" Jacky had come across to Belfast with a girl; he hoped to get her into bed by the time they were back in Glasgow. "Look at him. He's a disaster." Afterward, he waited by the stage door for the singer to come out, standing in the freezing cold with his hands rammed into his pockets. It was vital that he meet him, vital that he speak to him and ascertain the scope and grandeur of his dreams, and whether those dreams could include him or not. It was always Jacky's way: having no dreams of his own, he tended to attach himself to the orbit of another like an aberrant satellite.

Jacky was part of a public relations firm, a hole-in-the-corner affair with the improbable name of Ponchartrain & Lytton, as in Strachey. There was no actual Ponchartrain, just as there was no Lytton, but there was a company, consisting of Jacky and his mate, Reg, a displaced Englishman from Bath who'd come north in search of whisky and cheap drugs, of which Glasgow had plenty. With his one good suit, Jacky had gone to the bank and argued with the loans officer for two hours until Barclay's agreed to release the niggardly sum of fifteen hundred pounds. For collateral Jacky supplied his father's house, already repossessed by the mortgage broker and housing a family of Irish. Apart from the literal clothes on his back, he owned nothing, but within six months, his company had signed seven up-and-coming acts and had two more on a string while Jacky pondered whether or not to reel them in. And if their lack of solid cash flow required Reg and Jacky to live in squalor in a bedsit, no one was tactless enough to mention it, least of all Reg, who did the books and who assured Jacky that they'd break even any day now.

"You planning on making a career of that?" Jacky pounced on Simon as he came through the stage door. The wan street lighting reflected off of Simon's spectacles and hid his eyes from Jacky's view. Simon shifted his weight from one foot to another, anxious to be gone.

"Sorry, mate, but the car's waiting. I've got to get back. I've got work in the morning." Unlike his singing voice, the speaking voice was soft, almost accentless, surely not the voice of one destined to shake the recording industry to its foundations. He wasn't bad looking—already Jacky's imagination was making metaphorical nips and tucks—but he'd need something more than flashy piano playing and a good voice if he was going to make it.

"You'd do yourself a favor by listening, *mate*." Jacky thrust his business card into Simon's hand. "Give me a call in the morning and we'll discuss your career." It was Jacky's preferred method of initiating communication with a potential client: provide just enough to intrigue them but not enough to give the game away. Jacky could tell that this fellow, this Simon Duckworth, had *it*, that indefinable something that hucksters like himself were forever going on about. It was there; the lad had it in spades. "I think you could go places in this business. I could take you to America." It was the standard speech that Jacky gave to everyone, but this time, he believed it.

He left the girl in Glasgow and took the train back down to London, sitting up all night because the excitement jumping in his stomach wouldn't let him sleep. Hour after hour he watched the dark landscape sliding by and allowed himself to dream and wonder. Talent like Simon Duckworth didn't come along every day; in fact, Jacky had never seen a talent like Simon, ever. He had never met anybody who believed in what he was doing so thoroughly and absolutely, a musician for whom music was a living thing and not merely the means to fill his pockets. He would, Jacky knew, play and sing supposing there was no one in the audience at all.

The train stopped at Manchester long enough to take on passengers, a few weary night travelers like himself, all of them sleepy-eyed and silent. Jacky watched them as they passed: two women in their thirties, a couple with a sleeping child, an old man leaning on a stick. He waited 'til they'd passed through the compartment, sitting with his eyes closed and listening, but there was nothing much to hear, merely the usual complaints, exclamations about seats and who was sitting where. What was it about Simon Duckworth that had impressed him? He wasn't bad to look at, and with some decent clothes and grooming, he could even be beautiful. Get rid of the National Health specs, clean up the shaggy haircut, teach the lad how to shave properly… it could be done. It would take effort and a lot of gentle prodding—Jacky sensed intuitively that Simon would bolt instantly if anyone so much as shouted in his direction—he could be made into something marvelous.

THE Picador Club in San Francisco was a hole, a dingy space set entirely underground and boasting stuffed animal heads and blow-up plastic sex dolls as decor. Simon arrived off the European flight, exhausted, jet-lagged from hell to breakfast and wondering why he was even there. His new manager, Jacky Stride, set up the booking for him, convinced it would launch Simon Duckworth—or, as Jacky insisted on calling him now, *Abelard*—right into the pop music stratosphere.

He says I'm to change my name. Simon felt stupid even mentioning it. *He says if we're to go to America I've to have a stage name, you know, like people do.*

What people? Stephen seemed unconvinced. *Americans?*

It's what they do. Jacky says I'm to have a different name. It's a bit naff, I know.

What Jacky didn't understand—at least, in Simon's opinion—was that this was futile, that America and its screaming hordes of rock fans didn't give a toss for Simon Duckworth and his pub piano, for Stepney Simon in his flannel trousers and his navy blazer and his wire-rimmed granny specs. What America wanted was Elvis and Liberace, and The Beatles.

"It's all a show," Jacky said. "The whole bloody works of it, and that's what they expect from you, a show. Stop whining like a little baby. I broke my neck to get this gig for you." They were met at the airport by a bloke named Burl with chin whiskers as sharp and bright as cactus spines and a potent smell of whisky on his breath. Burl hired out a genuine San Francisco cable car to herald their arrival, and members of his staff had been busy all night long, painting an enormous banner that Burl had hung with great care: AMERICA WELCOMES ABELARD.

"I'm not riding in that fucking thing." Simon was nearly hysterical with uncharacteristic rage, exhausted and running on cocaine and diet pills and coffee. "You can fucking shove that up your arse," he told Jacky, but not in front of Burl. Simon had been too well brought up for that. He'd never be consciously rude to someone he'd just met. He'd had manners drilled into him by Nina, who'd never hesitate to cuff him round the ears if he forgot himself, if he embarrassed himself or her in front of company.

"You'll ride in it," Jacky said, "and you'll fucking well act like it's the best thing you've ever seen, do you hear me?" His dark eyes, of so stygian a hue they seemed almost black, twinkled with covert lights and his thin lips were fixed in an ever-present smile. He nodded toward Stephen, who had already chosen a seat near the window and was pretending not to hear the hissed argument mere feet away. "Even your pet yob knows the way it ought to be." And when Simon obediently chose a seat: "Good. Now sit there and keep your fucking trap shut."

"Why do you let him talk to you that way?" Stephen elected not to see the angry tears standing in Simon's eyes. "He's a bloody employee. He works for you, not the other way round."

"You don't understand." Simon exhaled on a sob. "You don't understand the way it is."

He had waited three weeks to call the number on the card given him by Jacky Stride that night in Belfast; Jacky answered on the first ring. They met at eleven in the morning in the lobby of the old Turkish baths in Bethnal Green. Simon was nervous and overdressed in his navy school blazer and fresh-pressed flannels; the hand he offered to Jacky was wet with perspiration. When Jacky suggested a steam, Simon panicked and ran; he'd reached the corner before Jacky caught up with him. *I wasn't trying anything. Honest. It's relaxing is all. Good for your health.*

I'm not allowed. My mum wouldn't like it. There's diseases in the water and things. The place had smelled like the men's lavatory in a public house, and Simon was assaulted by a barrage of memories, the feeling of a grown man's full weight on top of him, driving the breath from his body.

I'm an idiot. I don't think I can forgive myself. Jacky's contrite mask was flawless and absolute; he had no idea why Simon had run and he didn't care. *Would you come and have a cup of tea with me somewhere?* He took Simon to a Bangladeshi tea room and ordered scones and tea and they drank their way through two pots while Jacky spoke quietly and confidentially about Simon's potential as one of the great musical artists of the next decade. *The seventies could be yours, my lad. Oh, don't deny it. You know how talented you are. I know, and all.* Neil Armstrong had just walked on the moon; anything, Jacky said, was possible now. He gave Simon just enough to arouse his interest, and later that week, when Jacky called to invite Simon out for supper, Simon went immediately. Jacky chose The Bull & Finch, a posh restaurant near Canary Wharf; he picked Simon up in his own car, calling for him at Nina and Gerald's tiny terrace house as if Simon were the heir to the throne. Jacky's car was a Mercedes borrowed from a friend, a loan contingent upon Jacky finding suitable employment for the friend's younger sister, who fancied herself a go-go dancer—but it was impressive enough for Simon, who'd never seen anything like it. As they went into the restaurant, Jacky allowed his palm to rest lightly on Simon's lower back, just long enough to unsettle and—he hoped—arouse Simon. One thing Jacky knew was people: he was adept at discovering their hidden needs and exploiting them. He discerned an emptiness in Simon and an elemental sadness that ought to respond quite nicely to his overtures and, unless he was mistaken, the lad was as randy as a badger.

"Fuck me." Simon gaped as the waiter held his chair for him and draped the napkin across his lap. "This place is a bit flash, innit?"

"Do you like it?" Jacky glanced over the wine list and ordered a bottle of Bollinger. His mate, Reg, called it "knicker remover"; Jacky hoped he'd be able to ease Simon out of his Y-fronts before the night was over.

"It's... fuck." Simon's head might as well have been mounted on gimbals. "Are you sure?"

Jacky smiled. He fancied himself suddenly dark and sleek and handsome. *Oh yes. I've never been more sure.* "I like to enjoy myself, Simon. I hope you'll enjoy yourself tonight, too."

The tramcar formed part of a motorcade that wound its way through downtown San Francisco and into Haight-Ashbury. A local radio station organized a sort of booster rally, with hundreds of young people lining the roadways, holding placards and screaming as the tram rattled into sight. "How much did Jacky pay for that lot?" Simon wondered. Jacky never minded spending money, could always find more if he needed to. He'd splashed out plenty for their dinner that night at The Bull & Finch and, later, for the hotel room he'd rented for himself and Simon. *Are you sure you don't want me to take you home?*

I don't want to go home. I want to stay here with you. He was making his own decision, or so he thought. All evening they had driven round London in Jacky's car, with good music on the radio and Jacky's hand resting gently on Simon's thigh. When Jacky stopped in a car park near Regent's Canal, Simon was ready to shrug off his habitual caution. *You've made this evening so special for me, Simon. You really have.* Even Jacky's kiss was gentle, slow and considerate, deliberately calculated to ignite a slow fire. He was in control; Jacky was always in control. He'd booked the hotel in advance, knowing that, given the right inducement, Simon would agree to go to bed with him, and Simon did. It was what Simon did afterward that set Jacky back a bit. He'd imagined waking up with Simon in his arms, and he'd imagined that this metaphorical Simon would be not unlike a sleepy kitten, malleable and soft. He hadn't imagined he would wake up to find Simon sitting by the bed, fully dressed, waiting for a cab.

Where are you going?

I thought about what you said. I think you and I might work well together.

Where are you going? Come back to bed. He reached out and caught hold of Simon's wrist.

I'm going home. The smile Simon gave him was absolutely chilling. *Don't look so sad. Did you think you popped my cherry? Sorry, darling. Somebody got there first.*

"Money well spent, my lad." Jacky's fingers pinched Simon's elbow like a vise; the tramcar rattled over a set of train tracks, the whole frame wobbling dangerously. "Now stand up and wave to them and slap a smile on your gob, all right?"

Simon waved until his arm was tired. He waved until his face hurt from smiling. He smiled until it was too dark to see.

"IT FUCKING stinks in here." Simon, dressed in silver boots, a top hat, and a kilt, stomped back and forth behind the stage, busily working himself into what Clive, their drummer, called "a right lather." Lately Simon seemed to find more excuses than ever to throw a wobbler and scream the place down. "It fucking stinks in here, all right? Hello, is anybody listening to me, or am I fucking talking to myself?" Out front the audience was shuffling their chairs around and talking, clinking glasses. The knot in Simon's stomach expanded up into his chest, choking him, and he could taste bile at the back of his throat. *Do or die, my lad.* Jacky had spent months setting up this tour—months of sweat and hard labor, spending money that Simon hadn't even made. *If you fuck this up it's all our arses in the can, you hear me?*

"If you're gonna be sick," Jacky said, "go in the loo. Don't fucking puke on the floor." He turned over the racing form he was studying and penciled something on the back of it.

"How do I look?" Simon turned to Stephen, clasping the poet's clammy hands in his own. "You're nervous, too." He tried to laugh but it came out as a strangled noise. "What are you nervous for?"

"Did you ever think it would be like this?" Stephen was seized with a sudden fit of giggling. "Back in London, writing in the bedroom? Jesus *Christ.* Did you ever think…." He hugged Simon to him fiercely, rumpling the fancy costume and knocking Simon's hat askew. "You're gonna be brilliant," he said. "You're gonna be fucking *brilliant.*"

"Am I?" Simon clung to him for just a moment longer. "Are you sure? Stephen, I think I'm going to throw up. Have I got time to go to the loo? I'm going to be sick." But there was no more time. They were announcing him: *All the way from London, here for one night only at the Picador, you know this is the place to be, M&H Records is proud to present…*

"I'm sick," Simon said it again. "I don't think I can go on. I don't think I can do it."

"Too fucking late to worry now." Jacky laid aside the racing form and, seizing the collar of Simon's costume, shoved him forward onto the stage. The Klieg lights swept the wings and Simon suddenly shrugged off his customary cloak of diffidence. "I'm gonna do this." He wondered who he was talking to. "I can do this."

His stomach clenched itself like a fist as he stepped from the darkness of the wings and into the full glare of the spotlight. The

Picador's footlights were arranged so that Simon couldn't see the faces of the people sitting at the front and only the merest glimpse of those farther back. His approach had been heralded by a smattering of polite applause but now the entire room had gone deadly quiet. Simon sat down, got up again, adjusted the piano stool, sat back down, flexed his hands and coughed. "I'm glad to be here. Thank you all for coming. It's so nice of you to turn out." He'd written up a song list beforehand but had forgotten to bring it onstage with him; Clive slipped out from behind his kit and laid a sheet of paper on the piano. Simon thanked him with a shaky smile. "I think tonight we'll give you, ah, a taste of what we've been working on. We've been very busy writing songs." He reached out with his left foot, hunting for the pedals; something backstage dropped onto the floor with a loud clank and someone in the audience laughed nervously. "I think... ah, right. Well. I'll get on with it, then."

Eyes on the keys, he started slowly, giving them "Elemental Blues" followed by "My Ten-Ton Soul," a weepy, suicidal ballad that he and Stephen had written one particularly rainy weekend back in Stepney when Simon was depressed and Stephen was missing his family up in Orkney. Simon's voice was deep and beautiful, soulful and brave, but it wasn't what the Picador Club wanted. They weren't interested in soulful melodies; they wanted rock and roll. Several people in the front of the house got up and walked to the bar and two girls standing by the door started a loud conversation. Simon watched his own hands on the keys, watched his sturdy fingers reach and press and hesitate, but a silence hung around him, quivering and ectoplasmic; the audience, growing more and more disinterested, began to murmur and move about the room, clinking glasses and resuming their muted conversations. Simon's top hat was falling over one eye and he tried to shrug it up again, and his belt was suddenly too tight, cutting him in half. He was going to be sick, was going to sick up his dinner all over the piano keys and then slink back to London in absolute disgrace and have to kill himself. He'd have to change his name and move away. He'd have to take a job in a bank, or at the greengrocer's. He would never live it down.

When Simon was eight, he was chosen from all the music pupils at his school to play a complicated Chopin nocturne at the school's end-of-term show. From a class of seventeen, Simon was the only child who could play the piece to its completion, and it was a source of great pride to his mother that he had so distinguished himself. Nina bought him a blue suit for the occasion, with matching bow tie and short trousers, and took him to the barber to get a haircut. She trimmed his fingernails and scrubbed behind his ears until the skin there shone with an unnatural illumination. Everyone at Nina's work knew about the concert, and many of them had children at the same school, children not as musically astute as Simon, or as clever. Nina told everyone that Simon was a genius, that he'd be a concert pianist when he grew up, or play the nightclub circuit from London to Aberdeen and back again. "He's always had musical gifts, our Simon." Nina made sure everyone knew about it. "He gets his cleverness from my side of the family. I've always said it. He's a very clever lad."

There were the usual violin concertos played by polite Asian students, and a fat girl whose parents were from Bavaria played something on the accordion, and then there was a break for tea and sandwiches. Nina steered Simon away from the others and gave him a talking-to: *You're ever so much cleverer than the rest of them, do you hear me? I know you'll do right. I just know you're going to be brilliant.* Her scarlet fingernails dug into Simon's fleshy arm and her eyes were hard and bright. Her breath smelled of tea and cigarettes. *You'd never let your mum down, would you?*

I'm going to be sick, was all Simon could think to say. *I feel like I've got to vomit.*

Don't be stupid. Don't be such a baby.

The auditorium was hushed when Simon sat at the piano; he could hear the radiators clicking at the back, and the rustle of organza dresses, and the squeaking of some man's new leather shoes. He squinted down at Nina, sitting in the middle of the first row. His mother was smiling tightly, her teeth clenched behind her painted lips and her hands crushed together in her lap. *You'd never let your mum down, would you?*

Simon began to play. He played the piece from memory, easily negotiating the melody and adding creative flourishes and decorations, showing off. A burst of sweat bloomed on his forehead and slid inexorably toward his eyes; he faltered and began to lose the tempo and his fingers slipped on the keys. Nina's hands tightened, clutched each other, released and slid along the sides of her skirt. *You'd never let your mum down, would you?*

He was sweating furiously, a great effusion of moisture that oozed out from under his tight-fitting collar and slid down between his shoulder blades. The piano keys swam before his eyes as the torture went on and on; he could see Nina nodding and smiling, glancing nervously around her. Some of the other parents began to whisper; a woman sitting behind Nina tittered into her hand. Simon ended the nocturne with a final, decisive crash of chords and ran from the stage in tears. He stormed past his music teacher and his mother and out into the car, where he crawled under a lap rug on the floor.

I don't know how you could have made such a bollocks of it, was all Nina said.

A T THE intermission Simon rose from the piano and stalked backstage. He was sweating heavily, his costume askew and the top hat sliding down his forehead; between Simon's nervousness and the audience's disinterest, the first set had not gone well. "I'm not going back out there," he said. "They aren't fucking listening to me. All they fucking care about is talking and drinking. Fuck the lot of them. They can fuck off, and all."

Jacky Stride bore down on him and dragged him into the green room, sat him in a chair. The door was firmly closed between Simon and the others, but when Simon came back out, he was red-eyed and repentant, and Jacky was grimly smiling. Simon, seated at the piano for the second half, dispensed at once with weepy ballads and launched into "Do It or Don't," a true rock and roll rave-up. He followed with "Bite My Hand" and climbed onto the piano and waved his arms for the audience to sing along. He was dazzling and frenetic, dancing and banging a tambourine, running up and down the stage and, finally, bending double and lifting his kilt to expose his naked backside. Stephen had never seen this Simon: the man currently on the stage bore no resemblance to his shy, introverted friend—the man who, even in the company of other blokes, undressed in total darkness because being seen in his underwear embarrassed him.

"He's fucking wired," Al said to Stephen. Al was one of the roadies hired for the tour. "What's he on?"

"Three guesses," Stephen said. But it didn't matter: people had stopped talking, had stopped roaming round the room, had stopped whispering and laughing and lighting up cigarettes. They had eyes only for the stage and the man on it, the shy Englishman from Stepney who handled the piano like Chopin on drugs.

"He's gone mental," Al replied. "He's fucking *mental*."

In the end, Simon did everything that could possibly be done to win them over. He screamed and shouted; he danced on the piano; he sang and played his heart out. When at last he ran backstage, his fingers streaked in blood, he had won them. He had won them over.

"Take a fucking look at this, my lads." Flying home, Jacky handed around a copy of the San Francisco *Chronicle*: ABERLARD: HE WILL ROCK YOU! As soon as they landed in London, he whisked Simon away to some unknown destination in a limousine he'd hired just for the two of them.

"Getting a bit ahead of himself, isn't he?" Al waited with Stephen for their luggage at the arrivals carousel. "I mean, you do the other half, don't you? What's Jacky doing, taking him away like that?"

"He's not taking him away," Stephen replied. "He's been gone awhile." He knew that at least some of this was his fault, more or less, but, knowing what Simon wanted from him and what he expected, Stephen couldn't make himself give in. There was an intensity in Simon that frightened him, a need to manipulate most situations according to some inner script he was compelled to follow. He was no longer Stepney Simon. He was turning into a rock star.

5: *Sixpence for the Meter*

JACKY STRIDE made sure to be there when the designer's box arrived: monogrammed, exquisite, and tied with a pale blue ribbon, it could hardly be mistaken. It could be a monstrous box of flowers (which Simon loved and never got from anyone), except it was far too large. Curious that it should arrive in this place when everything that Simon needed always traveled with him, but Jacky knew what he was doing, and if Jacky thought Simon needed whatever was in the box, then that was that. Better that Simon should receive it here than somewhere far more public—a hotel lobby or a restaurant, perhaps. Lately Simon's moods had become dangerously unstable and he was liable to erupt in a fit of temper at any time, night or morning. When this occurred, he was transformed: quiet, biddable Simon Duckworth turned into someone nobody wanted to admit they knew, a shrieking parody of himself, red-faced and enraged. At other times he became ominously quiet and hid for hours in his dressing room or sat by himself on the airplane, eschewing any company, even Jacky's. Once, when Jacky, Stephen, and the others were sitting round the swimming pool at a California hotel, Simon had suddenly appeared, clad in a bulky white bathrobe. He marched past them and stopped at the edge of the pool, where he stood for some moments staring down into the water.

Simon, what are you doing? Stephen laid aside his book, curious. *Simon? Are you going to have a swim?*

Simon had turned and stared at him like he'd never seen him before. *Why?*

I'll go in with you.

Simon smiled. *I've just taken seventy-five Valium.*

Stephen stared at him, the significance of Simon's words suddenly penetrating his consciousness. *I think you should see a doctor.*

Simon jumped into the pool. Jacky—to his credit and Stephen's eternal shock—plunged in after him and hauled him out while Clive called an ambulance. Even after doctors pumped his stomach, Simon spent three days in hospital, hovering near death.

They were all standing round Simon's dressing room, watching the box as it was carried in, cradled in the arms of a delivery boy, who handled it with the sacerdotal reverence normally reserved for holy relics. Stephen was sitting by the door, drinking Schlitz and already half-pissed, but he would keep going until he couldn't feel his lips. Simon had been in a filthy mood all day, swearing at everyone, screaming obscenities. "I don't see why we've got to play in fucking *Biloxi*. What's in fucking Biloxi? An audience full of fat tobacco farmers and their ugly fucking sisters." Earlier, Simon had thrown a tantrum when a cup of tea arrived and it was cold. He flung the cup at Jacky, who smiled thinly and ordered them all out. Jacky could be heard screaming at Simon behind the closed door: "...fucking fat whining little *cunt*, don't you forget where you came from!" This was Jacky at his most restrained: so far on the tour (West Virginia to Maryland, briefly up to Delaware and back to Washington, D.C., then down along the eastern seaboard to the Deep South) Simon had sported a black eye, a fat lip, and had three pairs of spectacles broken. Jacky appeared late one afternoon with his arm suspended in a sling and one eye swollen shut.

"Love's young dream, innit?" Clive, the drummer, commented sourly to Stephen. "Wonder which one will kill the other? My money's on Simon."

Stephen watched Simon's eyes flicker to Jacky as the huge box landed in his lap. "What's this?" Simon burrowed through the snowdrift of tissue paper, lifting out a costume: a pair of trousers and a jumper, knit up of myriad parti-color patches.

"It's a Harlequin," someone said. "Ooooh, it's lovely." Stephen recognized it, an iconic form that decorated sundry consumer goods—pulp romances from America, sultana biscuits, a certain brand of matches that his mother often used to light the morning fire. The image reminded him of Pierrot pictures, the weeping clown standing all alone with his jumper sleeves drawn down, waiting in the rain.

"There's a hat—" Simon pulled it from the box, fitting it on his head; it sat at a curious angle, quivering like something shot from a sweets trolley in a restaurant. "What will Biloxi think?"

Biloxi wasn't thinking anything in particular, having seen its share of poncing madmen already. Twice a year the circus came around, shuffling its weary feet through town, dragging its scabby lions and its tired elephants behind it, and now and then some street preacher decided to rent himself a tent and host a big revival. There were no revival meetings just this minute and the circus had been three days gone when Simon and his lot rolled into town: no brightly colored banners snapping in the wind, just Simon and Stephen, Simon's mother, and Jacky Stride. The band and Simon rode up and down the Gulf coast in an ancient van, followed by a lorry that Jacky bought from an old man in West Virginia who had used it for hauling garbage; Clive the drummer and the sound men were made to ride with the equipment to ensure its safety.

Considering Simon's reception in America, there should have been a fleet of gleaming chartered vehicles and a bus for Simon and his mother, but there wasn't any money. The manager of the Picador Club in San Francisco paid the monumental sum of five hundred American dollars to Jacky for the privilege of watching Simon Duckworth leap over a piano, lodging and expenses extra. Jacky, to his credit, had screeched into the phone and got them some hotel rooms (they'd had to double up and share, and the contents of the minibar had been thoughtfully expunged well in advance of their arrival) and a couple of interviews with sympathetic music journalists. Simon was on his best behavior: congenial and warm, eminently forthcoming with details of his early life, his and Stephen's writing habits, their great friendship. Stephen came back to their rooms late in the day and heard Simon retching in the bathroom, but that was normal. Everyone was saying how this tour would make or break Simon Duckworth in America, and so what if Simon was a little terrified?

"I had it made especially for you," Jacky said. "He can do more if we want them, in different colors." Stephen noticed the judicious use of the royal "we"—but it wasn't Jacky who'd be wearing that outrageous getup; it wasn't Jacky who'd be made to go onstage looking like a freak. Stephen thought fondly of the days when Simon played the pubs, dressed in his old jeans and a clean white shirt, the spotlights glinting gently off his spectacles. So far on this tour, Simon had appeared in a fuzzy orange something; a suit of leather bondage gear, complete with dog collar; the costume of an eighteenth-century dueling fop; and a fluorescent pink and purple kilt with a yellow plastic sporran. As far as wardrobes went, Jacky was taking his cues from singers like David Bowie and Gary Glitter, echoing Bowie's Ziggy Stardust phase with silver capes and tall, extravagantly winged boots in rainbow hues. *You've got to get them to notice you,* Jacky had said. *Get their fucking eyes off each other and onto you, make them forget everything else.*

Stephen opened another Schlitz and the crowd dispersed, each member of the crew heading off to his or her appointed task. The sound men were already out front, checking cables and amps. "Don't you like it, Stephen?" Simon draped it over one arm in the manner of a Continental waiter with a tablecloth. But Stephen only smiled, fading back into the shadows, as time and circumstance had trained him to do. They had come a long way from writing songs in Nina's dingy Stepney kitchen, and Stephen ought to be glad of it, but instead, his inner eye seemed to be forever fixed upon the spectacle of Simon being dragged up from the bottom of the swimming pool, limp and choking, telling anyone who'd listen that he just wanted to die.

IT HAPPENED the same night Simon played Biloxi. He'd come offstage, exhausted but elated, and found three young men waiting in the wings for him. They were poorly dressed but clean, with the accents and demeanor of Mississippi farm boys, and Simon gladly signed his autograph for them, offered copies of his latest album, and shook their hands. He pretended not to understand when they sniggered amongst themselves, their hands half hiding their mouths: *You a fag, man?* He chatted and joked with them about rural life and told them how Stephen's father was a farmer, and he gave them all free tickets to the next night's concert in Tupelo. As far as Simon knew, that was the end of it.

He was lying in his bed asleep, tucked under the eaves of an old hotel; he'd had a fight with Jacky and kicked him out, and Jacky had gone downstairs to book himself another room. Nothing was amiss. He'd managed to drift off and he was dreaming about some talk he'd had with Gerald, and in the dream, it seemed that Gerald had been emptying eternal rubbish bins. A man came round the corner, wearing a Harlequin costume like the one Simon had worn onstage, but where the man's eyes should have been there were only smoking dark holes. Simon woke up abruptly, without his usual smooth transition between sleep and waking, and they were in his room. There were three of them, wearing black skiing masks or women's tights with holes cut out for the eyes. They didn't speak. At first he thought they might be fans or a party of revelers who'd mistaken his room for their own. He sat up and fumbled on the bedside table for his glasses.

"What do you want?"

You a fag, man? Is that what you are? A dirty little faggot?

He thought they meant to rob him, so he opened the nightstand, showed them where his wallet was. He raised his hands above his head to demonstrate that he had no violent intentions, but they ignored him. He tried to speak to them, but they didn't answer. *You can have my money; I don't mind. Look, I'll give it to you. I'll give you whatever you want.* They beat him with a horrible inevitability, and he curled into a fetal crouch and tried to keep away from them, tried to protect his face, shield his hands. He was terrified they'd break his fingers, snap his hands off at the wrists, destroy him. He'd do anything if it would make them go away. He'd try to reason with them, cajole them into clemency. *Listen, lads, I'm just like you. I hate this poncing nancy-boy rubbish as much as you do. Let's have a few cans and talk about it.* He had some absurd notion that he could explain himself and they would all be friends. It would all be perfectly fine. No one needed to get hurt. He imagined he'd sit round the hotel bar with them, and they'd all have a drink and laugh about it, and they'd take their masks off so he could see their faces. They'd be ordinary blokes. They'd be just like him.

They made a mask for him of blood and snot and the effluent of his own savaged body. He'd lain still on the carpet for what seemed like hours, and when the chambermaid came in to change the bed, she found him that way, bloodied and mute. His hands were tucked into his armpits, and his spectacles were smashed. Stephen found them underneath the nightstand, twisted and broken. Nothing serious, the doctor in Casualty said, but there was significant bruising on various parts of his body.

"They did this?" Stephen sat with Simon in the treatment room, holding his hand. "The men who attacked him, I mean."

The Casualty officer was young and seemed tired beyond his years. "No, these contusions are older than that—years, even a decade old." He indicated that Stephen should follow him down the hall. "The x-rays indicate a cracked collarbone—it's since healed, of course—and some evidence of blows to the head, but nothing that would cause lasting damage." The facial contusions wanted watching, did Simon have someone to stay with him?

"I'll stay with him," Stephen said. Jacky kept trying to get near Simon but Stephen was adamant, even savage: *If you lay one finger on him I'll kill you. I will. I'll bash your fucking head in. Now leave him alone.*

I've as much right to see him as you do. Now get out of the way.

After what you did to him? Get your kicks out of knocking him around, do you?

Jacky seemed genuinely puzzled at this accusation, and—surprisingly—rather hurt. *I don't know what you're talking about. I don't hit him. For Christ's sake! I'm in love with him. I'd never hurt him.* When Stephen finally relented, Jacky sat beside Simon's bed for a long time, holding his hand and talking quietly. Now and then he would reach out for Simon, bestowing some caress—a touch, a gentle kiss—and the sight of it went through Stephen like a spear. He carefully avoided examining his own reactions. It wasn't jealousy he felt, not as such. His tenderness toward Simon had always been passionate, almost violent, and now this feeling was redoubled because Simon had been hurt.

Jacky came out of Simon's room, his face wet. Stephen begrudged the Scotsman his tears, resented them bitterly, and was careful to look the other way. "He's asking for you. He wants you." When the Casualty officer released Simon into Stephen's care, Jacky was waiting. "You take care of him. Don't you let anything happen to him. If he gets hurt again, I swear to God, I'll fuckin' dile you. You hear me?"

Stephen nodded. Even Jacky's promise of a Glasgow smile had little effect. He would take care of Simon. He would make sure that nothing bad happened to him, that no one else could ever hurt him.

"Tell me what happened." Back at the hotel, Stephen sat with him, waiting for the drugs to take hold and lessen Simon's pain. "Did they say anything?"

Simon turned his face and stared at Stephen like he'd never seen him before. The bruises underneath his eyes seemed to deepen the eye sockets, turn them into empty holes. The flesh around Simon's mouth was taut and swollen, and his lips were marred with tiny blood-filled cracks. "Simon... please." He laid his palm on Simon's chest, hoping that this contact between them might elicit some response. Simon's breath lifted Stephen's hand and lowered it, and the thud of Simon's heart was regular and anticipated, but apart from that, there was nothing. Simon was absolutely mute, his expression reproachful, a supplication. Stephen wondered if he ought to call someone, arrange for psychiatric help, but he knew that such decisions were no longer his to make. Finally, he called Jacky Stride.

"I think we should get someone to help him."

"What?" It sounded like a party was going on in Jacky's hotel room; Stephen couldn't imagine why.

"He needs help. He needs to have the doctor."

"He's already had the doctor, for chrissakes. Leave him be." There were muffled noises in the background, a woman's laughter, and then Jacky came back on. "What he needs is rest. There's still the show in Tupelo and we can't back out of it. He's got to go on."

A pulse of anger boomed in Stephen's chest. "He can't go on, dammit. He won't even talk, let alone sing. What the hell do you think he is, a wind-up soldier?"

Jacky called out to someone in the room, told them to have themselves another, *Don't go yet, there's still lots to discuss.* "And listen, boyo: don't you say one fucking word about this to anyone. It's all I can do to keep this out of the fucking papers. Do you hear me?" And then, "He does that sometimes... he'll just stop talking. It's nothing to worry about. He'll come out of it, he always does." There was a pause, and when Jacky spoke again, his voice was quiet, dangerous: "I'm having it taken care of. Those fuckers aren't getting away with this. I'll make sure they get what's coming to them."

"What do you mean?" Stephen's palms were suddenly clammy. "You're not going to do anything, are you?"

"Not me personally," Jacky assured him. "But I know some lads who'll see to it that they get a nice little frightener."

Stephen wanted to ask him, *Are you sure that's a good idea,* but didn't think it worth the bother. Quietly, gently, he laid the phone back in the cradle and went to sit with Simon.

The day before they left to finish out the tour, Jacky handed Stephen a copy of the local newspaper. The headline read BILOXI BOYS DEAD IN FIERY CRASH, and underneath were mug shots of three nondescript young men, each wearing the same bewildered expression. "Sometimes you have to give these fuckwits a bit of a malky, by the way." He patted Stephen's shoulder and grinned. "Don't take on so. You look like a half-shut knife."

DESPITE his elective muteness, Simon was still able to sing, and so singing was what he did, every night for the rest of the tour. That the performances continue was very important: Simon's latest record had been released and had immediately zoomed to number one on the American pop charts, easing the way for Jacky to book another, entirely new series of concerts in America. But not "big" America—not New York or Los Angeles; Simon was now slowly playing his way south from Pennsylvania, stopping at places called Blue Balls and Intercourse, Ditch and Possum Trot and Pole. Jacky seemed to think that this leg of the tour warranted a change in wardrobe, and so Simon was outfitted as a cowboy, a mechanic, a lorry driver, and a Civil War foot soldier. Stephen thought these costumes lovely and in keeping with the album's theme, but nothing he said or did could make Simon talk or smile. His features seemed fixed in an expression of eternal soberness and he would occasionally turn his gaze to Stephen, watching him with the intensity of a hunted animal.

The only sound Simon made was while he was onstage, and it lasted only for the duration of the concert. As soon as Simon came off, he was surrounded by a veritable army of sycophants who toweled him off, who stripped the sodden costumes from his body and cleaned his spattered spectacles. All of this occurred in an eerie silence, as though these acolytes were engaged in the servicing of some obscure monarch. Simon would often seek out Stephen with his eyes, holding Stephen's gaze until the attendants left. Stephen was certain Simon was just about to speak to him, and sometimes Simon's mouth opened, as though he was testing the air on his tongue—but Simon would not speak. Apart from looking at him, Simon did nothing at all.

Tell me. Stephen slept next to him on top of the covers of Simon's hotel bed and sat with him during the day, waiting for Simon to tell him what had happened, to divulge whatever awful secret he was keeping jealously to himself. He and Jacky had attempted to file a report with the local police but Simon refused, sometimes with violent gestures, and so the plan was abandoned. *You can tell me. I'll listen, you know I will.*

The tour ended with a return to Mississippi, in a small town where the locals drove pickup trucks and drank Pabst Blue Ribbon and absolutely no one had ever heard of Abelard. There was a chain-link cage erected around the stage, and the local people hurled rubbish and empty bottles at Simon all throughout the show. Because of the cage, the bottles missed their target, which seemed to infuriate the audience. They screamed abuse and curses as Simon rested between sets, drinking from a water bottle that had been set out for him on the piano, his eyes fixed and steadfast on the keys. Jacky was fairly spitting with rage: by the time Simon played the final encore, the area immediately in front of the stage was awash in broken glass, bits of hot dog, and cigarette ends. Jacky screamed at the good ol' boy promoter until his voice gave out completely. "...sick and *fucking* tired of this fucking *bullshit*... call this an arena?" Stephen caught up with Jacky just outside the stage door; Jacky was furiously gulping from a bottle of throat solution and walking in circles.

"I think we should talk about Simon."

Jacky stared at him, gestured at his throat, and shrugged.

"He's tired, Jack. He's worn out. He could do worse now than a long rest."

Jacky looked at Stephen for a long time, then swallowed twice; it seemed to hurt him. "What have you got in mind?" His voice was little more than a whispered croak. For the first time, Stephen glimpsed something of Jacky's brutal loyalty to Simon, and it shocked him. It had always been the two of them, him and Simon, chasing down their dream together, but now it was different. Now it was Jacky and Simon.

"I thought we could probably rent a place in one of these little towns and just relax for a while."

Jacky's smooth face was expressionless. "You and him?"

"Well, unless—"

"Fine." Jacky turned to go and then suddenly turned back. He laid the bottle of throat tonic on the roof of a nearby car. "I know what you're thinking," he whispered. "You're thinking something daft and sentimental like your tender care will save him." His dark eyes played over Stephen's face. He looked every bit as tired as Simon did. "You think it will be like it was before, back there in Stepney, in the old days? Let me tell you something: he's set himself on a particular road, my lad. He's been on it all his life, long before me and long before you." He paused, glancing at the limo where Simon sat alone, staring ahead of him at nothing. The wash of neon from the roadhouse painted the lenses of Simon's spectacles in strange, hallucinatory colors. Simon's hands were lying on his knees, the fingers flickering now and then, a pattern of subtle movements. Simon was playing for an audience of one. "This road's going straight down and I very much doubt there's anything you or I can do to stop it."

"Simon needs a rest." Stephen felt as though he were asking permission, and he hated himself for it; Jacky Stride didn't own Simon, had no real say in what Simon did or where he went.

"We all need a rest," Jacky snapped. His face softened. "All right, go on, then. There's nothing happening right now that can't wait."

"Thank you," Stephen said. He was, he realized, absurdly grateful. "I promise you, I will take good care of him."

"Yeah?" Jacky stepped close to him, so close that there was barely a hand's breadth between their bodies. He and Stephen were of a height; at this proximity, they were gazing directly into each other's eyes. Jacky reached out and wrapped his palm around the nape of Stephen's neck, pulling Stephen's face close to his own. "And who's going to take care of you?"

His mouth was hot, beautifully deft, and the tip of his tongue slipped between Stephen's parted lips and retracted, quick as a thought. For a moment Stephen hesitated, shocked, then relented and gave himself to the caress. Jacky released him and stepped back, smiling. "Right," he whispered. "Thought as much." And just like that, he was gone. Stephen shrugged. What the hell. It was only rock and roll, wasn't it?

"It's all right now, yeah?" Stephen got into the limo and wrapped his arm round Simon's shoulders. "It'll be just like the old days, you and me." His lips burned with the impress of Jacky's kiss and he wondered if Simon had seen them. "We'll have ourselves a brilliant holiday, the two of us."

Simon didn't move, didn't try to cling to Stephen. He remained as still and silent as a stone.

STEPHEN was sitting in a rocking chair on the front porch of their hired lodgings, listening to the wind. Simon came outside to sit with him, even though the bright sunlight bothered him. Stephen had to fetch Simon's prescription sunglasses and put them on Simon's face, or Simon would sit there squinting into the harsh daylight like a weak-eyed winter animal. The spectacles were dark and shaped like rectangles, and they effectively hid Simon's soft brown eyes. "Are you hungry?" Stephen asked this three times daily, but Simon never answered him, and so Stephen made up plates of sandwiches and fruit, bread and cold meats and cheese. Simon obediently ate whatever Stephen put in front of him, without complaint. There were no servants here to tend them—Stephen didn't want that—but there was a curious pleasure in doing things for Simon and himself, in returning, however briefly, to a way of life they'd known years before in Stepney. Stephen found himself relishing this time alone with Simon, without the press of fans, without reporters nosing round and asking awkward questions. There were no flashbulbs popping in Simon's face, no Jacky Stride. But, to be honest, there was no Simon, either—just a silent stranger wearing Simon's face and Simon's body.

They had been here in this rented Mississippi farmhouse for a week, and Stephen had thus far tried everything to make Simon talk: pleading, begging, whispering. At night, he lay awake next to Simon and listened, straining his ears into the darkness, but Simon never murmured, not even in his dreams. When Stephen finally fell asleep in the wee hours of the morning, he dreamt that he and Simon were having a lengthy conversation about some complicated subject—but he woke to find Simon as silent as ever. Sometimes, Simon would be leaning over Stephen, looking down at him and waiting—for what? Perhaps he was waiting for Stephen to wake up and make his breakfast, even though Simon was in full possession of his faculties and could negotiate his way round any kitchen, if he needed to. What was he waiting for?

They got letters from Nina and from Gerald, together and separately. Nina wrote to say she was redoing all the living room in pale yellow and that she had bought new curtains. Gerald told Simon that his old Mini still ran as good as ever but was difficult to start in the mornings. Gerald had lumbago, and Nina's blood pressure kept going up and down, the result of her heavy smoking. They told him that sixty-six people had died in a stairway crush at a football game in Glasgow, and that three thousand people had fled Northern Ireland because of the ongoing violence, and that unemployment, according to the experts, was at an all-time postwar high. Simon wouldn't sit and answer the mail, so Stephen did it for him, writing cheery messages on Mississippi postcards and signing both their names, his and Simon's, at the bottom. They were an unwitting burlesque show, a two-man comedy act, played out over a slow and torturous and unbearably hot American landscape.

During the third week of their confinement (this was how Stephen began referring to it, in his own mind), Stephen acquired a piano from an antiques store in town and occupied himself by trying to pick out tunes on it. He could only play a few bars of "I'm in the Mood for Love" and so he played it over and over, the melody jagged and ugly and halting. *I'm in the—mood for—love... I'm in the—mood for... love...* Finally he felt Simon's weight compress the piano bench, Simon's thigh against his own as Simon pushed him over to make room. While Simon played, Stephen merely watched, his hands lying in his lap, enthralled by the spectacle of music being poured from such a wrecked and ruined vessel.

When Simon stopped, he motioned that Stephen should put his hands on the keys; Simon then laid his own hands on top, and they played in this fashion for a while, with Simon's small fingers compressing Stephen's longer ones, showing him the notes, imprinting the music on his sense memory. In this way Stephen played "Lay Down, Sally" and "Lady Madonna" and "Son of a Preacher Man." Even with Simon's expert guidance, he managed to play badly, but Simon laughed. It was silent laughter, with no sound save the errant rasp of his breath, a noise eerily like weeping. Perhaps, Stephen reasoned, Simon might talk if Stephen showed him how—like Simon's hands on top of Stephen's, pressing down the proper keys and making music. Perhaps Stephen could lend him words. Wasn't that what Stephen always did?

That night Simon lay beside him, his body rising and falling with his breaths while the crickets poured their plaintive music into the dark. "I wish I knew what you were thinking." Stephen flipped his pillow over, searching for an elusive cool patch, waiting for a decrease in temperature that never came. The night's heat lay over them like a smothering blanket, an invisible wall bearing down until even gravity seemed magnified to an untenable degree.

Simon reached out and traced the contours of Stephen's mouth with his fingertips, his touch gentle and butterfly-light. It tickled, and Stephen laughed, pulling away. "Are you trying to see how much torture I'll stand before I break? Is that it?" He caught hold of Simon's hand and slowly, deliberately, licked the palm and the delicate web between Simon's fingers. There was enough ambient light for him to see that this was affecting Simon and to know that he should stop, at least long enough to reconsider. The heat was doing things to him, making him slack and easy in his own skin, and he lay back on the bed and opened his arms to Simon, who did not speak but merely lay astride him, gazing down at him, his face beautiful and strange and somber in the moonlight. "Kiss me."

6: *Friday Night Madness*

STEPHEN hadn't played guitar since his school days back in Grimsby but he had found an old Gibson acoustic at an antiques store in town, and picking out fragments of the few tunes he knew helped fill the time—and it relaxed him while he sat on the front porch looking out over the tobacco fields. All day long, Japanese beetles flew themselves into the side of the house, and the cicadas chattered in the trees until Stephen was drugged with noise and heat. He sucked back whatever cold drinks he could lay his hands on: lemonade and Pepsi, or the pissy American beer that he'd grown fond of. He picked his guitar and drank Pabst Blue Ribbon and listened to the beetles killing themselves against the shed. He could hear Simon rattling around inside the house, a series of low noises just below the cicadas and the beetles, and then the screen door opened and Simon was standing on the porch, barefoot and wearing a pair of athletic shorts. His nose, badly sunburned, was red and peeling and so was his forehead. He squinted at Stephen, holding out an empty pitcher. "There's no ice."

Stephen twanged on his guitar so hard that the "A" string snapped; the rocking chair was still rocking as he leapt at Simon. His hands cupped Simon's face and two of his fingers found their way into Simon's mouth. "You said something."

Simon pushed Stephen's hand away, regarding him queerly. "Of course I did." He seemed surprised. "Are you all right?"

At first Stephen thought he was joking—that Simon was just having him on, taking the piss out of him. "Simon, you haven't uttered a word for weeks." Not precisely true, since Simon had been singing, but singing wasn't the same as talking. Wasn't it true that people who had speech impediments—like stuttering—could sing, and some of them brilliantly? Singing was too easy for Simon, a way to avoid the exigencies of everyday life. Simon would probably sing his way through hell if he had to.

"You must be daft." Simon scratched at his peeling forehead and his red nose. "I've been talking all this time—where the hell have you been?" And in that moment—in that awful moment, a realization so piercing and so cogent spilled across his features. Simon's expression slid right off his face. The pitcher, falling endlessly like a slow film, shattered at his feet. "When I was a lad, my dad's friend raped me." His face jerked and shuddered, searching for the right configuration of features. "It was in the men's at this club in Glasgow. I went in there to take a piss." His mouth worked soundlessly for a moment. "He held me down and raped me."

He turned abruptly and went back into the house and Stephen went after him. Simon's feet were cut and bleeding—had he stepped in broken glass?—and he left bloody footprints behind him, a trail for Stephen to follow. "Simon—" Stephen's voice bounced off the walls, fighting with the cicada noises and the ceiling fan. "Jesus Christ, Simon, just stay there, don't move." Stephen reached him at last, skidding to his knees in Simon's blood. There was so much blood, and literary Stephen was reminded of that scene from *Tender is the Night*: Nicole hiding in the bathroom while the party went on around her, shuddering alone with a pile of bloodstained sheets.

"Where have I been?" Simon kept asking this over and over while Stephen searched the local phonebook for a doctor. There were dozens of doctors listed; Stephen couldn't decide which one to choose. For such a rural area, there was an astonishing array of podiatrists and gynecologists, psychiatrists and dentists. Simon sat on the bathroom floor, waiting, and Stephen sat with him, holding on to him while the doctor—an elderly man with tufts of silvery hair growing out his nostrils—stitched up his torn and bleeding feet. The doctor's suture thread was drawn through Simon's flesh again and again, and made a wooden sort of pain, like bared teeth biting on a stick. Stephen thought about old cowboy movies, the sort he liked to look at on Saturday afternoons at the pictures: lean and stringy men with bullet wounds, biting on a piece of wood or leather or stupefied with alcohol. All the Grimsby lads loved the Westerns, especially the ones with Clint Eastwood and his slitted eyes. "Chinese Clint," the lads would say, because they knew it irritated Stephen, who hid up in his bedroom and practiced squinting in front of his mirror. "What's wrong with your eyes?" his mother asked. "Have you got something in your eyes?" Stephen went to school with a kerchief round his neck like Clint, until Marion Flatt asked him if it was a nappy.

That was the trouble with Grimsby: you couldn't have any fun with anything or you'd get laughed at. There was no room to be even a little different; there was no place for anything besides the kind of grinding normalcy that typified life in the North, and so Stephen hid all the poems he ever wrote, shoving them underneath his mattress. Where was poetry, in Grimsby? Where was it, in Orkney? He couldn't ever imagine telling his father—the stolid herdsman—that he'd written a sonnet, nor could he divulge such to his mother, who worked very hard and had done all her life. Poetry was something written in the birthday card you gave your grandmother, or something uttered by the vicar who saw your mortal remains into the ground.

Simon bore the doctor's ministrations in silence, but when the last stitch was in, he excused himself politely, crawled over to the toilet, and hung over the bowl for some time, vomiting. The doctor didn't even blink. "Fifty dollars," he said to Stephen. "And I don't usually make house calls." Stephen peeled off an American fifty-dollar bill and gave it to him along with a bottle of beer, which the doctor downed in one thirsty swallow, belching his thanks at the end. He wrote a prescription for Valium and gave it to Stephen without another word, stepping neatly over the broken pitcher on the porch.

"DID you tell anyone after it happened? Your mum?" Stephen forced himself to speak softly, convinced that a shout would cause the world around them to shatter like an egg. "Did you see a doctor?" They were inside the house now, and the day's oppressive heat had given way to a hellacious thunderstorm that rattled the window glass and lit up the tobacco fields like a strobe light. Simon lay tumbled against Stephen on the couch, his head resting on Stephen's shoulder, his arm round Stephen's waist; his bandaged feet gleamed white in the interrupted darkness. His glasses were on the coffee table, unattended: without them, he looked younger, more vulnerable, and his face was streaked with drying tears.

Stephen's arm tightened round him. "Please tell me."

"I was up in Glasgow, visiting my father." *Come up and see your old dad this weekend, eh? It'll be just us lads. We'll have a grand time.* "He'd moved up there, after the divorce. He asked me to come and stay. He'd got permission to take me out of school, even." *I'm playing in a band, now. Eh, that'd be a treat for you, wouldn't it? Make it a busman's holiday. Just you and me.* "I went into the loo, during the break." *Watch out for the splash... when you get your dick out.* "My.... Gus, his name was." He'd expected, after all this time, that talking about it would be easier—that the horror of it would eventually wear away. His heart thudded in his chest and his throat was tight—not with tears, nor with anything like sorrow. He was angry, and this surprised him. He hadn't expected to be so angry. He hadn't anticipated rage. "He pushed me down on the floor."

"Simon, you don't have to—"

"He pushed me down on the floor." He continued as if Stephen hadn't spoken. "I think he'd his knee in my back. It felt like that, anyway." His voice sounded dry and cold and utterly without emotion. He recited the details of his own corruption like a recipe. "He got my trousers down and he—" His throat closed, as though gripped by an invisible hand. "It really, really hurt." He spoke with an effort. "After he was done with me, he got up and washed his hands at the sink." Whistling, grinning at himself in the mirror, combing his hair. "He walked away and left me there on the floor. I don't know how I got dressed. I don't really remember much about it. The next thing I remember is being on the train, on my way back down to London. I was bleeding. I kept... I kept having to go in the loo on the train and check... you know, myself. I put paper up there, to soak up the blood." He disposed of the bloodied lavatory tissue, flushing it away, watching carefully to be sure it all went, washing his hands and scrubbing under his fingernails. "I thought maybe it would never stop. I remember thinking I was a girl now. He'd made me into a girl, what he'd done. I thought I'd bleed all the time, like a girl, when they get their periods. I wondered how I was going to tell Mum."

"Tell her what he'd done, you mean?"

"No. Tell her that I'd been changed into a girl and she'd have to… that she'd no son anymore." He turned his head and looked at Stephen carefully. "I thought if I kept quiet about it, she might not notice. She might not… be bothered."

They sat in silence for a while and listened to the rain drumming on the roof, and counted the intervals between lightning and thunder. "Does anyone else know?" Stephen felt old, as if eons had slipped by without his noticing. "Have you told anyone?"

"My mum still doesn't know. Jacky knows. I told him after we… I told him."

I won't hurt you, I promise. It can be really good. I'll show you.

Not that… I don't want to do that. He hadn't needed to say anything more: Jacky, with his unusual acuity for such things, had immediately understood.

Somebody hurt you. Tell me who the bastard is and I'll gut him.

Nobody. Someone my dad knew, ages ago. It's nothing.

Jacky had wanted to find Gus, had mentioned a private investigator he knew in East Kilbride, a chap by the name of Chisholm. *Chiz'll find him. If the bastard is still alive, Chiz'll track him down and fucking dile him.*

I don't know where he is. I don't know.

"My father lives in Glasgow," Simon finally said. "I get money from him every birthday." Even now, with his first album soaring up the charts and a second tour of America under his belt, he still got a card from Roger every April, with a five-pound note inside. Even seeing Roger's crabbed and miserable handwriting hurt. Simon was forever torn between love and resentment, between wanting his father's embrace and hating the mere mention of his name. Simon sometimes lay awake at night wishing to be crushed in his father's embrace, to feel his dad's arms go round him. He fantasized this so frequently that he had memorized a sort of script, and if he chanced to meet Roger ever again, he'd know exactly what to do. If Roger ever called for him, he'd go, instantly and without question.

LESLIE worked in the little shop where Stephen went to get bread and pickles and potato chips and jam. There was an antiques store attached to it, and a rental place that lent out musical instruments, the same place where Stephen rented the guitar he'd been using and found the beat-up old piano that he had shifted out to the farmhouse where he and Simon were staying.

Leslie was American and blonde, with prominent breasts that appeared to be forever overflowing the cups of her brassiere and a peculiar knock-kneed gait that would eventually come to remind Stephen of an old horse his father had once owned. She was slender and sunburned, with a spray of freckles across her nose, and had sticking plasters on both knees. She was seventeen, blue-eyed and beautiful, with a fetching Southern twang. She flirted shamelessly with Stephen across the counter whenever he went into the shop, asked him how Simon was, and dropped broad hints about coming over there some afternoon with beer. She was a perfect American dream girl, a dusty Southern blonde in the middle of a little nowhere town in Mississippi. It was so completely perfect, like something from a book, like something from one of Stephen's poems, like the lyrics to a song they hadn't written yet.

Leslie arrived one day just after five, driving her father's pickup truck and wearing a short floral dress and battered plastic sandals. She was chewing bubblegum and her hair was pulled back into a ponytail, and she looked about fourteen. Simon wasn't keen on Leslie being there: as far as he knew, this holiday was just for him and Stephen, and bringing a girl along was not quite cricket. He didn't try to hide his displeasure.

What d'you want her for? You might have asked me first.

Stephen was patting aftershave into his cheeks and neck and grunting a little as it stung the small cuts his razor always made. *I thought you might like a little company.*

Simon was angry—not tantrum angry, not Jacky Stride coaxing him into a hissy fit angry, but really, genuinely angry. He couldn't know how much he sounded like Roger when he was annoyed, or how much he looked like him. *I didn't come here because I want fucking company! That's why you're here. For Christ's sake! Why do I want a fucking girl here? Tell me why, would you?*

Stephen turned on him: *Right. You were thinking you'd keep me all to yourself. Thinking you'd get me to take it up the arse. Is that it?*

He regretted it as soon as it was out of his mouth, but it was already much too late. Simon slammed the door so hard it bounced in the frame and the whole wall of the flimsy cottage shuddered. *Fuck you, and all.*

When Simon was twelve, he was friends with Andrew, a boy who lived in Mile End Road and whose father—a successful plumber with a thriving business—sometimes did a bit of work for Nina. Andrew's chief attraction for Simon was his substantial record collection and the fact that he not only appreciated Simon's jokes but also encouraged him in the kind of schoolboy pranks that often got them both into trouble. Simon, a natural mimic, had a talent for doing "voices" and swiftly became renowned as a playground comic, adept at imitating teachers and other authority figures, to general amusement. During half terms and at weekends, he and Andrew spent their time listening to records and reading the popular music papers and speculating on which American acts they'd most like to see in concert. Being Andrew's friend was a bit of a risk because, even in those days, there was something about Andrew that excited certain suspicions in his parents. He had a way of talking that caused adult heads to swivel immediately in his direction; his gestures were broad and frequent and he had a habit of waving his hands dramatically when he spoke. It was whispered that Andrew's parents had even taken him away to Switzerland for treatment at a highly specialized clinic, but for what, no one knew. A girl at school whose father was a child psychologist said that Andrew was taking electric shock treatment, but no one could figure out why.

One hot July afternoon, he and Simon had just come inside; they had been chasing each other with the hose and were soaking wet. *We'll get changed in my room,* Andrew said. *I can lend you some of my things until yours are dry.* He was mightily interested in seeing Simon with his clothes off. *Go on, then. Get your wet kit off. I don't mind.* He and Simon quickly graduated from looking to touching and from there to kissing. The first time Simon ever came in the presence of another person was with Andrew: lying on his back in Andrew's bed late at night after his parents were asleep and letting Andrew touch him. Eventually Nina expressed concern over how much time Simon and Andrew spent together and put a stop to it; a year later Andrew went to live with an uncle in France, and the last Simon heard, he was working in a restaurant on the Côte d'Azur. He had changed his name to Angelil.

When Simon and Andrew were together, there was no room for anybody else; theirs was a universe of two. They liked the same things and explored the same topics of discussion; they borrowed one another's clothes and always arrived at the same conclusions about things. One day after school, Simon went to Andrew's house and found him going over *New Music Weekly* with a boy named Nigel, and was incensed. *What's he doing here? What do you want him for?* While Andrew was occupied elsewhere in the house, he sidled up to Nigel and hissed at him: *You'd best be off, mate. We don't want you here.*

Simon was sitting on the front porch, rocking savagely in the rocking chair, his bulky arms folded on his chest. Leslie, sensitive to Simon's body language, sat down beside him. *You want I should just go on home?*

Stephen's in the house. He wouldn't look at her.

I'm Leslie.

I know who you are. In direct contravention of everything Nina had ever taught him about manners, he ignored her outstretched hand. *I know why you're here. Stephen's in the house.* He wouldn't call it jealousy, this thing he felt, because that would be hitting far too close to the truth. He hated that she was here, that Stephen had invited her, hated that she might come between them, might separate the clinging strands of what they had together. He wouldn't call it jealousy. He would call it a dozen other things instead.

Stephen made spaghetti because spaghetti was the only thing that Stephen knew how to make, that and sausages with chips and mushy peas. He made spaghetti with hamburger and tomato sauce out of a tin and lots of stringy cheese and it was almost edible. It was almost good. And there was red wine and brandy for after dinner, and by the time they got to pie and coffee, Simon was himself again.

"…and there she was, sitting on the end of my fucking bed. I'm completely blind without my glasses, right? And so I say to her, 'Who the fuck are you?' and she says, 'Don't you know me? I'm your wife'."

Stephen and Leslie laughed on cue, like actors in a film, and Simon realized that somewhere along the way he'd been shut out. It was no longer him and Stephen against the world: on one side there was him, and on the other, Stephen and Leslie.

"That's what she said: 'I'm your wife'." But the joke had already wilted and there was no point in trying to resurrect it. For the rest of the evening, he was acutely aware of himself as an outsider, the usurper in their midst, a skeleton at their love feast. He wondered what Leslie would think about certain things that he might tell her.

Kiss me. And Simon had, more than once, until the heat between them rose and overflowed, shattering them both to pieces. Afterward, he and Stephen lay together, sweaty and ecstatic.

We probably shouldn't tell anybody, Stephen said. *They wouldn't get it. They wouldn't dig this sort of thing, you know?*

Simon was hurt and pretended not to be. *Sure, I get it. It's fine. No need for true confessions, right?*

It wasn't Stephen's fault, what happened in the end. In the end, it wasn't Stephen's fault at all, but such things happen in the world. Three days later—it was just that quick—Leslie had become a fixture in the house, and late one afternoon, Simon came back from an impromptu swim to hear them giggling together behind the bedroom door.

No, don't. No.

Don't you like it? Stephen's voice, clear and resonant. There was still something of Lincolnshire in his voice, and something else that was not quite Orkney. Simon listened in the hallway, hovering as close to the bedroom as he dared. *Don't you like it when I do that?*

Simon tried to occupy himself but couldn't quiet his mind to anything. He wandered into the living room and sat at the piano, playing chords and scales and little bits of things he knew, things he might make up. He tried not to listen, but the walls were thin and he could hear them in there, and he knew what they were doing. He knew Stephen was fucking her and he wondered what she looked like naked: did she have tan lines where her bikini swimsuit cupped her nubile teenaged body? Stephen was coltish and lanky, still not finished growing into his body: his hands were lean and brown, and his skinny chest was nearly hairless. He grabbed Simon's hair that night, held Simon's head that first time, as his body sighed and shifted under Simon's eager mouth.

Yes, Stephen had said. He was so quiet when it happened, not at all like Simon expected. *Yes. Oh yes, please.* That very first time, it always replayed itself for him, a strip of celluloid shuddering its images against an inner eye: here is Stephen, and here is Simon. Here are two bodies joined in space, all naked hands and eyes and open mouths embracing: *I love you, I love you.*

When they left Mississippi, Leslie went with them. That was Stephen's first genuine mistake.

7: *Locked Out*

SIMON was back in Britain nearly a week when the telephone in his new flat rang one night after supper. Simon had been in the flat exactly twice since he bought it; the flat and the furniture in it was Jacky's idea. Jacky said a budding superstar couldn't keep on living at his mother's house. As soon as the music papers and the popular press got hold of it, Simon would be put down for a bleeding mother's boy. "It's all bad enough," Jacky said. "You looking the way you do—you move like a cunt onstage, do you know that? No, we've got to undo the damage while we can." He'd taken Simon round the area, looking at housing estates, until Simon finally settled on the top floor of a renovated Hindu temple. Jacky thought it was brilliant and wanted Simon to pose for pictures in a turban and one of Gerald's old bathrobes. "The press'll think you've converted," Jacky said. "It'll be brilliant."

Instead, Simon went out and bought sufficient furniture to fill the cavernous space: a fashionable sofa and a brace of leather chairs, some tasteful coffee tables and an enormous stereo. He got a tank and stocked it with tropical fish, most of which quickly up and died. Every morning Simon would wake up to find a few more brightly-colored carcasses floating on the surface of the water. When the last of his surgeonfish finally kicked it, he was inconsolable. "They're bloody *fish*, for fucksakes," Jacky said. "Why are you getting your knickers in a twist?" But he went down to the shops while Simon was away and secretly replaced every one of the dead fish. Jacky was pleased that Simon was talking again, that he was himself again after that nasty business on the tour and then being holed up in Mississippi with that Lincolnshire yob. He had too much invested in Simon; it was to his benefit to keep Simon pliable and complacent. Jacky had set his management fees at an exorbitant twenty-three percent, and had already begun to squirrel away money against the day when Simon lost his voice or topped himself.

It was Nina on the phone. Simon wondered if something happened to Gerald; his stepfather wasn't getting any younger and he smoked as much as Nina. "It's your father."

"What's wrong with Gerald?"

"Not Gerald."

It occurred to Simon that she meant Roger—but Simon hadn't seen Roger in ages, ever since that disastrous weekend so many years ago in Glasgow. Simon had assumed he'd never see Roger again. "What does he want?"

Roger was dying, and there was little time left. It wasn't really such a long trip up to Glasgow and perhaps Simon was headed up north anyway, seeing as how he was just about to embark on a domestic tour, starting at London and working his way north. "What does he *want?*" Simon asked again.

"Just to see you." She didn't add any undue sentiment, and Simon was grateful. He knew the circumstances of their divorce; he knew he was the reason why his father left. He had no more bitterness left in him, as far as Roger was concerned. He recited this to himself as often as necessary, like a catechism. Roger couldn't do anything to him now. He inquired after Gerald and the health of Nina's two cats, and when his mother rang off to see to the washing-up, he called Stephen. Stephen had also found himself a flat, not too far from Simon but far enough so it didn't seem that they were unduly attached to one another, and also so that Jacky Stride wouldn't get jealous. Stephen was living with Leslie, a backwoods naïf who was so impressed with him that she followed him back to Britain with nothing but the clothes on her back. Stephen was appropriately galvanized by Simon's news.

"Can you... I mean, if you're not busy... I hate to take the train." Simon had a hard time getting the words out of his mouth. He had no illusions that a road trip with Stephen would be any kind of joyride, or that they would be able to recapture the blessed friendship of their early days. The presence of Leslie in Stephen's life effectively nullified any hopes Simon might have had in that direction. He wondered what would happen if she knew the truth. *Does he tell you that he loves you? I guess you know I fucked him first.* "You can drive."

Jacky had gone on to Glasgow ahead of them to investigate the venues for Simon's latest tour and to terrify a few promoters with his usual raging screed. Stephen came to Simon's flat the next morning without his girlfriend, for which Simon was grateful. He was afraid that Leslie would be too loud so early in the morning, and would want to stop all along the way to purchase coffee, and would smoke in Simon's car. Simon's new car was a Ford with a tidy leather interior; his only concession to his nascent fame was a state-of-the-art car stereo, well-stocked with all his favorite tapes.

Leslie's personal candor was of the unfortunate sort; she was clearly used to expressing herself in the plainest of terms. She called Jacky an "asshole" and said that Nina stuck to Simon like "shit on a wet blanket." She told Stephen that Simon was a "silly faggot" and his mother's house in Stepney was "a dump." She had the plainest contempt for England as a country and for the English as a people, and she wanted to go back to Mississippi as soon as Stephen could be persuaded to marry her. She asked him every day when he intended to buy her an engagement ring, and when he protested that they'd only just met, she told him he was a "dummy." *You asshole, you're dumb as a stump.* Stephen hadn't quite worked up the nerve to take her home to Orkney; he couldn't imagine what Leslie would make of his father's farm, the scruffy sheep, or his mother's reddened, work-worn hands.

"Are you all right?" But Stephen didn't press to ask anything further than this. Whatever Simon had to tell him would keep until they got to Glasgow—but the moment the car pulled out onto the motorway, Simon started to talk. He talked incessantly, as if he was making up for whatever time he had recently spent in silence. He talked about his parents and a grandmother who gave him a bicycle many years ago; he talked about the hard-faced shop girls when he used to ride the tram and how Nina gave him a chip butty for dinner every day while he was at school. He talked until Stephen wanted to stuff his mouth with something, just to shut him up. Just outside of York, Simon asked him to pull into a petrol station so he could use the lav. Stephen waited while Simon went inside and wondered just how long it took for someone to have a quick piss and maybe get a drink of water. He found his way round back and pushed open the lavatory door.

It's ten o'clock in the morning, Stephen thought, and *This is like a film or something.* Simon was crouched on the floor beside the toilet, sucking several lines of fine white powder up his nose. Stephen wasn't a total innocent: he understood the way the music business worked and he had seen this sort of thing before. *But it's ten o'clock in the morning.* Simon raised his head and smiled, lifting himself back onto his feet. "Can't a bloke get some privacy round here?" Simon's eyes were much too bright, and his familiar gap-toothed smile was somehow sinister. Stephen wondered how much coke it took to get Simon up in the morning; he wondered how much coke Jacky had to keep on hand in order to make Simon go onstage.

All the way to Glasgow, Simon was happy: drumming his fingers on the armrest, singing along with the tape player, much too loud. Perhaps it was merely false courage and perhaps Simon was entitled to it, but his drug-induced happiness grated on Stephen's nerves. Perhaps Simon was better off left in silence, as he'd been in Mississippi, or perhaps he should have just stayed in America, far beyond the reach of Jacky or Roger or anyone. Jacky would be waiting for them in Glasgow; Simon's proximity would draw Jacky near, like infection rising to the surface of a wound.

"HE'S IN here." The nurse was impossibly young, too young to be presiding over a scene like this. Simon had never seen such an array of noisy, flickering equipment. Roger looked nothing like Simon remembered. His bones showed through the imperfect papyrus flesh and the ends of his narrow fingers were blue. There were others here as well, grouped round Roger's hospital bed. A gigantic young man with reddish hair hovered close to Roger, guarding him; he had the thick shoulders and powerful forearms of a blacksmith. He spoke first, before any of the others could get a word in.

"So you're him." His eyes flickered over Simon's jeans, his leather jacket. "You're Abelard."

Simon started toward him, then faltered when he recognized that there was no welcome for him in the young man's eyes. "I'm Simon—Simon Duckworth."

"Are you, now?" The big ginger moved to clasp Roger's shoulder, claiming him.

"I bought your record." One of Roger's children, a red-haired girl, started toward Simon but was held back by one of the others. "I wanted to go to the concert but Mummy wouldn't let me."

"Dad's not well," the big young man said. "He's not up to having visitors."

"Oh, piss off, Mick." One of the others spoke, an older girl. "You don't bloody own him."

Simon tried again. "We're brothers. I'm your brother. Well, half brother." The others raised their heads to stare at him for a moment, then went back to whispering among themselves, casting covert glances at Simon. Stephen moved to stand behind Simon, shadowing him protectively. He hovered close, reading the subtle temperature of Simon's body with his own. Roger's voice erupted into the room like a sudden blast of static from a disused radio.

"Where's Doris?" He sounded petulant, and his once-powerful voice was the weak, desiccated voice of an old man. "Why isn't Doris here?"

"Dad—" Simon lurched forward, reached for him. Roger's hand was thin and burning hot, the skin of his fingers worn almost transparent by the heat of his illness. Simon turned the hand over in his grasp, seeking the network of fine lines stretching Roger's palm; he studied them, looking for himself in this palimpsest of flesh. "I've come to see you—my friend Stephen's here with me. You've not met Stephen yet. You'd like him, Dad. He's ever so nice."

Roger blinked, uncomprehending. "Where's Doris? Why isn't Doris here?"

Simon's back began to tremble. The shudders wrapped themselves around his torso and ran down into his legs like water.

"Dad, I've come up from London... I've come up to see you." Simon held Roger's hand so tightly, the small bones of the fingers creaked.

"Doris ought to be here. There'll be nothing for tea." Roger peered at Simon for a moment. "I knew," he said. He caught hold of Simon's sleeve and yanked on it. "I knew Gus went in after you." He sounded like a man who had recently seen a wonder. "I knew what he was doing." He rose off his pillow, holding Simon with his wiry strength. "I should have gone in after you. That's what I should have done. I should have gone." He gazed at Simon, his forehead creased in concentration, then closed his eyes and seemed to lapse into unconsciousness. Simon's face prickled; he fumbled with the zipper on his jacket. It was, Stephen thought, like watching a building fall down in slow motion.

"He's very ill, Simon." Stephen made his voice as gentle as he could. "He doesn't know what he's saying." *I knew Gus went in after you... I knew what he was doing.* He had no business commenting on someone else's family, even someone he knew as well as Simon, but Roger had clearly implicated himself. He was to blame for what had happened to Simon then and for everything that had happened to Simon since.

Simon began to back away, smiling the smile that Stephen knew so well, the one that meant Simon was dying of shame, and clinging desperately to whatever shreds of dignity he could muster. It was horrible to watch, and Stephen burned with embarrassment for Simon's sake. And then Simon fled, blundering past the phalanx of Roger's children and out into the corridor. Mick exchanged a long look with one of his brothers standing by the window: a tall, thin man with wide blue eyes and a crooked jaw and great big ears. "What'd I tell you? Turned and ran like I knew he would. Fucking little poofter."

"You've made him cry!" The youngest girl, the one who said she'd bought Simon's record, was red-faced, angry. "You've made him cry and now he'll never come back."

Stephen hesitated, on the verge of saying something to them, something poisonous and succinct, but changed his mind. He turned and went after Simon and found him in the car park, staring out over

Castle Street, his arms crossed on his chest. "We should go somewhere."

Simon didn't look at him. "Where? Where should we go? Hm? I'm open to ideas." His eyes were squinting behind his glasses, as if in response to some inner pain and his mouth trembled. "Did you hear what he said, in there?" The words sounded strange and far away. "Jesus Christ, Stephen, he knew. He knew I was in that lavatory being raped and he didn't do a fucking thing about it."

"I'm sorry." It was pathetic, and Stephen knew it. "I'm so sorry." He reached out, not caring who saw them.

"No." Simon backed away. "Someone will see."

"I don't give a toss," Stephen retorted. "The whole fucking lot of them can go fuck themselves."

Simon took his glasses off and pinched the bridge of his nose, squinting. "I want to go somewhere," he said. "I want to go somewhere and dance."

THE music was loud, pounding a savage pulse into Stephen's bones. He didn't know the song and he didn't care; he was compelled to dance to it like a man possessed. There was a theme in the club that night, with many of the patrons in costume or wearing masks, all dancing furiously under the strobe lights. "Simon." Stephen reached toward him; his own arm seemed impossibly long. "Simon, let's get a beer." He jerked his head in the direction of the bar and Simon followed him. But there was a long line of punters waiting to be served, so Simon tugged Stephen after him into the men's room. He hid them both in the same cubicle and crouched down, using the closed lid as a workspace, cutting lines with a credit card, manipulating the thin white powder with a deftness that some part of Stephen's mind admired.

"Here—have a go." He nudged Stephen to take the first line. The lights were alive and the music was deep inside Stephen's cells, pulsing with the rhythm of his heart. He felt sharp and impossibly alive, as if he could fly just by thinking about it.

"Good?" Simon's face was close to his, and Simon's head was somehow separate from his body, jigging insanely about like a swollen mask. "Don't worry—I won't let you get too fucked up." He pulled Stephen out onto the floor and they danced, close—too close— together. The lights were inside Stephen's head and in his belly, and it was only natural that he grab Simon, pull their bodies together, kiss him deeply like he meant it. Simon was slippery and hard to hold, but Stephen had bold new powers now. Simon tasted like stale hospital air and cigarette smoke, and a deeper tang of something that was probably cocaine. Stephen yanked Simon hard against him and danced them both into a frenzy, rubbing himself on Simon, touching him, kissing him. He was powerfully aroused, his cock straining against the front of his trousers, his body thrumming like the taut strings of a plucked guitar. If Simon touched him, just *there*, he would come like a freight train. *Close...* he saw the expression on Simon's face, the way Simon's eyes were squeezed shut. *Simon's getting close.* He wanted to make that happen, but it was all some sort of bizarre dream; it wasn't really happening. Simon's fingers were digging into his forearms, hard, and Simon was shuddering, falling against him, eyes closed and mouth open in ecstasy. Stephen held on, his fingers digging into Simon's shoulders, and came and came, his body heaving with his release, shuddering. He was dimly aware of Simon, crouched against the wall with his hands over his face, and some part of his mind wondered why.

"Where the *fuck* have you been?" Jacky was there; Jacky had tracked them down. He shoved them apart and planted himself in front of them. "Have you been in here with him all this time?"

Stephen found Jacky extremely funny right now. He couldn't stop laughing. Jacky took a swing at him, but Stephen danced back out of reach, and when he turned around again, Jacky had gone, taking Simon with him.

Stephen woke up in his hotel room alone. There were fifteen phone messages from Simon, all of a similar variety, and one from Leslie.

Stephen picked the one from Leslie and erased the rest.

8: *Moses, Get Your Gun*

SIMON was sitting in the bathtub nursing a nosebleed and a hangover. Jacky was on the phone in the other room, shouting at someone in the Netherlands about ticket prices and how much champagne Simon wanted in the dressing room: *I've got him in the Oderhaus for next month and they're giving us whatever we want. You'd best smarten up, mate.* Stephen came into the bathroom with Leslie close behind him, smiling her American smile; her blonde hair was pulled up on top of her head, and she wore a white maxidress embroidered with little yellow flowers. Stephen was smiling broadly and smelled of bourbon. "Guess what, man? I'm married." He laughed at Simon's shocked expression. "We did it, me and Leslie. Tied the knot. What do you think of that?"

Simon stared at him, a piece of bloody tissue paper held up to his nose. "We're touring next month. What were you thinking?"

Leslie made an irritated noise and flounced out of the bathroom. Stephen glanced after her but made no move to follow. "I figured why not? Why not do it and get it over with, right? It's like going to the dentist, isn't it? You've just got to nerve yourself and do it."

"Going to the fucking dentist?" Simon balled up the piece of tissue and threw it in the bin, then stood up out of the bath water. "Going to the *dentist*?" He reached for the bath sheet that was hanging on a hook and wrapped it round his middle. "Jesus Christ, Stephen. You could have mentioned it." He went through to the next room, a huge and beautifully furnished bedroom that featured a genuine medieval bed purported to have once belonged to Catherine of Aragon, which was so high off the ground that a set of steps were needed in order to reach it. The room had been decorated around the bed, and the walls were hung with watered silk and precious works of art. Someone had done a portrait of Simon in the style of Gainsborough, sitting on a satin cushion and petting a big-eyed spaniel while a harpsichord languished in the background. Jacky's presence was evident everywhere in the room: a desk had been set up against the far wall, ostensibly for late night work, and a trio of telephones kept close company with a Telex machine. A trouser press occupied the space directly in front of the huge double wardrobe on the other side of the room, and a great many pairs of Jacky's sedate leather shoes were showing from within the giant cabinet.

"It wasn't planned." Stephen shrugged and fumbled at his trouser pockets; there seemed nowhere to put his hands. "It just seemed like the right thing to do."

Simon sat in front of the oak dressing table and swiftly cut several lines on a mirror that was laid flat in front of him. He turned around and offered the straw to Stephen, who shook his head. "We're going on tour. I expect you to come with us."

"Of course!" Stephen tried for effusive and failed. "You know that—there was never any question. It's just that Leslie… she and I… we really made a connection in America. You know how it is."

Simon's dark eyes held Stephen in the mirror. "Yeah," he said finally. "I know how it is."

Stephen looked utterly forlorn. "Aren't you going to congratulate me?"

"Congratulations," Simon said woodenly. He turned back to his cocaine straw.

ONE tequila, two tequila, three tequila, floor. And a lot of pills. *It's easier this way*, and so clichéd it might as well be Hollywood, but Simon didn't care. He was floating somewhere else: he was in the Netherlands, in the Oderhaus, and the whores were crawling on the stage, calling out his name.

Stephen's phone rang while he and Leslie were in bed. They'd been married approximately twenty hours and had consummated their infant union at least a dozen times. Leslie had certain distinct ideas about how matters should proceed, and she wasn't shy about guiding Stephen in the right direction, should his instincts falter. "Oh, leave it," she said when the phone rang. "That fag can babysit himself for once." She surfaced from underneath the covers with her blonde hair all over her face; Stephen was already on the line. "So what happened, did he break a nail or something?"

Stephen thought it might be a wrong number at first: the person on the other end was slurring his words as badly as any drunk. "Who's this? I can't hear you."

"I bet you never thought you'd get a call like this from me."

"Simon?" Stephen's heart began slamming into his ribs like a demented trip hammer. Leslie was purring, drawing her fingers slowly up and down his back. "Simon, what's wrong?"

"It was easy. I should have done it ages ago." A pause; Stephen could hear him breathing. "I gotta go now."

"No, Simon, stay on the phone—what did you do? Tell me." Stephen groped around the floor until he found his trousers. "Just stay there, 'til—"

"I gotta hang up now, Stephen." Simon was getting fainter, as though talking through a tube. "I'm really tired."

A click, and then the dial tone was a steady hum in Stephen's ear, a flat line.

He was talking to his father. He was sitting with his father by the banks of a placid-flowing river, and his father was young again, alive and interested in him. His father was showing him how to tie the fishing line so the hook wouldn't slip off in the water. He was fishing with his father in the small canal that ran behind their house in Stepney. When he peered into the water, he didn't see his father: he only saw himself, wearing a peculiar fleshy mask with exaggerated nose and ears and great big glasses. Somewhere in the distance there was a faint noise like applause and there were people running, a lot of people running fast.

"Aren't you worried it'll end up in the papers?"

"I'll deal with it later. Get Knacker Phil for me. He'll know what to do." Jacky's voice came close to Simon. "Simon... wake up now." Jacky held on to him with icy fingers. Simon felt someone tugging at him, pestering him, checking his pulse and lifting up his eyelids. Why wouldn't they leave him alone? It was like being fitted for a costume, but what costume was he being fitted for in this place?

You're not going up there again—you were only there last weekend. Simon was fifteen and, despite everything, he wanted to spend some time with Roger. *Why do you have to be running off to see him all the time? What's the matter with Gerald? You said you liked Gerald.* Nina didn't understand, and all her arguments were good for nothing. Gerald was good and kind and Simon loved him, but Gerald was his stepfather—an imitation, a stand-in, not the real thing. *He's at that age*—Roger explained it to Nina on the phone one night. *He wants his dad.* But Nina kept at him, until Simon felt like a traitor for even mentioning Roger's name, for even thinking of him. He penned secret letters to Roger and mailed them on his way to school, but Roger only assumed the letters were a plea for extra pocket money and sent Simon a check for twenty pounds. Nina was outraged: *Why are you asking him for money? We don't want his money!* She tore the check in pieces in front of Simon's face. She invented excuses as to why she needed him at home—the car should be washed and Gerald was busy, or the garden needed mulching. On the rare occasions Simon went north for a visit, Nina purposely took the long way round to the station so that Simon missed the last train to Glasgow. She didn't bother to hide her glee as she took him home again. *Don't know why you want to go up there anyway, him and his fancy women. He never liked you. Any chance he got to get a little dig at you, he'd take it.*

Simon never complained out loud as he was relentlessly pulled in two directions. His father wanted to see him, and his dad's wife, Doris, was always nice to him—but Nina made certain of Simon's loyalties. She reminded him of all she'd done for him, and all that Gerald, in his turn, had done. In the end, Simon stayed with her, and in time, the visits to his father ceased altogether. At Christmas and on his birthday he received a card from Doris and his father, with a five-pound note inside and a happy face drawn under all their signatures: *From Dad and Doris, Mick and Patrick and Judy and Desmond.*

Nina liked to sit with Simon in the evenings and listen to him play the piano while Gerald read the papers and the knickers dried on a line up near the ceiling. "Play that bit you played last night," she'd say, or, "Do 'The Blue Danube'," and Simon always listened. He obeyed his mother, because his mother had been good to him. His mother gave him everything, and he should have been grateful. "Your dad never liked you," Nina always said. She knew that she could bind him to her side with words. She could sway him with her sacrifice, with all the things she did for him and all the ways she made him pay the never-ending debt. Over the years, the gap between Simon and his father grew until it was nearly impenetrable, until it would take a death in the family—his father's or his own—to mend the breach.

Simon woke to a darkness full of little noises, none of which he recognized. Without his spectacles he was profoundly myopic, and his night-blind eyes could just make out the dim rectangle of the window frame across the room. It wasn't his room—this wasn't his bed—and there was something in his throat, something sharp that hurt, that brought tears to his eyes whenever he tried to swallow.

Put it in your mouth. You don't have to do anything. Just lick it. His mind cast itself back to all those years ago in Stepney, with his friend Andrew, the two of them locked in Andrew's bedroom on a rainy Saturday afternoon, pretending to read Beano comics. Andrew's prepubescent cock was the size of a thumb, little and wobbly and uncut (Nina had insisted Simon be circumcised even as Roger protested that his family would think they'd converted and become Jewish) and smelling of piss. *Just lick it and see what happens.* So Simon did; it tasted of nothing much except perhaps raw meat, and was faintly wet.

Stephen's naked body had writhed and shifted under him that night in Mississippi as Simon rode him to completion, their skins slick with sweat. Stephen grunted when he came and held onto Simon's shoulders, hard fingers digging into the tender muscle, his cheek laid against Simon's, his breath in Simon's ear: *I love you.*

He blinked, trying to bring the strange room into focus but unable to see much without his glasses. If he turned his head to the right, he saw a shiny metal pole hung with plastic bags; to the left was a wooden chair and Jacky, sound asleep. From outside in the corridor came the occasional noise of the intercom, paging nurses and doctors, and various quiet conversations. Someone rolled a cart full of bottles past Simon's door and someone in another room woke and called out briefly. *I'm in hospital.* Simon wondered where Stephen was, wondered why he hadn't come, and then he remembered. *Guess what, man? I'm married.*

Jacky stirred and woke. "Simon."

"Yes." It took effort to pronounce the word in an empty room.

Jacky leaned forward and took Simon's hand in both of his, kissed it. "You're awake. Thank God." He hesitated for just a moment then climbed onto Simon's bed and wrapped Simon in his arms. "Don't ever do that again," he whispered, his cheek pressed against Simon's head. "Please don't do that. I don't know what I'd do if I lost you. I don't know what I would do." As unlike Jacky as it sounded, he meant it.

"He married her." Simon held his hands out in front of him, flexed the fingers. "Stephen. He married that American girl."

Jacky was silent for a moment, one hand moving absently in Simon's hair. "Would you like to go away for a bit?" he asked. "For a trip—you know, a holiday. Just the two of us."

"Me and you?"

"Yes. Who'd you think I meant?" It was hardly an indictment—Jacky's voice was teasing, gentle—but Simon wondered. It wasn't possible to know Jacky all the way through, not really. There were areas of himself that he kept hidden, buried so deeply that even he had forgotten they were there.

"Where would we go?"

Jacky stiffened, his arms tightening around Simon. "I don't know." There was defiance in it. "Go to the Caribbean, perhaps. Don't you fancy lying out on the beach, getting a nice tan?" And, when Simon didn't answer, "It's just an idea. It's not carved in stone or anything. We haven't got to go anywhere. I only thought—"

"It's not that." Simon looked up at him, but the room was too dark to see him properly. "I appreciate it. I really do."

"I'm not him." His frustration seeped into his voice, the Gorbals brogue thick with anger and sadness. "I'm not ever going to be him... you do realize that?" He abruptly rolled off the bed, went to stand by the window, his back to Simon and the room. "I realize the two of you have this magical history together." His shoulders rose, his back hunched under the expensive suit coat. "You're some sort of joined entity." He laughed bitterly. "I wonder where that leaves me."

Simon was quiet. "You jumped in after me."

Jacky turned to look at him. "I did, yeah." He shrugged. "What was I supposed to do? You'd have drowned and we'd be out a bundle of dosh." He grinned. "It's not like I can bloody sing." The grin faded away. "Simon, why'd you do it?"

Simon clenched his hands so hard his tendons creaked.

"Don't say you don't know," Jacky warned.

"Sometimes I wonder if they know." Simon's voice was very small. "Sometimes I wonder if they can see what I'm really like... how fucked up I am. I'm not that talented, when you get right down to it. I could have gone a lot farther if I'd only stuck with the lessons." Recognized as a prodigy by his first piano teacher, Simon had won a scholarship to the prestigious Royal Academy, an hour's journey on the Underground—but he was fourteen, and the Shirelles were much more interesting than Shostakovich, so he hadn't really bothered. "It's only luck. You know that, Jack, and so do I. Luck and—"

"A Lincolnshire lout," Jacky put in. He raised a hand to forestall Simon's protest. "I don't care for him but he writes a good lyric. He's a bit too casual for my taste but... he has his uses." He came to sit on the bed. "That's not it, though. There's more to it."

Simon's gaze slid away. "I don't...."

"You took seventy-five Valium and jumped into a fucking swimming pool, Simon. You said you wanted to die."

Simon picked at a loose thread on the blanket. "I did."

"What made you feel that way?"

The door opened and a nursing sister stepped through. She smiled at Jacky, told them she was going to take Simon's pulse. Jacky stood to one side as she recorded the results in Simon's chart, then smiled thinly while she fussed around the bed, smoothing the sheets and fluffing Simon's pillows. By the time she left, the moment for intimate conversation had passed. Jacky looked at his watch. "They're probably going to boot me out in a minute, so I'd best be getting along." He leaned down and gave Simon a lingering kiss. "Think about my offer, eh? You could do with a holiday."

"Thanks, Jacky."

The Scotsman's dark eyes filled inexplicably with tears. "Will you warn me next time?" he asked. "If you think you can't manage, will you at least give me some notice so I can stop you?"

"Of course." Simon's gaze was guileless and open. An hour after Jacky left the hospital, Simon smashed a glass bottle containing mineral water and used it to slash his wrists.

9: *Lunatic Blues*

WHEN the car pulled up in front of the huge double columns, Simon refused to get out. When Jacky cajoled him, promising him the moon, Simon stared right through him until the two burly security guards hired to accompany Simon everywhere had to lift him bodily out of the limo and carry him in the door. The media were told that Abelard had gone out of the country on holiday—a useful fiction, since the last time Simon checked, Southgate was still in London, and London was still in the UK. But that was neither here nor there, and anyway, Jacky picked this place in consultation with Gerald and Nina so that Simon could have his own room and a bit of privacy. Jacky assumed that Nina trusted him enough to choose a lunatic asylum for her son, but she and Gerald had already been here and had a look round. She wasn't stupid enough to say that Simon would like it. She knew they were under a deadline, all of them—Nina, Gerald, Jacky, and Simon—to get this over with and get on with things before the tour started, before the fans started screaming for their money back. To avoid a scandal, it was crucial that this entire charade be accomplished as swiftly and painlessly as possible.

Simon's admissions report said that he was suffering from depression "and related problems," but no mention was made there—or anywhere else—about Simon's suicide attempts. Jacky paid out a considerable amount of money to make sure that absolutely nothing about Simon's hospitalization ended up on the front page of the *Sun* or any of the other gossip mags. Simon began protesting his confinement immediately.

"I can't stay here." Simon got up from the chair and paced anxiously back and forth. "I have to leave now." He couldn't stop looking at his hands; his hands were bothering him more than usual today. He couldn't bear to look at them: their small size, the bruised and broken fingernails, the calluses. He was herded into another room with Jacky and Gerald and Nina, and the door was closed behind them. The sign on the door said "INTAKE."

"Simon, why do you keep looking at your hands?" The doctor was female, tall and slender and blonde, quite beautiful in a Scandinavian sort of way. Simon thought that her hands were larger than his, and this irritated him, made him feel paranoid. "Simon?"

"I can't stay here." His hands were lying on his lap; they looked like two small, naked crabs. Other people knew it and were laughing at him. Everyone knew the truth about him—that he was nothing but a filthy little poof, a girl, a horrible mistake, the ugliest thing that ever walked. He shoved his hands into his pockets. Everyone was looking at him, so he was very careful to appear normal, to control his facial expressions, to make his mood seem interested and quietly somber. He appeared perfectly all right—there were no scars on him, no cut marks on his wrists, no outward indication of the charcoal that the Casualty officer filled his stomach with the night he was brought to the hospital. He didn't remember the stomach pump or the way his heart flatlined three times before the doctors were able to bring him back. He didn't remember the three days he'd spent in a coma so profound that his doctors doubted whether he'd ever surface to consciousness.

When he tried to remember that night, he received only fleeting impressions—a metallic taste in his mouth, a telephone ringing in the distance, Stephen's voice. *Guess what, man? I'm married.* The broken water bottle, that was more immediate, and he'd remembered to cut lengthwise instead of across the wrist, for depth of penetration, for maximum achievable damage. The sharp, bright pain had startled him and the blood had sprung up, welling through his fingers and pooling on the floor. He knew he had to lie there, had to stand it and not reach for the call button, but there had been so much blood, and the weakness made a strange pain around his heart.

Simon turned to Jacky. "Have you ever really looked at hands? I mean, really looked at people's hands?" Simon took his own hands out of his pockets and looked at them closely. "They're too small. They're way too small." The clinic radio was playing Elton John, *Madman*

Across the Water, or maybe it was inside Simon's head. *Is the nightmare black, or are the windows painted?*

"We have a very good common room, where he can be with other people," the doctor said to Nina.

"I don't want to be with other people," Simon snapped, "and stop fucking talking about me like I'm not even in the room." He wondered if the clinic had a research library. He wanted to look up hand sizes for different populations, different ethnic groups. He wanted to examine photographs, compare himself to others, see if he was normal. "I saw a Jamaican once who had enormous hands. My hands are small. They're too fucking small. That's the problem." *Watch out for the splash, by the way. When you get your dick out—*

Jacky leaned close to him. "Would you stop it with the fucking hand thing? For five minutes? Please?" Jacky was very nervous; there were concert dates booked all over the UK as preparation for Simon's next American tour. Tickets had already been sold; fans would be expecting to see Abelard, not some simpering madman with a hand fixation. "There's nothing wrong with you," Jacky hissed, "except that you're a flaming head case!"

But Gerald had as much as he could take. "He didn't try to top himself because his fucking hands are small!" He stalked out of the consulting room; Simon saw him through the window, lighting up a cigarette. Gerald's hands were normal; Simon would like to have hands like Gerald. Could a pair of hands be transplanted from one person to another? Maybe Gerald would swap hands with him if he asked.

"Where's Stephen?" Simon looked from Jacky to his mother to the doctor. "Why isn't Stephen here?" Stephen's hands were beautiful: lean and tanned and graceful. *Touch me like this; oh God don't stop.* But Stephen didn't want that, at least not from him. Stephen only wanted it from Leslie and Simon would do well to remember it.

STEPHEN was sitting at the typewriter when he heard Leslie's tread in the upstairs hallway. His hands hovered over the keys and he waited. She knew not to bother him when he was working, but the term didn't mean the same to her as it meant to him. For Leslie, "work" involved physical labor of some sort, and sitting behind a desk, tapping tentatively at typewriter keys, didn't count. Her footsteps went past his door, paused, then came back again; Stephen laid aside the sheaf of paper.

"Stephen?" She tapped on the door, then eased it open. "Somebody wants you on the phone."

"On the phone?"

She sighed and rolled her eyes. "Yes." The initial euphoria of their marriage had quickly vanished, and was replaced by a lingering resentment that had everything to do with Leslie's belief that she had been grievously misled. She thought she was marrying a genius, a rock star's personal amanuensis, but instead, she'd landed an unassuming farmer's son, unhappily saddled with a penchant for words and the blight of a poetic soul. She'd imagined they would spend their days in blissful harmony, smoking pot and spending Stephen's money—but Stephen wasn't the least bit materialistic and his favorite mind-altering substance was beer. She had envisioned their nights as an eternal splendor of connubial bliss, but this, too, was not the case. Stephen's writing took precedence over sex, which was so infrequent that Leslie wondered if Stephen had something wrong with him. Acting on the advice of various women's magazines, she had attempted to seduce her husband by appearing in his study clad in nothing but a bikini bottom. Stephen, engrossed in the scansion of a lyric, had mutely waved her away. She had begun to suspect he was seeing someone else on the side.

"Who is it?" Stephen took the pencil out of his mouth long enough to speak. "Did they say?"

"I don't know. Some old man. You better come and talk to him. He sounds like he's off his rocker."

Gerald was as upset as Stephen had ever heard, and the tremor in his voice struck Stephen through with sharpest apprehension. "It's Simon. I thought you ought to know: he's in the hospital." And, when Stephen asked which one, Gerald was curiously evasive. "A… private facility in Southgate. We thought it best to keep things mum."

The only hospital Stephen knew of in Southgate was a psychiatric institution. "Oh, my God." His skin prickled with sudden cold. "He's in a mental hospital?" Not Simon... not Stepney Simon, who'd buoyed Stephen up through the languishing hell of their early years... not Simon, who'd met Stephen at the train that first night as if he were a long-lost friend returning from some interminable exile. Not Simon. Not ever.

"What happened?" *Guess what, man? I'm married.* He saw himself, Leslie in tow, standing in front of Simon's bathtub and proclaiming it, this aberrant gospel. The memory of it, that night and the hasty marriage, was curiously juxtaposed with the image of Simon's hurt, astonished face, his features slowly suffused with the realization of what Stephen had done.

He'd called her that night and went to pick her up, telling her only that he'd a surprise for her. She met him at the door in a flowered dress and a picture hat, her blonde hair combed into girlish ringlets, a bouquet of daisies slowly wilting between her sweating hands. How had she known? He'd only ever alluded to the possibility of marriage, had made no firm plans in that direction. He drove them to the council office and married her in front of the clerk, without sufficient notice or even a ring. *I'll buy you a dozen rings. I will.*

Their wedding night was uneventful, but that was no surprise, seeing as how they'd had each other before. She stroked him to hardness and climbed on top and Stephen made all the requisite sounds, grimaced in all the right places. Perhaps it wasn't significant; perhaps it wasn't anything. He hadn't meant to marry her—but the interlude with Simon on the dance floor had frightened him. It was one thing to indulge in a little bit of rub-and-tug, a friendly mutual wank in the dark... and he cared about Simon, he really did.

He did.

SIMON was sitting in one corner of the common room, glaring resentfully at the other occupants. His hands were covered with dark mittens, safe from prying eyes. Jacky was sitting on a sofa, not precisely next to Simon but close enough to intercept him if he did anything stupid. No one in the common room cared that Simon was there—he was not even a minor celebrity in this place, and he shared the common room at that moment with an earl, two dukes, a member of Parliament, and a rather horsey-faced princess of the current reigning monarchy.

"Take those bloody mittens off." Jacky edged toward Simon, who edged away, clutching his hands underneath his armpits. "You look daft."

"I'm in a mental hospital," Simon replied, simply. "I am daft."

"You're not making this easy on anyone."

Simon shrugged. "I don't give a toss." He stared at Jacky for a moment, but the Scotsman was unmoved. "Did you bring me any?"

"I did not."

"Why the hell not? Do you think I fucking like it in here?" Simon's raised voice elicited little or nothing from the other inmates. The earl continued with his needlepoint; the princess was pasting photos in a scrapbook. There were no photos of other people in her book, only horses; Simon had heard it rumored that she'd been incarcerated because of her attempted intimacy with a spotted gelding.

"Listen." Jacky wanted to grab the front of Simon's shirt and shake him but a large male nurse was watching with gimlet eyes from across the room. "That's what got you in here in the first place, right? You saw an opportunity and you jumped in with both fucking nostrils."

There was some small disturbance at the entrance to the common room; Stephen was standing there, alone, without Leslie. He seemed relieved that Simon still looked like Simon, that he didn't look mental or anything; he said nothing about the mittens. Stephen had a box of chocolates underneath one arm and a big bouquet of flowers. *Guess what, man? I'm married.* It was Jacky's voice that Simon heard, not Stephen's.

"You should tell him," Jacky said. He moved over to sit next to Simon, a proprietary gesture. No one invited Stephen to sit down.

"Simon, you should tell him." He nudged Simon with an elbow in the ribs. "Go on, tell him."

Jacky had coached him on what to say and how to say it, convinced him that it was necessary, that such a move on his part was only natural, and that things had run their course. *Does he think you're going to write songs with him forever?*

Simon didn't even look at him. "I think we should work with other people." The mittens clenched and unclenched in his lap. "I think you should go now."

"What do you mean?" Stephen was white to the lips. "We're a team, we—"

"Not anymore, you're not." Jacky took Stephen by the elbow.

"Simon—" Stephen reached for him, but Simon wouldn't look him in the eye. Simon wouldn't acknowledge him. Simon wouldn't pretend that he existed, not even for a moment. None of this was real; this wasn't Simon's face but some distorted mask, some costume that Jacky had forced on him. "Simon, you can't let him—" The door closed in his face, with Simon on the other side of it.

"He won't bother you again," Jacky said. Simon opened up the chocolates, offering the box to Jacky, who declined. Simon proceeded then to eat them all, one after another, until the box was empty. Then he got up and went into the bathroom. The whole common room could hear him retching noisily behind the door.

"WHY is his picture on the cover and not yours?" Leslie was in the habit of bringing home various popular magazines: *Rolling Stone* (Simon wearing a pair of custom-made spectacles that looked like a neon sign); *16* ("Abelard's Hot Secrets!!!"); *Hit Parader* (Simon in a wide-brimmed hat and diamante spectacles wearing a long red scarf); *Melody Maker* ("Abelard's A Teen Pop Idol!"); and a loaf of bread. The bread was for what Leslie thought were cravings (she was certain that she was already pregnant) and the magazines were for Stephen to look at so he'd get angry. Leslie believed that Stephen was allowing

Simon and Jacky to take too much of the credit for the songs that Stephen wrote with Simon. "Go up there," she said, "and tell that fucker that you want half."

Stephen was already getting half—his contract with the record company stipulated this—but Leslie didn't seem to listen. She insisted that Stephen take her on as his manager. (She was already his manager in every way that mattered, whether he liked it or not.) Leslie insisted on Simon's lesser role: "All he does is write the music." Her latest thing was Simon and how he had deserted Stephen. Once she got wound up, she could go for hours on this subject, running down everything about Simon, from his clothes to the glasses that he wore, to the state of Nina's house in Stepney and the car that she and Gerald drove. "For all I know, he probably doesn't even write the music. Maybe he gets someone else to do it."

But Stephen remembered Simon in their early days, crouched over the battered upright in Nina's front room for hours at a time, working out the music for Stephen's lyrics. No, Simon had paid his dues as far as this business was concerned. "He's worked as hard as anybody."

"Worked his ass off like you? Oh, right. He's God knows where getting pampered by his asshole manager while you're waiting around for the next handout." Leslie angrily flipped the pages of her magazine, steadily eating bread from the bag at her elbow. "Do my tits look bigger to you?" She cupped them in her hands; they were exactly the same size as always.

"I'm not sure," Stephen lied. The truth was, he didn't really care—with a pang of horror, he realized that he didn't care about Leslie and probably never had. He found her in an antiques store in Mississippi, when the cicadas were loud in the trees and Simon wasn't talking. Leslie was the one who sold him the piano that he brought back to their rented lodgings to see if he could get Simon to make some sort of sound, anything at all. *You're English, aren't you?* She'd appealed to him, standing there behind the counter with her hair in little-girl pigtails and with her chipped pink fingernails. She'd had plasters on both knees; her bare arms were sunburned and brown. When she bent down to retrieve the ledger from underneath the counter, Stephen saw the curve of her breasts and felt a hot lust go simmering along his thighs. When Stephen went back to the UK, Leslie went with him. Stephen remembered Simon's surprised expression when she boarded the transatlantic flight, the inquisitive lift of Simon's brows: *What's up with the bird?*

If Leslie became pregnant, Stephen would have to stay with her and help her raise the child... he'd have to support them both. His face prickled; the room was suddenly too warm. Leslie was still flipping through her magazine; the bag of bread was nearly empty. "Look at him," she said, pointing to a *Rolling Stone* cover of Simon sitting on a park bench next to Jacky. "Fucking asshole."

Stephen thought he might be sick.

10: *We Sometimes Fall*

THERE was a piano in the common room—of course there was, they were civilized people—and a moat around the hospital with a tiny, rounded bridge to get over, and an antique wooden door with iron straps. Simon liked to play the piano (it was the only time he took the mittens off) but he never thought about crossing the water to go anywhere. These days, he wasn't allowed to go anywhere at all, and if he knew what was good for him, Simon would stay put and listen to the doctors and take those goddamned mittens off, and eventually—if he was obedient and very, very good—they might let him out. Then he could go on tour across America with Jacky and make back the money that had been wasted while he was fucking about in this goddamned place. It's bad enough, Jacky said, that Simon had to behave like a childish cunt, but couldn't he have kept it to himself? It was all over the newspapers now, every gory detail exposed for the eyes of the world: *Abelard Suicide Drama* and *Pop Singer Tries to Top Himself* and *Abelard's Mum Says Success Has Ruined Her Lad.*

It was all rubbish, of course—Simon was "ruined" long before success—but people believed it, even the patients in the hospital believed it, which was why Simon played the piano like he did: all day long, from daylight to literal dark. He played every song that he and Stephen had so far written, and he played them over and over, starting at the beginning of his repertoire with songs like "Baby Gone Blues" and "Jeans Girl" to "I'm Digging It" and "Go Away." His perennial favorite was a weepy ballad that he used to perform very early in his career when he was still playing folk festivals and bingo halls, a very long, very gloomy song called "My Ten-Ton Soul." Simon liked it so much that he incorporated it as both a warm-up song and a closer, and sometimes he varied the tempo, making it fast and racy or slow and suicidal, like he was. He'd launch into "My Ten-Ton Soul" if anyone came near to talk to him, or if the nurses tried to make him stop, or if anyone entered the sacred circle of space that he had designated around the piano. When the lyrics that Stephen wrote weren't quite enough, Simon would add more words of his own devising, thus stretching the song out for half an hour or more, a stadium rock relic of astonishing extravagance. He had been here for a little over three months, receiving treatment for his addictions (cocaine, marijuana, Quaaludes, alcohol, and diet pills) and other difficulties—something his doctors termed his "comorbid conditions."

At first, the other residents of the asylum didn't seem to mind: the spectacle of a rock star (albeit a newly minted one) playing the hospital's homely, beat-up instrument had been interesting, even somewhat cheering. But Simon had been playing every day for nine days straight, and it was beginning to wear on everyone's nerves. The matron came out several times to ask Simon to please stop, but he refused to acknowledge her presence. The earl had started making murderous pictures in his needlepoint, and twice the horsey princess screamed at Simon and was led away weeping. The staff had no idea what to do. Simon's mum and Gerald had gone to Spain on holiday so that Nina's nerves could recover and Jacky had gone across to Amsterdam and couldn't be reached. "He's driving everyone mental," the matron said. She and the doctor were closeted in her office with the door closed, but the sound of Simon's incessant playing still reached them clearly. "We have to make him stop."

It took four strong men to drag Simon away from the piano. He was physically restrained with leather straps and injected with enough Thorazine to stop a moving train. With the exception of his rape when he was thirteen, this was the single most humiliating thing he'd ever had to endure. He lay in his bed and drooled on himself, drifting in and out of a strange, dreamless sleep. He felt like someone was chasing him through a dark forest, and he wasn't allowed to stop or rest. He must keep going, moving doggedly forward whether he wanted to or not, because the thing that was pursuing him wanted to kill him and eat his insides out. Always there were the same confusing images: a steel cup full of cold water held before his face, and stairs leading down to a cellar, and the smell of mold.

"Simon?"

There was a hand on his forehead, soothing him, a cool hand with long fingers. He knew that hand and he wanted to look at it, but it was so hard to force his eyes open. It was easier to let go, slide back down into sleep again. He forced himself to speak through dry lips, a mouth as parched as the desert. "It was metal... steel. She was giving me a drink from it. Drink up, make it better." But the drugs had taken it out of him; he couldn't make himself understood at all. When he tried to remember—when he tried to articulate these memories—his mind seemed to be full of a furiously buzzing blankness, a swarm of invisible bees. Why was Stephen here? Hadn't Jacky driven Stephen away? Jacky didn't want Stephen... didn't want Simon working with Stephen, didn't want Simon anywhere near him. Yet the mind's eye, with its unerring instinct for sentiment, drew relentlessly on the past. Here was Stephen in Nina's Stepney kitchen, up to his elbows in soapy water. Here was Simon, perched on the table, legs swinging, chattering happily to Stephen about the records he was going to buy. Here were Simon and Stephen, languid on a rainy Sunday afternoon, watching the football and listlessly pestering each other the way young men did when they couldn't speak the truth of their affections.

"What is it?" Stephen wasn't sure this man was really Simon. He wondered whether the hospital staff had secretly moved Simon elsewhere and put this man in his place.

Simon's lips were moving. "Kill me."

After the nurses cleaned him up and took off the restraints, Stephen was allowed to wheel Simon outside so he could have some fresh air. There were several sturdy guards stationed round the garden who would raise the alarm if Stephen tried to take him away. But Simon didn't have the physical strength or the presence of mind to go anywhere. Stephen was shocked at what Simon had become and horrified at what the hospital had done to him. He parked Simon's wheelchair near a lilac tree and sat on a bench so they could talk.

"Leslie says hi. She made me come and see you." It wasn't true: Leslie had hurled accusations at him, accused him of loving Simon instead of her. She'd threatened to go back to America if he didn't start behaving as a husband should. "How are you?"

Simon didn't answer. He was staring off into the middle distance, and his eyes were glazed. In their struggle to get him away from the piano, the staff had broken his glasses and he hadn't got a spare set with him. The drugs were making him hazy, uncoordinated. Stephen picked up Simon's hand and stroked the back and palm, over and under, moving slowly. Perhaps Simon couldn't feel this, either, but Stephen would keep doing it until Simon told him to stop.

Simon's fingers tightened around Stephen's hand. "I'm sorry." There were livid scratch marks on his wrists and forearms, even though his fingernails were bitten nearly to the quick. "I shouldn't have got you into this." His voice was an unsteady twang, like an out-of-tune guitar. His normally steady gaze was wobbling all over the place. "I shouldn't have got you down from Orkney. None of it would have happened."

"Don't be stupid." Stephen combed his fingers through Simon's disheveled brown hair. "I'd be nowhere without you." It was the sort of thing you were expected to say under such circumstances, and besides, if Stephen had stayed in Orkney, he'd have ended up working at the local chicken hatchery or raising sheep with his father. He'd come home at dinnertime from his boring job and sit at the table to eat sausages and peas, and he'd probably succumb to the dubious charms of some local girl, be obliged to impregnate her with a succession of squalling infants that he didn't want and had no time for. All at once he saw himself on top of Leslie, her skinny legs spread on either side of him, her breasts jiggling as he fucked her—fucked her with his eyes closed, pretending he was somewhere else.

"There's things I don't remember, only bits of it." Simon wouldn't look at him, pretended instead to be absorbed in the badminton game occurring the other side of the moat. "I'd been crying—screaming the house down, really—she was giving me a drink of water. Her hands were always so cool."

There was something in the way he said it that made Stephen's hackles rise. It reminded him of Davy, back home in Orkney. Davy did the shearing for Stephen's father, working from dawn to dusk and sleeping in the stable with the animals. He claimed a supersensory communication with them and said that lying on their straw the night before he was to shear them made them calmer. Stephen's father dismissed this as a "load of old shite" but at the same time appreciated Davy's delicate touch and the fact that none of "his" sheep suffered the nicks and cuts that were all too common in less-skilled shearers. Davy was so good with the sheep that Stephen's father often had him back to help with the lambing.

One evening in very early spring, Davy came up to the house and asked for Mr. Abednego. "It's the little one." He referred to a small ewe that Stephen's mother had named Delicious, on account of her resemblance to the cartoon sheep that graced a certain brand of biscuits. "She's straining awful hard but the lamb still isn't coming. I think we ought to get Doctor Finlay." But Finlay (the vet) had gone to Mull to help another farmer whose ewes were also lambing; he wouldn't be back for days. Davy, Stephen, and his father had gone to the stable and waited as the ewe, clearly in distress, withdrew from them, her breathing labored, her gaze glassy and unfocused. The amniotic sac surrounding her unborn lamb was just visible between her hind legs, and bulged from her body with each shuddering contraction. Stephen had never seen a living creature die, but he sat with Davy and his father and watched as the light fled from her eyes and, afterward, he wept and was ashamed of his sorrow.

Stephen saw the light going out of Simon's eyes and felt the threat of tears. "You'll be home soon enough."

Simon laughed, a noise like breaking glass. "Fuck that."

Stephen swiftly turned Simon's face and kissed him, square on the mouth; the kiss tingled in the soles of Stephen's feet and crackled in the roots of his hair. Simon's hands clutched at his jacket as he returned the kiss: sloppy, eager, desperate. His mouth tasted strange; his saliva had an odd tang—probably the Thorazine. Simon slumped against his chest. "You should go now," he said. "You should go home to Leslie." But Stephen couldn't; he knew that now. The only person he could ever possibly go home to was Simon.

Simon was Stephen's word for home.

11: **My Ten-Ton Soul**

IT WASN'T like Simon had never been to a funeral before. There was the time his grandmother died when he was twelve, and a couple years before that, a classmate had died of some rare childhood cancer. He'd become adept at crying on cue, at pretending to be affected, even if the person wasn't anyone he knew particularly. But this was different—this was Roger. His father was dead now, there was no way around it. There was no way around the open grave. The others hated him, he was certain of it. He kept trying to meet Mick's gaze, but Mick wouldn't look at him. Mick huddled close to his wife and their small daughter, his broad back bent against the cold.

The priest was stalking round Roger's grave, black vestments fluttering in the wind like the wings of a carrion crow. Why Catholic? Had Roger converted? It was difficult for Simon to believe: his father never had any religion, never went to church. But Roger's widow was a Catholic, wasn't she? Simon never asked. After his hospitalization, he received a card in the mail from Doris, informing him that masses were being said at the St. Columba's Church. He didn't know what to do with it, so he used it as a bookmark in a book that he started reading and never finished. He often wondered about it: when masses were said for someone, was the person actually mentioned by name? *In the name of the father and the son and Simon Duckworth...* Maybe it was a task that fell to lesser members of the seminary—priests in training, acolytes, or friars—or assigned as penance if one failed to properly observe various of the holy tenets. *His cassock came above his knees during cricket practice, Father. It was a shocking spectacle.* Simon imagined this exchange taking place inside a darkened space, a library or confessional. *Above his knees? Well, he can say the masses for Simon Duckworth, then. Serves him right.*

The casket—his father's casket—was going down into the ground. Roger's mortal remains were effectively conveyed into the underworld, there to await the resurrection; Simon wondered if the dead could feel the presence of the living, the impress of a beloved foot as the ground above their coffin was trod by mourners. He imagined his father could hear the beat of his heart, a misplaced metronome. Why wasn't Stephen here? He was sick with a bad cold, he was in bed asleep somewhere, snoring noisily with his mouth open—the image was comforting. Someone in this world, at least, was still alive. The clods of dirt surprised him, hitting the casket noisily like stones hurled down from a great distance. The mourners filed past the grave, dropping fistfuls of earth down onto Roger's coffin. It must be a Catholic thing; he had never seen this done before. (This noise would stay inside his head forever, and subconsciously inform the cadence of his music.) Simon found himself bending, his fingers clenched around a clod of earth. He saw Roger, sitting by the canal out back of their old house, fitting a worm to the hook for him. The worm was wriggling in his grasp, still alive, still sticky with dark earth. His father's fingers, too, were dark and clenched around the edges of his vision, holding him, squeezing his thoughts.

There was a sort of wake afterward, at Roger's house. The mourners all got back into their cars and drove away—quickly, as though fleeing the scene of a crime. Simon didn't have his car there, and no one invited him to ride with them, so he walked down to the nearest cross street and hailed a cab. The driver was cynical and middle-aged and perilously lean, with a toothpick hanging out the side of his mouth. His greying hair was slicked back over his head like a greasy helmet; his hands on the wheel were stained with nicotine, the fingernails much bitten and abused. He had a tattoo of an anchor on his left forearm, or maybe a skull; the ink had faded and was in the process of being devoured by the skin, so it was hard to tell. He grunted when Simon told him the address, hauling the cab into gear with a subdued savagery. He lit a cigarette, and the pungent smoke filled the whole inside of the cab. Something like relief rolled over Simon, something comforting and familiar, the sort of emotion he felt when he saw washing on a clothesline or a group of old women talking. The smell recalled Nina's homely kitchen and the dim house of his grandparents back in Stepney.

"Care to make a few bob extra?" He reached forward and laid his hand on the cabbie's shoulder, feeling the muscles knot and flex beneath his fingers. The driver turned his head but didn't speak; obviously he had done this sort of thing before. He pulled in behind a deserted warehouse whose windows had been beaten out, whose rusted railway tracks went halfway to nowhere. He insisted on payment before doing anything: twenty quid.

Simon pressed the bills into his hand. He wasn't sure what he ought to do there in the back seat of the cab, alone, so he pressed himself back against the dark upholstery, waiting. The door flew open and he felt the cabbie fumbling with his trousers, then his cock was engulfed in heat and wetness. He deliberately kept his hands away from the cabbie's greasy head, unwilling to spoil the illusion. *It isn't Gus, it isn't Gus, it's him, it's Stephen.* He squeezed his eyes tight shut and imagined he was lying somewhere with Stephen, and Stephen was the one doing this. He was lying on an Orkney beach on a warm summer night, lulled by the sound of the sea, and he and Stephen were naked together. The moon gleamed on Stephen's naked torso and his tanned legs; he smiled and caressed Simon's cheek before leaning in to kiss him.

Simon came with a grunt, curiously unsatisfied. The cabbie straightened up, turned aside and spat on the ground, wiping his mouth on the back of his hand. Without another word, he went round to the front and slid back into his seat. His eyes flickered up to Simon's in the rearview mirror. "Where to, again?"

"My father's dead." There was a nasty taste in Simon's mouth. "My father's just been buried."

The cabbie lit a cigarette. "Where to?"

Simon sat back in the seat and zipped up his fly. "Hamiltonhill Road."

AS SOON as Roger married Doris, Nina put a stop to Simon's visits. "I won't have you going up there to that house," she said, "consorting with his fancy women on the side." Simon wondered where Nina had got that idea: Roger had no women on the side and Doris (despite her kindness to him and her innate good nature) wasn't what Simon would have called fancy. She was short and wide, with big hips and hair that couldn't decide whether it was red or orange. She had perpetual eczema on her hands, a result of the near-constant washing that her job required (Doris was a nurse). He couldn't figure out why his mother hated the thought of her, since Doris wasn't now and couldn't ever be a threat to Nina, and anyway, it was Nina who finished with Roger and not the other way round. Who knew how long she'd been seeing Gerald on the sly? Roger was away all day up the gas company, working, and Gerald had good reason to pay daily visits to the house, him being the postman.

The last time Simon had been here was with Stephen on their way to visit Roger in the hospital. "You need to have a cuppa and a bite to eat before you head back on the road," Doris had said. "You'll be starving." Simon was too buzzed on coke to eat, but Stephen was famished, so they sat together in Doris's pale yellow kitchen and looked at photographs: Roger with swim trunks on, smiling on a foreign beach; Roger and Doris on their wedding day, Roger looking dapper in a suit and Doris surprisingly pretty in a pale pink dress with a crown of daisies in her hair. Doris turned another page and there was Simon, sitting on the railing of a bridge with Roger, fishing in the old canal that ran behind their house in Stepney. Some were pictures that even Simon hadn't seen and didn't remember: a Christmas photo of Simon at a school concert, his diminutive hands spread on the piano keys, his face turned to the camera, features frozen in an attitude of expectation.

The cabbie dropped Simon at the door and he somehow found his way inside, pushing past the relatives that thronged the foyer and the fleet of gleaming cars that formed a steely gauntlet up and down the street. He remembered the proper protocols, his manners driven into him by Nina. He found Doris in the kitchen making tea. He touched the knot of his tie nervously, running an uncertain hand through his hair. "Auntie Doris?" He always called her that.

"Oh Simon! Dear Simon—" She reached for him and hauled him into her embrace, squeezing him so tight that Simon thought he heard his bones crack. "I'm so glad you came."

The word gave Simon a moment's worth of difficulty, thinking of the cabbie, but he shrugged it off. He allowed Doris to kiss his cheeks and look him over with a critical eye. "You've not been well," Doris said. "I can see the dark rings underneath your eyes."

"It's nothing." But she already knew he'd been in a lunatic asylum. "I've had the flu." He should hate this woman, and he would if Doris were to blame, but Doris wasn't, he knew this now. His parents' marriage was over long before Roger ever met Doris, or even before Nina had met Gerald bringing the post round every morning and smiling at her over the shrubbery. Gerald, too, had been married before, to a foreign woman. No one knew what happened to her and no one ever asked; Gerald never mentioned it.

"He loved you, Simon." The kettle shrilled, and Doris moved to shut it off. Simon could hear the others talking loudly in the sitting room; he hoped they would leave him alone, at least until he had said what was in his mind.

"I loved him—" The news of his father's death had come while he was in the psychiatric hospital. Remembering it now nearly choked him. *Mr. Duckworth, I'm afraid it's bad news.* "I know we never—" *Your father's died, Mr. Duckworth. His wife asked us to relay the news.*

The swinging door banged back on its hinges. "It's Abelard!" The small red-haired girl was there, one of Roger's children, Mick's younger sister, little what's-her-name. "Abelard's here!" She lunged at Simon and grabbed one of his hands. "Will you play the piano for us later?"

"Darling, bring the teapot into the sitting room. I'll be there in a minute." Doris reached quickly into a drawer and took the scrapbook out: a thick book with dense grey paper, every page bulging with mementoes. Roger kept everything: every newspaper clipping, every photograph and concert program. "He wanted you to have this. He made it for you, when he was ill, when he…." She trailed off, unable to continue, turning away to hide her tears. Simon pretended to be looking at the scrapbook. He didn't belong there; he should never have come. He wasn't a part of this; this whole thing was Roger's life, not his. It was nothing to do with him.

"I really ought to go. I've got to get the train back home, you know how it is." A lame and cowardly excuse and Simon knew it, but he'd die if he stayed there. He couldn't bear the telescoping glances of his father's other family, of Mick and his brothers and sisters and their friends. He couldn't meet their collective gazes, Mick and Peter and the quiet one called Billy. Doris said Mick could drive him to the station to get his train, but Simon refused. "I'll call you on the weekend and see how you're doing." Simon kissed his stepmother on the cheek and tucked a wad of banknotes quietly into the pocket of her cardigan, taking the scrapbook with him and exiting by the back door. He left the house behind him in the gathering dark. It was at least a couple miles' walk to the station but he didn't mind. In fact, he welcomed it. He intended to look through the scrapbook while he was on the train; he wanted to look at it. But he was horribly tired and a bit strung out and the clacking and swaying of the train was quite hypnotic. He slept soundly all the way to London, waking with a start at King's Cross station.

He left the scrapbook on the train.

12: **Don't Jump the Queue**

London, 1981

"I DON'T like the way he looks." Simon wasn't trying to be difficult, but he had a headache and he wasn't in any mood for this. Not for the first time, he wanted to talk to Stephen, but ever since their split nearly ten years before, it was harder than ever to track down his old writing partner. It was rumored—although Simon had no proof of this—that Stephen had gone to Australia. He was little more than an occasional figure on the contemporary music scene, appearing only reluctantly and vanishing again as quickly as he was able. Now and then, word of him would surface in connection with some other musician, some up-and-coming band, but Simon never heard from him and Stephen made no effort to contact him. Their music, so laboriously crafted years ago in Nina's Stepney kitchen, had dispersed into the world: there was literally nowhere anyone could go without hearing Simon Duckworth's voice on some radio, somewhere. Simon has been famous for a long time.

"You can't leave him sitting there all day," Jacky said. They were in Jacky's office—Jacky's swanky new office, bought with Simon's money and filled with such gorgeous treasures as would make a looting Cossack drool: Aubusson carpets and tapestry chairs and Old Masters carefully framed in gold and silver, sofas upholstered with the skins of rare jungle animals.

The new lyricist that Jacky found was named Johnny Slaughter, which couldn't possibly be his real name but it was. Even funnier, Johnny's father was a butcher in Philadelphia, the owner of a posh little meat shop on Society Hill. Johnny pretended to come from the hard side of Philadelphia, but really, he grew up in the suburbs, in a gated modern community located a comfortable distance from the city. With his head of bubbly blond curls, he resembled a man-sized cherub, or one of the Renaissance *putti*, somehow stretched and elongated. His face was almost painfully red and boiled-looking, like a small animal that had been left too long in the sun, and he was forever wandering about doing yoga breathing exercises designed to increase his sexual prowess. He could roll a marijuana cigarette faster than anybody and consumed only the very best in modern ganja. Johnny had made his name as a lyricist writing for bands like Tensile Pistol, Poverty's Arse, and the Socket Queens. At the age of twenty-three, he, along with the members of the Tobash Trio, wrote "Moon Over Memphis," which captured the prestigious International Songwriting Competition's first prize. Since then, Johnny had been a very hot commodity.

"At least go talk to him," Jacky said. He wasn't quite wheedling. He hadn't enough imagination to suppose that he might put Simon's career in jeopardy, or that Simon and Johnny would write anything together besides rubbish. He had been seduced by the idea of it, by Johnny Slaughter's vast angelic visage and his bubbly golden curls.

Johnny towered over Simon, a great colossus of a man with a face like God's personal anointed. He was at least a full foot taller than Simon, with enormous hands and feet. "Simon Duckworth." Unlike the rest of him, Johnny's voice was soft and raspy, the result of laryngeal nodules that would eventually render him entirely mute but which presently made him sound rather like Bob Dylan. "Fuck, man. It's a total mind fuck. The people need this music." His smile revealed a myriad of gold teeth. "The world is moving towards this all the time, you know? It's the Great Brotherhood. Want to see my scar? I've been marked, man." He pulled down the stretchy fabric of his roll-neck shirt, exposing his pink chest. Someone had engraved the words *Rita's Tits* into his skin; the words were old and faded, and appeared to have been done with a Biro. It wasn't quite a tattoo. Johnny's smiling face and strange inscription reminded Simon of something sinister: men in masks, the slow and certain descent of an individual darkness. He shivered, forced himself to concentrate.

"Put your money where your mouth is, eh?" He couldn't believe he said that. He had never seen so many gold teeth, not even among the Gypsies who frequently camped in Victoria Park near Simon's old home. He'd been briefly involved with a Gypsy girl named Lola with the most beautiful breasts Simon had ever seen, smooth and white with rosy nipples. She'd been equally enthralled with him, exclaiming over the bulge of muscle at his biceps and his strong shoulders. The first time they made love, she pulled Simon into her and rode him like a polo pony. There were few people in Simon's life who'd ever boosted his self-esteem as much as Lola. He was shattered when her family had abruptly left for Yorkshire without so much as a by-your-leave.

Simon was acutely aware of his own physical imperfections, especially his working-class teeth: serviceable but hardly glamorous, with gaps and faint misalignments. Nina could never afford the time to take him to the dentist's when he was young and Simon, wealthy enough now to buy whatever he wanted, couldn't imagine willingly subjecting himself to the dentist's chair. There would be anesthetic, and for a time he would be unconscious: unable to move, unable to respond or help himself. His old insecurities, never far away, came roaring to the surface. What was Johnny Slaughter thinking as he watched Simon? Simon was clean-shaven and wearing a suit and tie; his shoes were polished and he looked like a youngish bank executive rather than a rock star.

"I loved the album, man." Johnny reached into his briefcase and extracted a copy of *Abelard*, Simon's first album. The cover sported Simon's spectacled face staring mournfully at nothing. "I keep a copy of it everywhere. I keep one in my car on tape. I know the kinds of things you're saying—I totally get that. It's about control, and power." He offered the album to Simon. "Would you sign this for me?"

Simon's pen traced his name without hesitation. Wasn't this what it was all about? Hadn't he waited years for the opportunity to inscribe his name on record sleeves for legions of adoring fans? Didn't he love it when they screamed his name, no matter where in the world he went? He never needed worry about money or status or any of it, ever again. He was richer than God. Everybody knew his name. He'd come a long way from frying sausages in Nina's grimy Stepney kitchen, from crouching over his shabby white piano in the front room and teasing music out of Stephen's words. He'd gone as far as anybody could go. He was a legend.

"Wait a sec." Johnny held the album up to him. "You made a mistake there." He pointed to the place where Simon's pen had been. Instead of signing "Abelard," Simon had written Stephen Abednego's name.

WHEN Simon opened the door, it was late and raining. He remembered hearing Jacky counsel him against opening the door to strangers: *Hire some fucking big American to stand security detail,* he'd said. *You don't need to open doors to people. You're Abelard.* "Stephen." Simon, like Stephen, was older now, would be thirty-four at his next birthday, nearly middle-aged. He'd traded his spectacles for contact lenses, revealing his long-lashed brown eyes—but there was a pervasive sadness about him, a melancholy that hadn't been there before, and something haggard in his face. He drew Stephen into the warm and lighted foyer, took his sopping coat away. "You've got balls, being out on a night like this. How's Leslie?"

"She...." His heart slammed into his ribs. "She threw me out."

Simon stared at him. "Fuck me," he said. He caught hold of Stephen's arm. "Are you all right?"

Stephen laughed gently, and for a moment, it was just the way it had always been: the two of them, together, like in the old days. "We've been divorced for... must be eight years now."

"Eight years." Simon mulled this over. "Do you need... I mean, do you... you can stay here, you know. You can always... look, come in."

A tall man with a froth of golden curls was sitting at Simon's piano, his back to them. He didn't look up or acknowledge Stephen's presence but went on playing softly, a tinkling melody like an antique music box. "We're gonna be working for a bit," Simon said. It gave Stephen an uneasy pang. "I mean, don't wait up."

Stephen helped himself to a bottle of Smirnoff from Simon's liquor cabinet, and around one in the morning, he wandered out to see what was keeping Simon. Simon was sitting at the piano playing something very soft and slow and very beautiful, singing words that Stephen didn't write. With regular practice Simon's voice had deepened, become richer and more nuanced than it had been in his early days; listening to it now brought tears to Stephen's eyes and he had to turn away for a moment to compose himself.

"You didn't used to take so long to write when it was us," Stephen said. He wasn't really all that drunk, merely jealous, and he wanted to be boorish and rude. The tall blond man was sitting on the sofa with his eyes squeezed shut like he was in pain, a marijuana cigarette burning unheeded between his fingers, filling the room with its pungent smoke. "So what's this," Stephen asked, "the honeymoon?" He waved the bottle at Johnny, whose blue eyes were open now in his boiled-looking face. "Wanna drink, do you?"

"My God." Johnny snuffed out the spliff and got to his feet, stood swaying for a moment. "Stephen Abednego. Oh my God. You wrote the lyrics for 'Radio Baby'. I thought—" He broke off, his expression shuttered. "I've been writing some things. I'm really into Dylan, his early stuff, you know?" Without asking, he launched into a long, breathless recitation, delivered in a voice he apparently thought was like Bob Dylan but which actually sounded like someone dying of emphysema. Stephen was reminded of John Keats on his deathbed in Rome, smothering in his own body fluids. "We gotta break the ties/that keep us from being kind/we're all behind/we gotta rewind." He beat time against his thigh with his free hand, his head bobbing at the end of his neck like one of those felt dogs that people put in the back window of their cars. "What do you think?" he asked Stephen. "Do you dig it?"

"It's brilliant," Stephen lied. He went back into Simon's bedroom and shut the door.

"HE'S a nice fellow." Simon, dressed in a dark blue jogging suit, his shoes kicked off, leaned on his elbow, gazing down at Stephen. "He used to write television adverts." He giggled a little bit. They were lying on Simon's huge, four-poster bed in Simon's enormous, rock-star bedroom. The presence of Jacky Stride had been erased since the last time Stephen was here: there were no more Telex machines; no giant desk; no rows of gleaming shoes, faintly beetlelike, grinning from the open wardrobe. The tabloids and the gossip rags had been splattered with supposed quotes from Simon: WHY I FIRED MY MANAGER, but Stephen knew better. Simon would never fire Jacky. He needed Jacky the same way some people needed to be hurt in order to experience sexual satisfaction. It was more likely that Jacky had been the one to move on.

"You remember that advert for Joneses washing soap? 'Don't let the laundry kill your wife'." Simon sang a phrase or two. "He wrote that."

"McCartney's been after me to write songs," Stephen said. It wasn't true, but it could have been, because Stephen's gift for writing had brought him significant fame quite independent of Simon. "I've been up to my arse lately. Hardly time to breathe." Simon's dark eyes with their long lashes were beautiful; Stephen reached up and touched Simon's cheek, feeling the slight rasp of stubble against his fingers. "I should have never married her," he whispered.

"You haven't got to explain." Simon caught hold of Stephen's hand and kissed the palm. Then, holding Stephen with his gaze, he took each of Stephen's fingers into his mouth and sucked. The effect was shattering and immediate: Stephen grunted softly and rolled onto his back, his whole body trembling. Simon's hand slid over his torso, expertly located a nipple and began stroking slow circles round it. Stephen's cock twitched and began to fill with blood; his back arched and he reached out to pull Simon toward him. Their clothed bodies met in the middle of Simon's enormous bed; their mouths met, too, in a clash of lips and teeth. Simon's hands were on his head, cradling his face and Simon was kissing him—so good, so good—like he had never left, like nothing had ever changed between them, like Stephen had never gone away. Stephen got both hands up under Simon's jacket, keening aloud when his palms met warm skin. There were too many clothes between them, so he wrestled and tugged until Simon leaned away from him and pulled off the top of his tracksuit, baring his torso.

"You're beautiful," Stephen whispered, but there was a sorrow in it akin to desperate prayer. "Oh God, you're beautiful."

"Oh God, I'm not," Simon retorted, "but at this moment, I don't really give a fuck." He fell silent as Stephen traced a long, slow path from his navel to the base of his throat, leaning in to press his opened mouth over the bulge of Simon's larynx. He tongued the flesh under Simon's jaw, working his way back to Simon's mouth as Simon's hands came up, unbuttoning his shirt and pushing the garment off his shoulders.

They lay together for a time, exploring bodies that the intervening years had altered. Simon was heavier, bulkier through the chest and shoulders, with powerful thighs and arms; Stephen was as slender as he had ever been but there were new lines around his eyes and a certain world-weary knowledge in the way he carried himself. Like Simon, his hair was cut short and his right earlobe had been recently pierced to accept an earring. A tiny, five-pointed star had been tattooed into his lower back by a girl in Singapore who spoke no English but whose skill with the needle was unrivalled. Stephen had submitted to her ministrations in the pale grey light of dawn, lying prone on a narrow wooden table in a small room located at the back of a drugstore. It had hurt him more than anything ever had before in his life but he accepted the pain, wanted it, even entered into it as a kind of spiritual ordeal.

His experiences, like Simon's, had been many and various, and in their travels round the world he, too, had enjoyed intimate encounters with lovers whose names and faces he didn't really remember. The only thing that stayed was the memory of pleasure commensurately taken, of nights and afternoons and early mornings spent in pursuit of an elusive ecstasy that, once found, split him wide open. He regretted nothing.

"What do you want?" Simon asked, his voice rendered voluptuous by sexual longing.

Stephen leaned in and licked the corner of Simon's mouth. "I want to make you come."

He lifted Simon's heavy cock and stroked the head with his lower lip. Simon grunted, an explosive out-breath, and fisted the sheets as Stephen swallowed the blood-hot organ, sucking Simon's cock deep into his mouth. Stephen stroked him hard, rhythmically, swirling his tongue around the head, working Simon until he teetered on the edge of orgasm and then backing off. He climbed on top of Simon, felt Simon's arms go round him and Simon's mouth on his and they were moving together as the world sped up and he was dimly aware of the bed squeaking and Simon's body heaving underneath him and Simon crying out as the orgasm took him. Stephen's own release tingled in the soles of his feet and the curve of his back and for one eternal moment he hung there, absolutely silent.

He yelled and writhed and shouted as it throbbed out of him and he didn't care who heard; God only knew what Simon's servants thought. His body shuddered and rippled and finally came to rest on top of Simon, who held Stephen with his strong arms and kissed him.

"I love you." He reached out and smoothed Simon's sweat-damp hair off his brow. "Simon. Oh, God." His breath went in and out of him and he lay with Simon's arms around him and Simon's face close to his. It occurred to him that some primeval question had been posed—and answered—but not what such things meant.

"DON'T let the laundry kill your wife," Stephen sang gently, just under his breath. "Let the Joneses help." They lay in each other's arms, gazing up at the night sky through the glass ceiling. The ceiling, like the bed, was a recent addition to the room. Someone else would have mirrors on the walls, mirrors above the bed, but he knew Simon couldn't bear this. After all these years, Stephen knew Simon still couldn't stand looking at himself.

"Stephen."

It was very late, perhaps three in the morning, but Stephen was still awake, his body humming with the pleasure they had shared. "Mm."

"What are we… are we—I mean, you and I… are we going to say anything?"

Stephen had been dozing, dreaming of white sands and a foreign beach somewhere. "Say?" He awoke with a start. "Say about what?"

"About us, Stephen."

"About us." Stephen sat up, his desire for sleep suddenly flown. "You mean—"

"I mean about you and me, being together—for fuck's sake, Stephen!" Simon leapt out of bed, naked and angry. "You know? You and me? Together? Fucking each other? Here, Stephen, and when we were in the States, and in Orkney, and all the other times. Or have you already forgotten?" He yanked a dressing gown off the back of a chair and pulled it on, belting it savagely round his waist.

"I didn't think we were going to be public—I mean, there's your career to think about." It was a feeble excuse and he knew it. He should have been ashamed to even say it, but the idea of a public declaration terrified him. "What will people think? Imagine if the newspapers get hold of it."

"That isn't it." Simon's voice sounded like it was coming out of someone else's mouth. "That isn't it at all. Tell me the truth. You should tell me the truth. Goddammit, Stephen, I deserve that much."

Stephen was back there again—in Nina's kitchen, with the smell of grease hanging in the air and the knickers drying on a makeshift clothesline up near the ceiling. "I don't think—I don't want to do that."

"You already did it."

"I realize that, Simon, but—"

Simon carried on, as if he hadn't even heard Stephen. "With me, just now. And this wasn't the first time. There have been lots of times, Stephen, regardless of what you think people know about you and me."

The back of Stephen's neck prickled unpleasantly. "What do you mean, what people know? What people? I've not said anything." He cast his memory back, wondering if he'd ever said anything to a journalist or a casual acquaintance that might have been misconstrued.

"In my mother's house, back in Stepney, in the house in Mississippi, in the back of the fucking bus, for Christ's sake."

"That wasn't...." Stephen's eyes felt hot. "That was a hand job. It's not the same thing." This argument was specious, and he knew it. It had been much more than merely a hand job.

You know I love you. You know that, right?

Don't talk so much. We're almost in Biloxi. Hurry up.

Simon seemed incredulous. "You really are looking for the fucking exit, aren't you?"

"Simon, I think the bloody world of you, you know that." Someone stirred elsewhere in the house; a door closed quietly. Had some member of Simon's staff been listening? Was their conversation being recorded? "I just don't want that."

"You don't want what?"

"I don't want to be...." Something warm and infinitely precious was slipping inexorably away. In a moment it would be gone forever and there would be nothing he could do. "I don't want to be a... poof."

"Is that what I am?" Simon swallowed; Stephen could see the ripple of his throat, a pale blur of movement in the darkness. "To you? To anybody?"

"I didn't mean—"

"I don't give a fuck!" Simon was suddenly shouting. "I don't care. Fucking Christ, Stephen! I thought we were something to each other." He was crying, swiping at his face. "You don't want to be a poof? You don't want to be a fag? Is that it?"

"Simon—" Stephen started toward him, thinking that touching him would help, but Simon slapped his hand away.

"Get out."

"Don't be childish."

"Fuck you." Simon turned away, went to flip on a light. He sat on the edge of the bed and cut several lines of coke in rapid succession. "This is such bullshit."

"Simon." Stephen reached out a hand, but Simon shrugged him off.

"I'm good enough to fuck but that's the end of it?" He bent and swiftly inhaled the lines, one after another, pressing the back of his wrist against his nose, then went to the small bar set into a far wall and poured two fingers of whiskey into a crystal glass. "I'm only just good enough to fuck."

Stephen was silent for a long moment; then he threw back the bedclothes and stood up, searching for his underpants. He dressed himself quickly, eager to get away, to put this entire episode behind him. "I understand that you're angry with me." He raised his arms, let them fall by his sides.

"Angry with you?" Simon shook his head. "You just don't get it, do you?"

"Look, you know how I feel about you." Stephen's hands clenched into fists. "You've always known. I just don't see why we've got to announce it to the whole bloody world."

"No, let's not announce it." Simon cut another line. "Let's be ashamed of loving each other." He laughed mirthlessly. "You know, if this were a film, we'd be screaming at each other now. We're too bloody civilized, aren't we?" Stephen tugged his shirt on over his head and reached out, but Simon shrugged him off. "No. It's not that easy. I'm not letting you take the easy way out." He went back to the bar and splashed some more whiskey into a glass. "Want a drink, Stephen?" Simon held the glass out to him. "How about we toast the death of our immortal friendship? Christ, that's bleedin' poetic, that is. That's like something you'd say."

Out of everything Simon had said, this seemed to hurt the most. Stephen's face crumpled, his body tensed as if warding off a violent blow. "Yeah." The muscles in his throat worked as he swallowed. "I suppose it is."

"Go away, Stephen." Simon tossed back the whiskey and poured another. "Go the fuck away."

"Simon, try to understand."

"Get out."

Stephen stood there for a long time, watching Simon cut lines and drink. He had the idea that Simon would eventually say something, apologize for the argument, tell him to stay, but Simon didn't. Simon seemed to forget that Stephen was even in the room.

Stephen went out to the foyer and stood for a long time, one hand pressed against the front door, waiting, but Simon never appeared.

THE first time Simon ever got high was at an industry party held in the basement of someone's house in Mile End. There were train tracks running behind the house and all night long they heard the clack of metal wheels on track while the stereo blared stoner hits and people passed a joint around. Simon was shaky, weak from hunger and his latest diet and a long stint on the road, playing dives at every whistle stop between Liverpool and Putney. He sat between Stephen and some noisy red-haired girl named Chase and watched Jacky cut lines with expert ease. Chase's blouse rode low over her breasts and she was braless, as far as Simon could see. Her hip-hugger jeans exposed a smooth expanse of taut white belly and a ruby bellybutton ring shaped like an oriental dragon. She kept her hand on Simon's knee and squeezed it when she talked; sometimes she was even talking to him. She rolled a joint with one hand and licked the paper with her shiny red lips and Simon was simultaneously aroused and embarrassed. "Here—" She lit the joint and sucked on it, held it out to him. "Go for it."

"Like this." Stephen was a veteran of many hazy Orkney nights, lying in a farmer's field and smoking: the pot of his childhood was indigenous, grown under special lights in some local yob's bedroom, and potent. "Hold it in."

Simon had smoked his share of purloined cigarettes, stolen from Nina late at night when she and Gerald were asleep, or purchased on the sly from a school friend. He never liked the way tobacco burned his throat and seared his vocal cords. He took a drag and blinked back tears, struggling to hold the smoke in. "I don't think it's working," he said. "I don't feel anything much."

The room dilated beyond the expanse of paneled walls and dirty carpet; the music suddenly was everywhere, Jefferson Airplane singing "White Rabbit." The music worked its way inside of him, slid down his throat and deep into his belly and warmed the base of his spine. "I can't stop anything," Simon whispered. Chase's eyes were blue, with golden rings around the pupils, golden rings like a field of summer flowers. "It's got nothing much to do with me."

"Of course it does," she whispered. She straddled Simon's thighs and looked at him. "Everything's to do with you." She took his hands and laid them on her naked waist and Simon touched the ruby bellybutton ring, the oriental dragon with its flaming eyes. Her mouth was warm and wet and open, sloppy kisses and her long red hair falling into his face. She took his glasses off and laid them on the coffee table. "You're gonna be a star, you are. Yes, you are. You're going to be ever so famous." She pressed her lips into the base of his throat and hummed *famous famous famous* and smiled against his skin. Simon looked at Stephen, and suddenly Stephen's face was close to his and they were smiling at each other.

"It's lovely," Stephen said. "It's so lovely being here." His long fingers brushed against Simon's cheek. "It's just lovely, that's what it is."

The room was moving; Chase tugged on Simon's hands and pulled him to his feet. "Come in here with me." She caught hold of Stephen's wrist and pulled him after her. The corridor was long and dark and narrow, claustrophobic, and led into a dingy bedroom with an old-style four-poster bed piled high with satin pillows. Chase's pubic hair was red and so was the hair underneath her arms; she sat on Stephen and rode him, sucking on his fingers. Stephen was naked, young, beautiful, and strange, and he grunted as she pleasured him. He turned his head and gazed at Simon, saw himself reflected in Simon's myopic stare.

"You haven't got your glasses on," Stephen said, right before he came.

"You lads are so fucking hot together." Chase pulled Simon on top of her, pulled him into her, and he found Stephen's hand and brought it to his mouth, sucking on Stephen's index finger.

"That one's mine," he said. He turned Stephen's face to his and kissed him, and it was warm and safe and good; it felt like coming home. They shared another joint, the three of them, and it pulsed and boomed inside of Simon like a living thing. There was some business with Chase and the two of them, he and Stephen, underneath the covers, and Simon wasn't sure whose hands were on him or who was kissing him, but he came so hard he saw stars.

It was late or early when he woke, and Chase was gone but Stephen still lay beside him, sleeping with his arm thrown over his eyes. Simon got dressed and went to the bathroom; Jacky was asleep in the bathtub with Chase on top of him, wearing his shirt. "What time is it?" he asked no one in particular. "I need to know what time it is."

"It's really early." The girl was blonde, Chase's friend; her name was Monica. "People think it's late, but it's actually very early." The music on the stereo was jazz, soft and muted, a looping melody without words. She combed his chest hair with her long red fingernails. "Time is subjective that way."

"I want to experience it all," Simon told her. "All of it, the good and the bad. I want to know what it's all about."

Her blonde hair made a curtain around her face as she snorted several lines in quick succession off a piece of broken mirror. "It's not seven years' bad luck," she said. "It's not quite seven years."

"Your nose is bleeding." He caught the trickle of it on his fingers. "It's redder than you might expect." There were noises from the bathroom, Jacky shouting something, and the blonde girl was gazing at Simon with a strange expression.

"I don't believe I know you," she said. "I don't believe we've even met, have we? I don't believe we've been introduced. I don't believe in God or the Devil. I don't believe I even know you." Her head slammed into the arm of the sofa and her body thrashed spasmodically, her heels drumming against the floor. She stared at Simon with glassy eyes and tried to say something, but all she could manage was a disconnected grunting.

"I need someone to help me," Simon whispered. He cleared his throat and shouted. Jacky came running, and Stephen and Chase, the red-haired girl who'd fucked them both in someone else's bedroom. "I need someone to help me," Simon said. He caught the blonde girl underneath the arms and tried to hold her still but the convulsions were too strong.

"Call the doctor," Stephen said. "Call an ambulance."

Jacky slapped the phone away. "Are you off your fucking head?"

"She's having fits," Simon said. "She's got to have the doctor." The room was waking up; people were standing round them, looking at the blonde girl.

"She's got to have the doctor," Simon said again. "She's ill."

He was led to a waiting police car with handcuffs on and Jacky cursing behind him. The ambulance lights washed red over Simon's face, over the lenses of his spectacles, lighting them from inside. He shivered in Jacky's borrowed coat under fluorescent lights while the detectives asked him questions: had he given her cocaine? Had he watched her take cocaine? Did he know the girl? The younger of the two detectives, a constable named Collins, asked him for his autograph: *I know you. You're Abelard.*

"Now you've fucking torn it," Jacky said. In the early light, his face was pale and strained with dark rings underneath his eyes. "This'll be in all the fucking papers, just you wait and see."

"She would have died unless we'd called the doctor," Simon said. It was later in the evening, and he and Jacky were huddled in a booth at the Lancaster Grill, eating sausages and chips.

"She's already dead," Jacky told him. He shoveled chips into his mouth with the stolid regularity of a machine. "I called the hospital. She died this morning." He stared at Simon and burst suddenly and noisily into tears; it shocked Simon more than anything ever had. "She died this morning."

SIMON cut cocaine in straight lines on the glass top of his coffee table; it wasn't quite morning. Apart from his servants, who knew enough to keep to their rooms, he was entirely alone in the house, and there was silence except for the ticking of a French Empire mantel clock that echoed eerily in the cavernous living room. He had already taken enough cocaine to keep him up for three days straight, but he couldn't seem to stop and, left on his own this way, he had no idea what to do. He had no idea about anything at all. He dialed Jacky's number and got his answering machine: too late, he realized that Jacky was in America, holidaying with the parents of some rich girl that he hoped to marry for her money. He couldn't call his mother because she and Gerald were in Australia. There were any number of servants and functionaries he could call, all of whom would come immediately, but what he wanted was someone to talk to, someone not dependent on him for a paycheck or two weeks off at Christmas.

He breathed on the glass tabletop and drew a heart. *Look, this is what I think about when I see you.* He and Stephen, sitting on the top of a bus on a cold December day, dressed in pea jackets and donkey scarves, on their way home from… where? It had been so long ago, a country far away now in the imagination, but Simon could see them both so clearly: Stephen at seventeen, skinny and fey and young, green eyes sparkling with laughter, his whole being animated, happy to be there. And Simon, twenty years old…

"Twenty years old." He spoke aloud to the empty air. "You were seventeen and I was twenty." They'd gotten home in the early dark, their noses and their ears red with cold. Nina and Gerald had gone to play cards with another couple, the husband of someone from Gerald's work. He and Stephen made sausages and chips for tea, and mushy peas out of a tin and HP sauce and soft white bread thickly spread with butter. Afterward they'd watched *Steptoe and Son* and did the washing-up together, Simon washing and Stephen drying. The cold kitchen windows steamed with the moisture from the sink; Simon reached up with one soapy hand and drew a heart. "This is what I think about when I see you." Immediately he regretted having said it; Stephen would think he was soft—but Stephen merely smiled and said nothing at all. Simon let the subject drop. Maybe, he'd thought Stephen would be more receptive later and he could speak freely then, but he knew this would never happen. Even talking about something as mundane as the weather was difficult for Simon; he could only ever really express himself under the influence of some mind-altering substance. "That was a funny one, wasn't it?" He scrubbed the frying pan harder than necessary, trying for a cheer he didn't feel. "'There's always brass about! You've got to shout for it!'"

"Simon." Stephen tried to get him to stop scrubbing. "What you said before…."

"And he was always talking about the horse, about the horse being hungry." Simon kept his gaze down so Stephen couldn't see his eyes and pretended vexation with a spot of burned sausage that had clung to the bottom of the pan. "'He's a dumb animal!' God, it's a laugh. I like that show."

Stephen grabbed his arm and held on. "It's not you."

"That bird with the cigarette, at the beginning. The way he was rolling his eyes, Christ!"

"Simon, would you just—" Stephen caught hold of him by the upper arms and shook him gently. Simon leapt violently backward, crashing into the far wall.

"Don't." He held his hands out in front of him. "Don't."

Stephen moved toward him, intending to apologize.

"No. Don't move, I said. Please. Please don't." Simon sank down on his haunches and tucked his hands into his armpits. "Just give me a minute." He laughed, but there was no warmth in it, no humor. "Didn't mean to give you a turn. Sorry. I didn't mean—you can't just—"

Stephen lowered himself to the kitchen floor and sat down, some feet from where Simon was. "Was it because I grabbed you?"

"It's like a short in a wire," Simon said conversationally, "isn't it? Like something snaps in my brain, like something—" He swallowed hard, his gaze on the floor. "Forget what I said. Just forget it. It was mad. I wasn't thinking. I'm mental." They'd left the telly on in the other room: *Top of the Pops* was on—applause, and playful banter, the noise of electric guitars tuning up, Mott the Hoople. A drop of water fell from somewhere into the sink, and Simon jumped, recovered; he tried to smile.

"Tell me." It was phrase Stephen was to utter many, many times during the course of their relationship.

"It's fine," Simon said. "I'm fine." His mother's hands had always seemed enormous, the fingers infinitely gripping, spatulate; she gave him water afterward to drink, in a metal cup that tasted of cold and Stepney water.

THERE was a big sensation in the papers that time about the girl who had died at the party: ABELARD FRONT MAN DUCKWORTH IN DRUGS BUST. But there had never been any bust and Simon was never arrested, even though the girl had died. He'd gone, of course, to the funeral, at Jacky's insistence: *It'll make you seem sympathetic to her family. The public love that sort of thing.* He'd driven there himself and stood at the back of the church and bowed his head when the prayers were said. Her mother was surprisingly young-looking, with the same blonde hair. She'd worn a chic black dress and a hat with a veil and dabbed her eyes with a handkerchief. If she recognized him, she gave no sign, and at the end of the service, she filed out, supported by her husband and the minister. *You should go to the cemetery, too,* Jacky said, *and let people see you there. Probably it's better if you could even cry a bit.* But Simon couldn't, and so he stood there watching as the coffin was lowered down and everybody wept. All he could think about was Chase, about her oriental dragon and the red hair underneath her arms. All he could think about was the blonde girl with the piece of broken mirror and the blood coming from her nose.

He'd never seen anyone die before, but she had died long before the ambulance had come. She'd died in Simon's arms, gazing up at him with open eyes and a surprised expression, and her body trembling through a dozen tiny seizures, one after the other. He'd never watched anyone die before, not really, although he'd seen his share of cinema and television deaths, all perfectly sane and sanitized. People died so clean on television; there was no agonizing final struggle, no fight for breath. There were no spasmodic gestures, the body releasing its feces and fluids, the breath exhaled on a final, ghastly rattle. The room was silent then, and Simon sat for what felt like ages with the dead girl in his arms, watching a silvery line of spittle slip from her opened mouth into her hair.

The paramedics are here. Stephen had touched his arm. *You've got to let them take her to hospital.* Stephen was crying, and his tears made his eyes glisten like green jewels in his pale, contorted face. Stephen was good, and beautiful, and none of this was his fault. None of this was Stephen's fault. Simon sat for hours in the police station, wearing his filthy clothing with the blonde girl's death on them. Jacky had been curiously comforting, sitting with his arm round Simon, holding his hand and talking to him.

It's not your fault. None of this is your fault. At seventeen Jacky had run with a gang of youths calling themselves the Butcher Boys; they all inhabited the same desolate, forgotten streets and laneways and faceless housing towers, and many of them never knew their fathers. They made pocket money playing dice and "fingers" after school, or waited for the younger boys and stole their dinner money. One of their opposite number, a brassy rich boy named Malcolm, had insulted Jacky one morning in the laneway behind the house. The Butcher Boys and Jacky waited for him that night, watched him put the milk bottles on the doorstep, and then they took him. They dragged him behind an abandoned building and beat him half to death and gave him a Glasgow Smile, slitting his mouth from ear to ear and leaving him to bleed there on the ground. It was later rumored that he hadn't survived the trip to the hospital but lay in his blood for two days before anyone found him and by then it was too late.

Did you kill him? Simon accepted the glass of whisky Jacky gave him and drank it, sitting in his bathrobe before the fire.

I never knew. I never asked. The police had come round the neighborhood, asking questions and taking names, but Jacky didn't even register on their radar. He'd had a talent, even then, for slipping under the wire, for escaping detection. He was adept at camouflage and blending in, of waiting patiently in hiding until the danger had passed. *I'd kill for you.* He said this quietly to Simon. He didn't even blink. *I'd kill anyone that tried to hurt you.* There was a livid, U-shaped scar on Jacky's lower back; Simon would later trace it with his fingers, memorizing it, remembering its curves as though it were a talisman, or a mandala.

Where'd it come from?

My father gave it me.

It tasted of salt and hatred.

13: *Third-Floor Bedsitter*

STEPHEN ABEDNEGO was somewhere in the wilds of Australia, somewhere beyond the reach of telephones, somewhere far away from anything remotely like society. It had been three months to the day since Simon shut him out; Australia was as far away from Simon as he could get. He took a small cabin at the very edge of the sea and all day long sat watching the waves as they rolled up on the shore. The waves were endless; they went on and on, and watching them, his mind was curiously empty, his body without sensation. He passed many hours this way, drifting in and out of something not unlike sleep, and the sun rose and set on him, a diurnal rhythm that marked the passage of his days.

There was a small shop at the end of the road where he went to purchase bread and chocolate, potato chips and ham, and occasional paperback novels with cowboys on the cover. He deliberately avoided doing anything that he used to do. He didn't write song lyrics or strum a guitar and he disciplined himself not to think about the life he left behind, about Leslie and their abortive marriage. Mostly, he tried not to think about Simon but he failed in this; he failed utterly. His dreams were full of Simon, and so erotically charged that it was very nearly painful. His every waking hour was similarly occupied and his long days in the hot Australian sun left him drugged, drunk with Simon's imagined presence. He couldn't stop thinking about his first night in London and how Simon met him at the train, and how Simon looked in daylight, the morning after their first coupling. He had never in his entire life felt anything as powerful as that and he understood now why his marriage to Leslie had failed, and why it couldn't have survived. He understood what people meant when they said they'd met their "soul mate," even as the sensible part of him cringed from such a florid term.

The water was pale blue, sunlit, as warm as blood, and comforting. He wasn't sure why he might need comfort; he wasn't sure why he sometimes woke now with tears on his cheeks, or why sadness seemed to overtake him at the most nebulous of moments. He swam a great deal and wept into an ocean made temperate by his tears. The notion that he might someday slip into it and never again surface was too near his thoughts.

I know you, man... I know you. He'd been in America; the heavy-rock group Tensile Pistol had asked him to write some lyrics for them, and he often tagged along when the band went out of town. He found himself seated on the bus next to a young music reporter called Stoneman with stringy hair and a straggling moustache and big sideburns long out-of-date. *You're Stephen Abednego. I know you.* He was a journalist for a music paper out of San Francisco, something called the *Vice*, and he'd been touring with Tensile Pistol since they started, off and on. *You're a fucking genius. How come you're not with Abelard?*

Stephen had become adept at spotting microphones, hidden cameras, and little tape recorders, but there was nothing, not even a notebook. *Our paths diverged.* He was proud of himself; he hadn't even had to think that one up.

Do you miss him?

They were in the middle of a crowded bar, and some of the lads from the band were having a bit of a rave-up near the jukebox. The music was loud and there were countless conversations taking place around them, but Stephen heard him. Stephen heard every word he said. *Dunno what you mean, mate.*

Are you sure?

Gotta go to the loo.

To his credit the journalist didn't follow him in but waited outside the door until Stephen reemerged, zipping up his fly. *Where is Abelard now?*

I don't know. I don't know where he is. He bit back the rest of it. There was no need to say more; indeed, there was no need to say anything at all. Any remark at all was fodder for the tabloid press, and he'd rather not be held up to ridicule. He had no comment about Simon; that door had closed in his face.

Whenever Stephen tried to remember that very first night, he could never recall who moved first—but someone did, and there was the taste of toothpaste from Simon's mouth and the quiver of Simon's warm breath against his cheek. *It's like kissing a girl,* Stephen thought. *It's like kissing anyone, really.* And the sensation of eager kisses, their noses bumping together, Simon's glasses cutting into Stephen's cheek. *I don't want to be a fag.* But he'd already done plenty of other things like that, things at parties, things with whores and groupies and hangers-on. He'd woken up in strange beds with half a dozen people and a funny taste in his mouth and reacted with a mental shrug. They were both so young—he was seventeen and Simon merely twenty—and at best, it was a bit of kissing and a hand job and a bit of clinging to each other in the dark. They were both so young. *We were young.* This was what he told himself, walking on his Australian beach and weeping into the blood-warm sea.

THE letter was addressed in an unfamiliar hand. He wondered if he should open it or not: *To Simon Duckworth, calling himself Abelard these days.* The envelope was white and ordinary, the postmark smudged with dirty fingerprints. The letter smelled like laundry soap. Simon called out for his butler, Nestor, a huge Jamaican with exquisite manners and an accent rich as butter toffee.

"What is it, Mr. Simon?" Nestor appeared from a side door as though summoned by magic. He was carrying a tea towel and a silver ladle. "Someone bothering you?" Nestor took the letter away to the kitchen and slit it open with a knife. "Just a letter, sir. There's nothing else in there." He was kind, but Simon still felt stupid. Perhaps he ought to hire someone to read his fan mail, like other people did. He could set up a little room here in his house and have someone in to open all his parcels and his letters. Isn't that what other people did?

The letter had been typed by hand on an old-style typewriter with a crooked letter L and a burr over the crossbar on the T.

Dear Abelard, my dearest darling Abelard, or Simple Simon, if that's what you're calling yourself these days. I'm trying to think of a way to say this that won't hurt your feelings... wait, what the hell am I saying? I want *to hurt your feelings.*

His fingers slipped a little on the telephone, but he got Jacky on the first ring. It was eight hours earlier where Jacky was, if Jacky really was in California, but Simon couldn't really remember, because the letter was messing with his head. Was he in California or New York? Where had Jacky said he was going?

You have to come.

I'm in fucking Long Island, Simon. You know this. What the bloody hell's the matter with you?

I got a nasty letter.

He was Abelard; he was a darling of old ladies and young girls. He didn't get insulting letters.

"Let me put a detective on it," Jacky told him, "and we'll see what he can come up with." There were party noises, music and glasses clinking. Simon was suddenly very thirsty.

"Where are you?" Simon asked.

"Long Island," Jacky said, "I already bloody told you. Long Island, New Fucking York, all right? Christ, you're like a child." There was laughter in the background. "Lock the bloody doors. You'll be fine."

Simon's eyes filled with tears he would not let fall. "Right, then. Thanks." He laid the receiver down.

His piano bench sat before a bank of windows, tall and glistening and empty as the eyes of a skull. He ought to do some work, ought to work on something. He summoned Nestor from the kitchen: *Shut the damned curtains, would you?* There were eyes fastened on the back of his neck, eyes forever watching him. There were strangers in the dark, creeping round his house, looking for a way in. What if the man who wrote the letter really knew where Simon lived? What if he decided to come and visit? What then? Simon should have changed the locks... he should have changed the locks and put extra deadbolts on the doors and steel shims in the windows, just in case. He ought to have secured the garage because sometimes crazy fans got in that way; look at what happened to Peter Locke after the Wembley concert last year, and wasn't that just a hoot for all concerned? Would Simon end up like that, beaten nearly to a bloody pulp with a claw hammer and left for dead? *I* want *to hurt your feelings.*

"Nestor." It came out as a squeak. He cleared his throat and tried again.

"Mr. Simon?"

"Could I have, um, whisky, scotch, something?"

The drink arrived on a silver tray; he downed it all in one go and asked for another. Nestor was circumspect: he never said a word, never betrayed himself with gestures or some aberrant expression. He was the perfect gentleman's gentleman; he was as silent as the grave.

Simon got up from the piano bench and went into the main foyer where the alarm box was. There was a row of blinking lights, blue and green and red, but he couldn't remember what it was supposed to look like, or which ones ought to be lit or not. He should have asked someone... he should have asked Jacky to check it for him before Jacky went to America, but Jacky would probably have said something nasty and Simon would have felt stupid. Simon often felt stupid around Jacky. What if it wasn't set? What if someone could get in? *Simple Simon, if that's what you're calling yourself these days.*

"Nestor."

"Mr. Simon."

"How do you... when is this...." Beads of sweat popped out on his forehead, his upper lip. Everything was going much too fast. "Can anyone get into the house?"

"I don't believe so, Mr. Simon." Nestor's posture said he would effectively dispose of any intruder. Nestor's huge biceps strained at the sleeves of his coat; his hands were enormous. Nestor could squeeze the life out of anyone; he could snap their bones like drinking straws. This thought didn't comfort Simon, who merely imagined Nestor doing it to him.

"I don't want anyone to come in," Simon said. "I need to be sure." A long shiver ran through him like icy claws skittering across his vitals. The imagery was very apt: Stephen would have liked it, would have said that it reminded him of T.S. Eliot, would laugh affectionately at Simon for coming up with it. Stephen should be here. Stephen shouldn't have gone away. So much of this was Stephen's fault. Simon tried to remember: what had they been fighting about? Stephen's wife had left him—good riddance to bad rubbish—and he and Stephen had argued about writing songs, or had that been a different time? The only thing that seemed to stick in Simon's memory was the slick sensory impetus of warm and willing flesh, the sounds that Stephen made, the way his body shuddered and flexed under Simon's hands and mouth. They had lain together afterward, tenderly, in each other's arms, and it had seemed to Simon that the whole world was his, or could be. *I don't want to be a poof... I don't want to be a fag.*

Simon sent Nestor off duty for the night and wandered into the living room. The window drapes were sinister to him, like the closed eyelids of blind men. He cut a few more lines on the coffee table and inhaled gratefully, immediately calmer and more centered, yet buzzing with a zestful energy. He made a circuit of the house, putting one foot deliberately in front of the other, counting his own footsteps as he walked, the journey transecting each room in the house. It was a ritual with him, to walk through them all and mark them with his presence. He needed to remind the house that he lived there, that this was his house, a sacred space. The cocaine hummed like a swarm of locusts in his head and his body felt transparent: if he held his own hand up to the light, he would be able to see the bones and vessels, the slow passage of blood moving through his veins. Without Stephen, the world had become a foreign place, and he did not belong in it; everything was baleful, monstrous. There was no symmetry; there was no peace.

He started the shower and stood for a long time under the hot water, letting it stream down on him. He imagined the water passing through a hole in the top of his head, passing into him and cleansing him. If he could only stay perfectly still, the water could get inside and wash him clean but he couldn't stop, not even for a moment. His hands were shaking and his body was vibrating and he knew he was being looked at. There were eyes and faces in the patterns of the tiles, on the floor and on the walls and on the ceiling. Each single drop of water was a minuscule face with tiny, staring eyes. Everything was judging him. He could never be correct. He would never know the answers.

You're a filthy boy. His mother's voice, Nina's voice, berating him. *I know what you were doing in your bedroom. I know what you were doing in there.* She'd been angry because of his pajamas, because he'd got through a week's worth of clean pajamas. *That's a filthy thing to do. You know it's filthy and still you do it, don't you? You're just like him. You're as bad as your father.*

Simon lay on his bed in the dark, vibrating with fear and panic and cocaine. He wanted Stephen—no one else could help him except Stephen. And Stephen wasn't there. He was twelve years old again and his parents were fighting bitterly outside his bedroom door and he was trying not to hear them. He was trying not to hear his father calling Nina horrible names, or Nina screaming at Roger. He was trying not to hear the sound of things being flung around the room. He clenched his hands together and breathed. Like everything else, this was merely another trial to get through; this was just another bump in the road. He closed his mind to every other thought besides the minute-by-minute counting of his breaths.

SIMON'S new car knew the streets of Stepney as well as his old one did. At ten past one in the morning and wide awake, he found himself driving near the old gasworks, motoring inexorably toward Mile End. There were four girls standing by a hoarding, smoking cigarettes. Simon pulled his car up and rolled the window down. "Can I have a word?"

"What word's that, dearie?" The girl was short and plump and blonde, wearing fishnet tights and platform shoes and a shiny orange jacket. She could be forty or she could be fourteen; it was always hard for him to tell.

Mum, there was a nice lady on the tram that said I'm going to be a handsome man.

What lady on the tram?

Simon had gone with Nina to the corner and pointed her out and Nina promptly boxed his ears. *Don't be so bloody stupid! Don't you even know a tramp when you see one?*

"How much for you to come back to mine?" He had a wallet full of bills, but wasn't quite certain about the etiquette in matters such as this. Did she get payment first, or did he wait 'til after? No one had ever explained it to him; it wasn't like he could run and ask Gerald about it, and anyway, he and Nina were on holiday in Spain. Simon liked to spread his money round: his newest single *Get Your Own Back* was one he'd written with Johnny Slaughter, and despite all odds, it was doing well. He was fairly flush now, more so than he'd ever been, and although he was frugal with his dosh, he didn't mind spreading it about when the situation warranted.

"Depends on what you want," the girl said. She leaned in close and smiled, the same smile she used for all the blokes. "You want French, you want oral, up the back, you want a knee-trembler or a shirt-lifter, round the world, fish supper, hummer, or the works? Which is it? I don't do nothing weird and kissing costs you extra."

Simon's face was hot; he was grateful for the dark. He was even more grateful that Nestor was off-shift and wouldn't be hovering in the doorway when Simon brought this girl home with him. "I want you to sleep with me."

She laughed uproariously. "That's what they all want, love. But I'm trying to set a price here." She frowned. "I think I must know you. Haven't we done business before?"

The other girls were muttering amongst themselves and casting a weather eye over Simon and his car. One of them called out, *All right there, Janice?*

Simon leaned forward into the light and showed her the face that routinely turned up on the cover of *Rolling Stone* and *People* and in the pages of all the gossip rags. "Flippin' heck," the girl said. "Is it really you?"

"I just want you to sleep with me," Simon said quietly. "Nothing fancy, nothing weird. Just sleep with me, all right?" He saw her mouth opening: "And keep it quiet, yeah?" It was ridiculous for him to even think it, but he no longer cared. This wasn't even about sex and it wouldn't have mattered if the girl had been a bloke. Simon was terrified to sleep alone, terrified to lie down on his bed and watch the advent of the evening's darkness, terrified that if he lay down willingly he would never wake again.

Her shiny vinyl skirt squeaked on his car's upholstery. She fastened her safety belt without being told and grinned at him. "Ooooh, this is nice. Aston Martin, isn't it?" Simon could just imagine what Jacky would say when he found out: *I could get you any bloody girl you wanted! What the fuck is the matter with you, for fucksake? Are you off your fucking head, or what?*

"I live in Windsor." Simon pulled out into traffic, eyes fixed on the road. "Is that all right? I'll bring you back to London in the morning." He was afraid that if he looked at the girl she might disappear.

"Oh, I don't mind, darling." She was pretty in an overblown sort of way, with full, pink lips and a round face both cherubic and knowing. She hadn't been completely ruined, not yet anyway. "I bet the rest of them back there are pissing themselves about now, especially if they got a look at you."

"You don't have to do anything" Simon ignored her comment; he didn't want to be Abelard tonight. "Just sleep beside me, that's all." He was trying not to think. Instead, he concentrated on the high-pitched roaring inside his head. "You don't even have to talk. Just sleep. That's all." For this privilege he would give her a thousand pounds.

"YOU'VE got ever so many lovely things," the girl said. She wandered round his bedroom, touching various objects, exclaiming over the gold records on the walls. "But it's tasteful, not over the top, like." She moved close to him, sliding her arms round his waist. "I'll make an exception for you," she purred. "You can kiss me if you want. You can do whatever you like."

"You can't tell anyone you've been here." Simon slipped away from her and sat on the end of the bed. "You can't say a word to anyone." Of course this was rubbish and they both knew it: as soon as she was back in London, she was off to the tabloids like a shot, and who could blame her? They'd pay a lot of dosh for dirt on Simon. The *Sun* and the *Weekly World News* had been speculating about his sexuality for years, but even the most veteran of their reporters hadn't been able to find out anything factual. A recent foray into the speculative had cost the *Sun* five hundred thousand pounds. *ABELARD TROUSERS SCANDAL: WHO'S IN AND WHO'S OUT?* The cover story purported to prove that a despondent Simon, fresh out of drug rehab, had taken a string of lovers both male and female, ostensibly to "soothe the pain of lyricist Stephen Abednego's abrupt departure from his life." Jacky, working in concert with Simon's lawyers, had sued them into silence, but both he and Simon knew it was merely a matter of time before someone—some passing acquaintance of Simon's or a hotel chambermaid, or someone in attendance at one of Simon's lavish parties—told everything they knew.

"Swear on the Bible, darling." Janice hovered by the bed, still fully clothed. She went down on her knees and reached for Simon's fly. "Let's get that big boy out for some fresh air, then."

Watch out for the splash, by the way...

"No." He pushed her hands away from his jeans. "Don't do that."

"Don't you want me to do you?" Her voice was amused; she sat back on her heels and smiled up at him. "You are paying me for it, or don't you remember?"

"Just sleep. That's what I said." His heart hammered in his throat. In a moment the panic would overwhelm him. "I just want you to sleep with me."

"You don't want me to do you?"

"No. I don't want you to... do that." He went abruptly into the bathroom and stripped to his underpants, cleaned his teeth with restrained savagery and dragged a brush through his hair. Stephen should have been there. What Simon wanted was Stephen. Stephen would make everything all right again; Stephen would make him safe.

Where had Stephen gone? He even tracked down Leslie in America and asked if she'd heard from Stephen. All he got was an earful of curses and the phone slammed down. It shouldn't be like this. It should be just the two of them, writing songs in Simon's old bedroom back in Stepney, watching football on the telly and teasing Nina at the breakfast table. It should be socks and knickers drying on a clothesline in the kitchen, and the smell of grease and cigarettes, and Gerald bellowing at them to shut the bloody hell up, he was trying to watch the news. He wondered if perhaps it was Nina who sent Stephen away, like she disposed of everyone who'd ever loved him, like she'd driven his father away and kept Simon entirely and jealously to herself.

"Are you coming out of there, love?"

The girl was sitting on his bed, rubbing her feet. He saw that her hair wasn't really blonde but had been dyed; her unguarded face was tired-looking, and she was at least thirty or perhaps even older. When Simon lay down, she took him into her arms, drawing his head down onto her shoulder. "There, there, darling. There, there." She smelled like tobacco smoke and sweat. "Now tell Janice what you want us to do, hmm?"

Simon pressed his eyelids shut so hard that he saw yellow spots. His heart hammered in his chest in double two-four time and he felt sick. "Tell me I'm a good boy." It came out as a tortured whisper. "Tell me I'm such an awfully good boy."

"Why of course you're a good boy. You're ever such a good boy. Why wouldn't you be?" She sat up and stared at him. "Don't you want me to...." She glanced around as if one of Simon's servants might any moment come bursting into the room. "Don't you want me to fuck you?" She reached for the front of Simon's shorts, but he caught her wrist, held on.

"No. I don't want you to do that." His grip tightened, the powerful piano player's hands crushing the bones in her wrist. "I want you to lie down. I want to lie with my head on your shoulder."

"All right, love." She wriggled her hand free. "Don't break my hand though, will you? I might need it later."

"Sorry." He flushed a deep red. "I'm sorry. I didn't mean it. I'll pay you extra if you want." He lay beside her awkwardly, his head on her shoulder. Janice put her arms around him.

"You're such a good lad." Her fingers drifted through his hair and she sighed. What was she thinking? That Simon was so much nicer than her usual johns? That his home was immaculately clean, that he himself was polite and well-attended, not hard up for dosh like some men, not interested in anything weird or dangerous. "You really are. I don't know if anybody realizes what a good lad you are. I wish I could tell them." Simon's fists unclenched and he slid his arm around her waist. Janice stroked his forehead, the planes of his cheeks, the point of his chin. "Mummy loves you ever so much. Yes, she does." In any other setting, with any other man, it would have been ridiculous; with Simon it was only sad. "You're Mummy's special angel. Yes, you are. Mummy's special angel."

Simon wept silently, his tears soaking into her blouse, his body heaving with unvoiced sobs.

IN THE morning when Simon woke, there was another letter, written on the same typewriter as before and bearing similar sentiments: *I saw you bring the girl into your car last night. I'll have you yet. I know where you live.* Simon called Nestor, who called the police.

A LONG line of people were waiting to see Simon, all of them with Abelard albums in their hands and some with T-shirts or posters and several even had autograph books, the likes of which Simon hadn't seen since he'd left school. The store manager set up a table for him, piled high with Abelard merchandise and flanked by two strapping employees that Simon knew were really private security. He was glad of them; he wished there were more of them, an enormous number, enough to form a veritable phalanx round him. *Stop being such a fucking baby.* He could hear Jacky's voice inside his head. *These are the people who made you. Now put your fucking chin up and smile.*

"You're Abelard."

"Yes, I'm so pleased to meet you. How are you today?" Simon's reaction was instant, polished, and very charming; it had been drilled into him by Jacky, who hired a professional acting coach to teach Simon how to loosen up in public.

"I'm great, but it looks like you're even better." The fan was a woman (Simon could clearly see breasts underneath her T-shirt) but she had made herself look as masculine as possible. Her hair was buzz-cut close to the sides of her squarish head; there was a ring in her bottom lip and an array of tattoos slithering up and down her plump forearms. She must have weighed 25 stone. She wore baggy dungarees held up with rainbow-striped braces and a pair of clunky workman's boots. "Let's go back to your place so I can fuck you through the mattress."

All the blood drained out of Simon's face; he was suddenly nauseous, struggling to control his reaction, even as Jacky's strident voice sounded inside his head. *I don't care what they fucking say or do. It's you up there and it's me, and remember: these bastards buy your records, so be nice to them.* "It was so nice of you to come today."

For some reason she found this violently amusing. "I haven't come yet, but I'm sure you can help me with that!" Someone giggled behind her and the middle of the line shifted uneasily.

Simon attempted to put the best possible face on it. "Have you come a long way today? I met one bloke who'd traveled down from Manchester." He held his hand out for her to shake but she ignored it.

"Come on, then." She opened her mouth and licked her top teeth suggestively. "Me and you. Let's go somewhere private. I want to eat choccy ice cream off your arse."

Simon's heart thudded painfully in his chest and he staggered backward, reaching out instinctively for something to hold onto. The store and everything in it retreated from his gaze, becoming small and indistinct, and he knew without question that he was going to faint. This was surprising, because Simon had never fainted in his life. The woman advanced on him, grinning insanely, and he saw that she had braces on her teeth. It was an odd sort of thing for him to notice, someone having braces on their teeth. It was very odd.

"Did you get my love letters?" She hissed it into his face, standing so close that Simon could make out each individual pore on her nose. "Simple Simon, calling himself Abelard these days...." *I want to hurt your feelings.*

Simon's fists clenched. "Get her away from me!" he shouted. "Get this bitch the fuck away from me, all right? What the fuck are you waiting for?" He was trembling violently, but with fear or rage, he couldn't tell.

"Right, that'll do." One of the burly shop assistants standing to either side of Simon moved in and hustled the woman away, but not before she leered at Simon over her shoulder. He watched as her buzz-cut head disappeared between the giant bodyguards, his hands shaking, his whole body trembling violently.

The HMV manager slipped through the crowd and murmured a question in Simon's ear: Was he all right? Did he need a moment to himself, some water, an aspirin?

"I'm fine." He forced himself to turn to the next girl in line and sign for her. She had some T-shirts, one from each of his tours, and an Abelard album and a book of postcards printed illegally in Japan. She was young, not more than seventeen, dark-eyed and lovely.

"Could you sign it for my gran, if you please? My name's Jin, and I love your music, too, but Gran really adores you."

Simon treated her to his gap-toothed smile. Would it be wrong of him to ask her home with him? Of course it would, and anyway, she was far too young; it wouldn't be right. He could just imagine Jacky's frothing rage when he found out. *It's all fucking bad enough! You want people to think you're a fucking pedo or something?* "There you go, love. Tell your gran hello for me, won't you?"

He wrapped up the session quickly and was escorted back to his car by the big young men. He scanned the crowd, but the woman was nowhere to be seen. "Thanks again for signing my things." The youngster, Jin, appeared at his elbow. "I know you're busy, and I really appreciate it. I really do." Her skin was the color of pale coffee, as smooth as satin; her dark, almond-shaped eyes glistened as she regarded him, the rings on his fingers and the gold chain at his wrist. She was clearly assessing him and that assessment didn't go far beyond a simple fuck, but Simon didn't care. He wrote his private number on a piece of card and handed it to her: *Call me sometime.*

"What about right now?" She laid one hand on his arm. At this proximity she was older than seventeen. She was old enough to know the difference.

Simon held the door open.

STEPHEN had never really been away from Simon. He'd gone home to Orkney now and then, visiting his family, and once, an awful Christmas week, during which he pined for Simon like a young girl pining for her lover. When the train finally pulled into Paddington Station, he bolted into Simon's arms and stuck to him: *I missed you awfully. God, I'm never going away again.* The truth was that Stephen needed Simon; in his own way, he was just as emotionally indigent, just as fragile.

Unlike solitary Simon, holed up in his Stepney bedroom with his record albums and his dreams, Stephen always had plenty of other lads to pal around with, but was never familiar with them, never intimate the way he was with Simon. Stephen never needed to say anything and yet he had wound up telling Simon all his secrets: that his parents slept in separate rooms at night and his father had a mistress in the village; that his sister at eleven years old still wet her bed; that his grandfather died in an insane asylum and Stephen often wondered if the same would happen to him.

His grandfather, Horace, wrote epic poetry in the style of Milton, full of heroic language and grand anapestic gestures. Yet Horace could never shake the persistent veil of melancholy that surrounded him. At twenty-two he tried to kill himself by driving the nib of a fountain pen into his carotid artery; at twenty-eight he tried again, this time with poison, but the dosage was too great and he vomited most of it away. He married at thirty, comparably late for his generation, but Stephen's grandmother was a sensible girl with her own career (she framed oil paintings in a shop in Lincoln) and she was able to take him in hand. She found work for him at a foundry where he kept the books and managed the offices and handled himself quite well for many years. Some of his poetry was published (under a pseudonym) and enjoyed a favorable if fleeting reputation. His wife gave birth to three daughters in succession and then a son, Stephen's father. Everything appeared astonishingly normal. Yet, when the old man retired from his position at the foundry, he began to wander. Late at night he could be seen straggling down the main road of the village, clad in his cap and nightshirt. The local constables apprehended him and brought him home, and Stephen's grandmother installed special locks on all the doors and windows. The old man discovered how to pick the locks and was off, wandering again. When questioned about it, he had no memory of what had happened in the night; he insisted that he'd slept quite well. Finally, he was caught crawling into a young girl's window in the early hours of the morning and remanded to the village jail and then to an asylum.

Stephen was horrified that he would end up the same way: wandering the roads at night, dressed in nothing but his underwear, unable to remember who he was or who he wanted to be. Who would run after him and bring him back to bed? Not his parents; surely not Leslie. He had imagined Simon forever at his side, had naturally assumed it would be Simon running after him, Simon taking him back home. He had thought they would be together always.

Stephen never wondered about Leslie in the same way; Leslie was an aberration, a ploy, a stratagem to make Simon pay attention to him and, ultimately, the means to reassure himself of his normalcy. He chose her because she was convenient and because she reminded him of his childhood friend Bernard, a spoiled boy whose parents owned a series of successful Orkney pubs. Bernard spent the greater part of the school year with his grandmother, but since she helped to run the family pubs, he was mostly free to do as he wished. He met Stephen shortly after Stephen's parents had moved the family to St. Margaret's Hope. *Come over to mine after school and I'll show you something.* Bernard moved in elevated circles, was rumored to have been kicked out of some fancy public school in England, except nobody knew why. Whatever Bernard wanted, he got; his bedroom was filled with expensive riding gear for the horses he never bothered with and various musical instruments and board games imported from America, some still sealed in their cases.

Have you seen Lisa Morry's tits? Give her a quid and she'll show them to you. She shows them to all the boys. Bernard stripped to his underwear and threw himself onto his bed, immediately began stroking himself with one hand down his pants. *Come on, get your kit off. Christ, I'm really packing it.* He paused to roll a joint, offered it to Stephen. *You gonna get off, or what?*

I've never... I don't do that.

Like fuck you don't. Bernard's eyes narrowed to slits; his hand sped up inside his underpants, working himself furiously. *Do you want me to do it?*

Stephen, curious, lay back on the bed, his trousers unzipped. *If you like.* The ceiling above Bernard's bed was white, stippled with brown spots where the roof had leaked. The bedspread was white as well, chenille, the kind with the little tufts of wool pulled through holes to make a pattern of roses in a cottage garden. *What's it feel like?*

Like you could die. It feels like you could die from it. Bernard put his hand into Stephen's pants, wrapped his fingers round Stephen's cock. It immediately hardened, stiff and swollen, beating with a pulse all its own. Stephen had dreams like this, and woke up with a damp spot in his pajamas and feelings of confusion and deep shame. Bernard's fingers were rough and callused but all it took was three or four strokes before Stephen came off with the best feeling he'd ever had in his life.

You can't tell anybody. Bernard knelt on top of him, his bony knees driving Stephen into the bed. *If you ever tell anybody, I'll kill you. Do you hear me? I'll kill you.*

SIMON'S butler Nestor sent the girl home the next morning. She was disappointed that Simon wouldn't touch her, wouldn't kiss her or have sex with her.

I don't understand why you brought me here. She was wearing expensive Japanese lingerie, decorated with strategic slits and bows. She was young and beautiful and her body was firm and taut, but Simon didn't touch her. It would have made him no different from Gus if he did that. Like most of her generation, she was sexually bold and her advances were difficult to refuse. She'd offered to do anything he wanted her to do. *You can give it to me up the arse. I heard that's what you like.* She had no idea the very notion horrified him, on account of what he'd been through.

I'd like you to sleep with me. I mean, I'd like you to sleep beside me. Please.

It should have made him ashamed, having to ask for it like that, but he was beyond shame now, beyond guilt. He wondered what Nina would say if she knew the sorts of things he was doing. He remembered the French girl and how he kissed her by the canal and put his tongue in her mouth. Perhaps it wasn't right, bringing Jin home with him and then simply lying beside her all night. She would tell her friends that Abelard was a nancy-boy. She'd tell them he was a poof. Thankfully, he hadn't had to face her at breakfast, since Nestor had slipped into Simon's bedroom early and extracted the girl, given her a hot breakfast, and sent her back to London with Simon's driver. In situations such as this, Simon had always been able to count on Nestor absolutely. He was the most reliable of all of Simon's employees.

Nestor made a pot of coffee and Simon helped himself to a cup, flicking through the newspapers idly. Jacky would prefer to keep Simon sheltered from the more salacious tabloids but Simon reminded him that he grew up in Stepney and didn't need sheltering. He didn't need to remind Jacky that being raped at age thirteen effectively obliterated whatever remnants of innocence he'd had left.

The front pages were all of a piece: FORMER ABELARD LYRICIST MISSING, POP STAR MUM; ABEDNEGO DEAD IN PLANE CRASH SAYS FORMER ABELARD STAFFER. There were first-person accounts from various Abelard "close pals" attesting that Stephen had gone back to Orkney, that he'd got religion, that he shaved his head and went to live in a commune or an ashram or a fisherman's hut on the Isle of Wight. No one really knew where Stephen was—

Simon included—but he was hardly dead, and even if he was, Simon would have heard something. Simon would have known if something horrible had happened to Stephen. He would have absolutely known.

The woman was outside his window. At first Simon couldn't believe it, but there she was, standing on his lawn as large as life, wearing a black T-shirt with the sleeves cut off and baggy black jeans and black Doc Martens. The front of her short-cropped hair had been dyed bright blue, and there were three shiny new safety pins through her left eyebrow. She saw Simon watching her and she grinned, winking at him. She clutched her enormous breasts and hefted them in her hands, as if gauging their individual weight. All the blood seemed to leave Simon's head; he was struck dumb. He laid his coffee cup down on the counter and walked deliberately toward the window. The woman blew a kiss. Simon raised both hands above his head, fists clenched, and brought them down on the glass. "Why don't you fuck off out of it?"

The glass shattered instantly, cutting Simon's hands and wrists. He watched in amazement as bright red drops spattered down onto the pale carpets. His blood was dripping onto his shoes, onto the floor, onto the legs of his trousers. His blood was running down his arms and dripping off his elbows when he lifted his hands. He felt weak, dizzy, helpless. The woman had disappeared.

"Mr. Simon, sir, what have you gone and done?" Strong hands caught him round the waist and half carried him into the kitchen, easily negotiating the curving wall that jutted out from the dining room, the bank of enormous windows looking out onto the garden, Simon's grand piano. Nestor wasn't slipping in Simon's blood. Why wasn't Nestor slipping? There was so much blood. Amazing that there should be. Where did it all come from? Jacky was going to be really pissed off that there was blood on the carpets... no, fuck Jacky, they were Simon's carpets and he could bleed on them if he wanted to... if he wanted to. "Mr. Simon, hold your arm above your heart, sir. You've got something cut in there."

He did what Nestor told him to do. Nestor seemed to know what to do. Nestor was calling 9-9-9. "I can probably drive to the hospital," Simon said. "There's no need to call."

Nestor's big face was grim. "Keep your hand above your heart. Do what I tell you!"

They were in Mississippi, he and Stephen, and it was hot, it was so incredibly hot and the cicadas calling all day long in the trees and the Japanese beetles killing themselves against the shed. The house was at the end of a dirt road, beside a tobacco field, and the trees around the house were tall. There were tall trees.

"Don't faint, now. Keep talking to me, Mr. Simon."

Simon felt ridiculous, sitting there with his hand above his head. It was like being back at school: *Please, miss, I know the answer.* Simon wasn't very good at school, did only what was necessary to pass his year and keep the teachers off his back. He had an aptitude for literature, for writing, and of course, for music, but his mind was always elsewhere. It irritated Roger to no end: *You've got to pull up your trousers, my lad, or you'll never get on in life.* There was a siren nearby, moving nearer, getting louder. The shattered window gaped at him like a row of savaged teeth; the woman was nowhere to be seen. He could just imagine the sorts of things Jacky would say when he found out: *Why didn't you just cut your bloody hands off and have done with it? You're a fucking idiot, you. What the fuck are we gonna do about your winter tour, for fucksake?*

"I cut my feet when we were in Mississippi." He kept his hand over his head. "Stephen and I. I dropped the water jug and it broke. It just shattered. I cut my feet on it and had to have the doctor."

There were men in his house and flashing lights were yelling a peculiar photon warning. One of the men was tall and thin, with ginger hair and pale eyelashes. He examined Simon's hand. "Keep that over your head, now."

His companion was small and dark and quick. He lifted Simon's other hand and something grated against the small bones inside Simon's hand. "He's got a shard in here. I'd rather not touch it." He shook his head at Simon. "You've done a right job on yourself, haven't you, mate?" A piece of jagged glass went completely through the palm and out the other side. It quivered with Simon's heartbeats. There was a girl at Simon's school who used to cut herself with a craft knife—open her wrists and forearms in the lunchroom and then bind them with a red handkerchief she wore tied around her arm. Simon sat next to her one dinnertime and watched her do it, watched her open herself up, watched red rivulets run down and pool on the table. She behaved as if Simon wasn't even there, as if she were entirely alone. She let her blood out onto the tabletop like a declaration: *See me.*

You don't care for being looked at, do you? Jacky, shortly after their first time together, said this to him. They'd been lying in bed at Simon's flat in the middle of a summer afternoon with the blinds open; the July sun streamed in, painting their bodies with heat.

It's like hands slapping at you, Simon told him. *Their eyes feel like hands.* Simon was warm, satisfied, his body drunk with sex and sunshine.

You never look people in the face.

I always look at you, Simon said.

But you didn't, Jacky countered. *Not the first time we met, you didn't.* He was forever on at Simon to loosen up, engage the crowd, talk to people and meet their eyes, but Simon simply couldn't do it. One night in San Francisco, shortly after Simon's appearance at the Picador Club, they'd attended an industry party, Simon and Jacky and Stephen. Jacky took Simon into the loo and offered him a little coke: *Just sniff it up your nose is all. Just a little bit. Everybody does it. It helps to loosen you up. People like you better when you can talk to them.* It wasn't like that night with Chase and Stephen, and the blonde-haired girl who'd died in Simon's arms. It was bright and clean and crisp like good Champagne, and it left a vivid tang on Simon's palate and made him feel wide awake and a little restless, eager to converse with anyone. He found himself pinned down by two young men in matching psychedelic T-shirts who told him they were surfers and brothers and twins. They were going up to Big Sur later on to catch some waves and maybe tour some of the local wineries—did Simon want to come? He talked to an actor who was also a bartender and who stripped sometimes at ladies' parties and for extra cash on weekends, but who really wanted to be on the soap operas.

Never tried it, have you? He deftly rolled a joint and offered it to Simon, who declined.

The coke was racing through Simon's veins; it made him feel invincible. *Soap operas? I used to watch Corrie with mum. Dunno if that's what you mean.*

Stripping. The actor cast a practiced eye over Simon's body. *Looks like you've got what it takes. You could make a pretty penny if you wanted to.*

Simon couldn't decide if the actor was making fun of him or not; he had one of those faces that always seemed to be grinning, or that intended to grin. *I don't think so. It's not for me.*

"Keep both hands above your head." The one with the ginger hair was helping Simon onto a stretcher; Nestor was on the telephone again, trying to reach Jacky. Nestor was shouting at someone: *She was right there in the yard, I saw the girl myself.*

SIMON woke to unfamiliar blue-tiled walls and a smell of germicide and disembodied voices coming over the PA. There was a refrigerator set against one of the blue-tiled walls; the refrigerator was squat and blue and humming. "That's A-sharp, that is."

A woman's face swam into his view and disappeared again: a nurse. He felt the cold metal of a stethoscope being pressed against his chest and he realized, with embarrassment, that he was quite naked under a standard hospital gown. His hands were bandaged. His glasses were gone. "You've been very, very lucky," she said. Her tone indicated he was a fool. "That piece of glass went right through your hand, right through. You're bloody lucky you didn't bleed to death."

He thought about that old joke: the man waking up from surgery and asking the doctor if he'd be able to play the piano.

Of course, I don't see why not.

Brilliant! I could never play before.

"I feel sick," he whispered.

"Well, turn onto your side if you feel like you're going to vomit."
She shoved a metal pan at him. "You think we'd nothing better to do in
this country. I don't know why folk can't be more careful."

Simon curled onto his side, trying in vain to pull the narrow
hospital sheet round his shoulders. He drifted for a while, and when he
woke up again, he was in a private room and Jacky was sitting by his
bed. "You stupid, stupid bastard," Jacky said. His face was wet; this
was one of the few times Simon had ever seen him cry. He climbed
onto the bed and took Simon into his arms, but the gesture seemed to
be more for Jacky's comfort than Simon's. "You're to have surgery,
did you know that?" He touched the thick wad of bandages covering
Simon's right hand from elbow to fingertips. "You've done something
serious, they think. Something in there's not right."

Simon's heart thudded painfully in his chest. "What do you
mean?" Riding in the ambulance with Nestor by his side, he'd done as
he'd been told and kept his hand high above his heart. The first finger
was cold to the touch and resisted Simon's attempts to bend it; the last
two fingers on the same hand were curled tightly toward the palm.
"Will I be able to play?"

Jacky's mouth compressed to a thin line and he looked away.
"Let's just concentrate on right now." He nodded several times in rapid
succession, as if obeying some inner goad. "That's all we can do."

"SIMON, I'm going to inject you with an anesthetic now and I want
you to start counting backwards from ten. You might taste onion or
garlic in the back of your throat. All right?" The anesthesiologist was a
trim Japanese man with round, wire-rimmed spectacles; his hands were
cool and dry as paper. Simon watched as a measure of syrupy yellow
liquid was decanted into the intravenous portal near his right elbow.
His hand and wrist were covered in pale blue surgical drapes and
carefully hidden from his view.

Jacky had given explicit instructions that under no circumstances
was Simon to be told the extent of his injuries. There were severe
lacerations to several of the tendons controlling his fingers, but the

surgeon was hopeful—that was the word he'd used when talking to Jacky, "hopeful"—that a complete repair could be effected and that, in time, Simon would regain full use of his hand.

How much time are we talking about? The man's the biggest rock star in the world. You do realize that, don't you? For once it wasn't anger in Jacky's voice but fear and empathy and genuine regret. Apart from the money and the adulation and the fame, there was, simply, the music, which was what had drawn Jacky to Simon in the first place. The sound of Simon's voice raised in song had pulled Jacky out of himself and into a dingy Dublin pub to watch a dumpy kid in black-rimmed Buddy Holly glasses sing his heart out. He had that same feeling every single time he watched Simon onstage, whether he was playing to an intimate BBC audience in a television studio or to fifty thousand at some huge American football stadium. Neither Simon nor any of his entourage knew that Jacky, overcome with emotion, openly wept when Simon played for twenty thousand at Wembley Stadium. Quite apart from Simon's future as a rock musician, Jacky was one of the few who stopped to consider Simon's future as a man.

Simon closed his eyes against the glare of the surgical lights and began to count. He reached six when a wall of blackness, moving with the assurance of a tsunami, ploughed into him and dragged him under.

14: *Seaside Rental*

HIS mother kept a little shop in the village and was down there during the day. Her loom was set up in the front window so she could watch the street, and often tourists would see her weaving and come in. *It's the best marketing ploy ever,* she said. *All I do is sit there and in they come, neat as you please.* She made wonderful things from wool: sweaters and caps and mittens, but also gorgeous handloomed shawls and decorative wall hangings. She'd studied at the Glasgow College of Art and Design and graduated at the head of her class. *Your mum's the Michelangelo of wool,* Stephen's father used to say. *There's nothing she can't do with it.*

The amount of traffic in and out of the shop during the day meant that Stephen's mother didn't come home at dinnertime, but Stephen and his sister Jane were old enough by then to fend for themselves, and anyway, Jane preferred to stay at school with her friends. The lunchroom offered a hot dinner almost every day, their mother said, and it wasn't worth it for Jane to trundle home and back again. It was better if she stayed at school. It was better all-round if they both stayed at school, but Stephen wasn't having any of it. By then he was of an age to spend his dinner money playing pool at the pub, or hide in the crawl space behind the girls' change room to peek at them through a hole in the wall. He wasn't interested in coming home to listen to his dad grumble about the sheep and pester him about what sort of job he would get when he left school. *Writing poems and making things up is all fine, but you've to earn a living, you know.*

And then one day Stephen did come home for dinner. He'd been chased by four thick-necked hooligans with nailed boots and straight razors in their pockets; he slipped away from school and came home by a different road. The house was silent; he let himself in. There was mail on the table and the kitchen clock ticked relentlessly above the old wood-and-oil stove. He'd just opened the fridge to make a sandwich when he heard someone walking around upstairs.

Dad? That you?

There was the low rumble of his father's voice and the sound of feminine giggling. Stephen's heart was booming in his chest as he mounted the stairs; he could barely breathe. *Dad, is that you?*

The door of his father's bedroom suddenly flew open and his father was there, and behind his father, lying naked in his parents' bed, was a woman.

Stephen's father was furious. *I thought you were staying at school for your dinner, and all!*

Mick MacDonald and his brothers said they'd pound me. They've got razors, Dad. His father didn't bother to say who the woman was and Stephen didn't ask. He had never been so shocked. He wanted to say something but he didn't dare, and he didn't know what to say or how he would find the courage to say it. In the end, he turned and went down the stairs and walked back to school by himself, and when Mick MacDonald met him outside the shop that afternoon and tried to bash him, Stephen balled up his skinny fists and beat him 'til he fell down. The images of his father's naked mistress and of Mick MacDonald's bloodied face were forever conflated in his mind. He remembered that the woman was blonde, and she had one black tooth in the front.

That's bloody Oedipal, Simon said when Stephen told him. Simon liked saying things that sounded intelligent and posh. Stephen's mother had come home that night from the shop as usual, had hung up her coat and gone into the kitchen and started frying sausages for their tea. Nothing was ever said about it then, or ever.

Girls are like that, his friend Bernard said. *They never do you right.* They were in Bernard's bedroom on a Saturday night, smoking marijuana that Bernard's cousin grew in his mum's greenhouse and listening to David Bowie on the stereo. Bernard was stripped to his underpants and wanking gently to the music. *I had Mona Degan last weekend. She fucks like a mink.* Bernard had hair underneath his arms and around his cock; he was proud of showing it off to anyone who cared to look. His cock was large and pendulous, as big as Stephen's dad's was, and grew instantly erect at the slightest provocation. *You can look but don't bloody touch it,* Bernard said. Stephen watched, amazed, as Bernard's penis filled with blood and flushed deep red. He sometimes woke at night to find his own cock hard, and lately there were morning stains upon his sheets, but that was all. When Maura gave him hand jobs on the swings, he came, but it was nothing much. He wondered if there was something wrong with him. Considering the books he'd read and the filthy talk around the school bathrooms, he'd expected something much more powerful than that: bursting fireworks and crashing cymbals, a pleasure so exquisitely painful that it could hardly be borne.

Stephen had just left school after a disappointing run; his attempt at the A-levels was a resounding nonstarter. He drifted in and out of diverse part-time jobs, earning barely enough to keep himself in lager. On the weekends he disappeared with Bernard, who had a car; they spent much of their time drugged or drunk or both, and enthusiastically screwed as many girls as could be found. Stephen caught the clap from a girl he knew in Inverness and had to tell his mother.

I've to see the doctor, Mum.

She'd been folding blankets to take down to the shop; he found her in the spare bedroom.

Not got a cold, have you? She felt his forehead like she used to do when he was little. *Or is it your tummy?* When he explained that he'd got a strange discharge *down below,* her face completely froze. Her hands sped up, moving restlessly among the blankets. *You should talk to your dad about that. I expect he's down the stable. Why don't you go down and talk to him? Your dad's the one to talk to about it.*

He had disappointed her; this knowledge stung him. He was just like his father. He could not be trusted. *Dad's...* His father had stood framed in the bedroom door, the day Stephen had caught him with his mistress. He'd stood stark naked in the doorway, and her behind him, giggling in the bed. Did his mother know? How could his mother not know? *Dad's busy. I don't know if he wants bothering... what should I ask the doctor for?*

Stephen, I don't have time for this. That was what she said, that she'd not got time for it. She made her embarrassment into his fault. Neither she nor Stephen's dad had ever told him anything; when he turned twelve, his mother opened his bedroom door early one morning and tossed a slender paperback volume onto his bed. *If you've any questions, ask me.* But he never did, and he never opened the book, but slid it into his bureau underneath his socks. The cover had a photograph of a barefoot girl in a flowered dress, wearing a garland of daisies round her neck, and a lad with Donny Osmond hair and platform shoes. Stephen complained bitterly to Bernard.

What's me mum think I am? A little kiddie?

Fuck the bloody lot of 'em, Bernard said. *I've had my tongue in Judy Buchan's cunt. It tastes like fish.* Stephen never knew whether to believe Bernard or not; on the other hand, Bernard seemed to know an awful lot about sex. *What you gotta do is get their knickers off. Then you get it hard and then you stick it in their hole, see?*

When Stephen told the doctor what was happening, the doctor laughed. It wasn't a nice laugh; it was the sort of laugh that said, *You filthy little bastard.* He told Stephen to go behind the screen and undress, take everything off so he could have a proper look. He handled Stephen's balls and squeezed the top of his cock like a tube of toothpaste. *You've got gonorrhea.* He wrote out a prescription for antibiotics. *Use a condom from now on. You can get some at the chemist's on the way out.*

Seventeen-year-old Stephen Abednego stayed off sick from work the next day and got sacked; he sat at the kitchen table for a fortnight, reading the newspaper and drinking tea. Bernard had gone to Southampton to visit relatives and Stephen's mother stayed away at the shop. He sat alone in the empty house, listlessly turning the pages of *New Music Weekly.* There were classifieds in the back: people looking for rides to this or that concert; someone selling an electric guitar; a bloke in Brighton who wanted to buy used records. There were adverts for hair tonic and sex pills and coy references to dirty magazines that could be had from Belgium or Amsterdam. There was a tiny little notice about song writing; Stephen tore it out and stuck it in his pocket, and forgot about it. He found it again when he was doing his laundry, and wrote a brief note to accompany some of his poems.

He got a job working as a checker in one of the local shops and started a brief flirtation with an older girl, a woman of twenty-six who was going through a divorce. She liked Stephen's green eyes and his shy smile and invited him back to her flat after work. She had a tiny waist and a lot of bright red hair and she showed him all sorts of things that even Bernard didn't know about, but Stephen stopped seeing her when she started talking marriage. *What are you saving yourself for?* she asked, scornfully.

I don't know. Something. Something else.

She kicked him out early one morning and he ended up walking home and got soaked in a downpour. There were sirens in the distance and the sound of a helicopter, circling somewhere nearby. He stopped in at a shop and someone said there had been an accident on the road from Burray. His mother was waiting for him at the door when he got home; her expression was stricken.

What is it? Stephen's wet clothes hung on him like grave clouts. *Is it Dad? Has something happened to Dad?*

I'm ever so sorry, lad. It's horrible, what's happened. It's just horrible.

No point in going to the accident site. The bodies had already been removed by a Highlands and Islands helicopter. The police had the road all cordoned off. There was nothing anyone could do. *It's Bernard, lad, do you understand? He's run his car off the road. He had Maura Firth in with him. They've both been killed.*

Seventeen-year-old Stephen Abednego stood beside their graves while the sky opened up and poured rain and the church brass band played "Nearer My God to Thee." Bernard's mother stood beside him and held onto his arm and cried. *You were his best friend, you were. He loved you like a brother. He loved you.* Stephen couldn't reconcile their tragic faces with the coffins going down into the ground. He kept seeing Bernard smoking dope with one hand down his underpants, wanking for all he was worth, and Maura beside Stephen on the playground swings, rubbing him through his grey school trousers. He came home from the funeral and found an envelope: a letter written on thick cream paper, asking him to come to London. *We find your poems esoteric in the extreme but they may yet have merit. Mr. Simon Duckworth will meet your train.*

Here was seventeen-year-old Stephen Abednego, and here was Simon Duckworth, standing on the train platform at King's Cross Station, waiting.

PIET was a sculptor of "found" objects; he made things from flotsam, things that came in on the tide, driftwood. "Whatever the sea brings, I make something of it," he said. Stephen met him on the beach one morning, and the sight of someone walking toward him in the distance annoyed him. When Stephen took the cottage, he was told that the beach was private, for his use alone; it had been a condition he insisted on. To see a figure moving toward him, even at a great distance, irritated him. He wanted no part of humanity.

What are you writing? Piet resembled a young Peter Lorre. There was something coy and nebulous in him, something held deeply in reserve, something not entirely to be trusted. *Are you writing a novel?*

The question startled Stephen: *How did you know?*

I live up there—Piet pointed up the beach. *I've seen your light burning late into the night.* The only ones who stayed up late, he said, were authors and insomniacs. *Which one are you?* And perhaps Stephen was lonely or perhaps he was merely bored, but conversation with Piet became a comfortable habit, along with impromptu fishing trips and meandering, drunken forays along the beach at night.

"Do you know what I love about this place?" Piet asked. "People come here to forget. They can forget who they are in the outside world. That's what this place does." They were sitting on the sand together, watching the sun set, and drinking from a bottle of Australian red that Piet brought with him. There was no hair on Piet's legs and no shadow of a beard to mar the smooth roundness of his cheeks.

Stephen asks, "Who were you in the outside world?"

Piet was silent for a long moment, gazing at the ocean. "I was... lost. I lost myself. That was a long time ago." He sighed, seeming to shake himself from a reverie. "What about a swim?"

Stephen laughed. "Now?" It was full dark, and the moon was shedding silvery light on the sea. "Aren't there sharks?"

"They'll eat me first." Piet had dimples. "I'm much more tender." Piet had small breasts, not even breasts, merely the suggestion of them, and no body hair. Piet asked, "Who are you trying to forget?"

Stephen, unpleasantly jarred by the question, couldn't help himself. "Are you a man or a woman?"

"Ah." Piet was curiously calm. "I wondered when we would get to that." He began swimming toward the shore, moving his arms and legs in languid circles. They sat together on the sand and drank from the wine bottle, passing it back and forth. The night was beautiful, the air very still. "I am... both. And neither."

"You'll have to explain," Stephen said. "Either that, or the wine's doing my head in."

"Somewhere during my mother's pregnancy, something unusual occurred. I was born the way I am. This is nothing I have done, nothing I have failed to do." Piet kept his eyes trained resolutely on the horizon. "My mother didn't sleep with the gardener, or look upon a goat under a full January moon. I enjoyed a sheltered childhood, free from prying questions or the well-meaning curiosity of the neighbors." He glanced at Stephen, just as quickly looked away. "I will always be grateful to my parents for their care and... sensitivity. It could have been so much worse. I have heard stories of others who... were not as fortunate as I."

Stephen reminded himself to breathe. "So have I."

"My parents named me Piet, which is easily transmuted to Pieter or Pieta, should I choose. I was raised as a boy, with toy cars and trucks and soldier dolls. We traveled a great deal, and I was exposed to the eminent museums of the world and introduced to art and great literature. And when I was about fourteen and my body began to change, they asked me how I should like to live my life: should I wish to have my body altered, to appear more male or more female? They allowed me to think on it, to ponder it as long as I wished."

"But you're—"

"Male." In the moonlight, his face was serene and beautiful; Stephen wondered what this serenity has cost him. "I am a man with breasts." He spread his hands, a theatrical gesture. "In the ancient world, a hermaphrodite was assumed to have godlike powers and a certain... prescience, an ability to see layers of meaning where others did not." Piet shrugged. "So. Make of it what you will. This is what I am. Perhaps everything I just said is the story I made up to comfort myself."

"You need to comfort yourself?"

Piet's large eyes were sad. "Don't you?" He wrapped his arms around his torso, hiding his small breasts from view. "Doesn't everyone?"

AT SIX thirty, two nights after their initial encounter, Stephen was walking up the beach toward Piet's house, carrying a bottle of very good wine and thinking about Piet and Piet's sculptures. Thus far he hadn't seen anything that Piet made, only because he hadn't yet been in Piet's house and Piet's house was where Piet worked. He very much wanted to get into Piet's house, to the point that even his most casual conversation hid a violent yearning, or tried to. Stephen refused to believe that what he felt for Piet was anything but friendship, two mates bound together in loneliness and looking for a bit of company. That curiosity and something else was forever nibbling at him with sharp and tiny teeth was hardly worth the mention: Piet would never be interested in him.

At 6:33 Stephen pushed open the silent screen door of Piet's house and found himself looking at Piet's profile, and at Piet's left arm, which had a rubber tourniquet around it. Stephen watched as Piet injected himself, watched as Piet's head drooped back against the cushions, watched as Piet sighed and untied the tourniquet, rubbing the bend of his elbow. He dropped the empty syringe into a wooden box on the table in front of him, and rolled down his sleeve. Piet was wearing a long-sleeved blue shirt and baggy beige hiking shorts; his feet were bare. He was smiling. The knot in Stephen's stomach grew until it was larger than the world. "I brought a bottle of wine," Stephen said. He couldn't make himself look at Piet's face, look into Piet's huge dark eyes. He wondered what was in the needle. He wanted to ask but knew he didn't have that right. People had their particular secrets and sometimes asking was the last thing you should do. *When I was a lad, my dad's friend raped me... he held me down and raped me.*

"Stephen, my dear friend, come in." Piet rose and came to greet him. "Welcome. I am so glad you could come."

"...THAT tree root there, for instance." Much later in the evening, and Piet was pointing with the handle of his knife, directing Stephen's gaze. "I found that wedged underneath a rock at low tide, just up there in the cove. It looked to me like Felix the Cat. Do you remember that cartoon? But I see faces in everything. Have some more wine." Some called them *devas*; Stephen read about it somewhere. "In driftwood, mostly, because those spirits have been so horribly battered, very much abused and damaged by the sea." Piet explained that their faces must be seen; when they chose to speak, it must have an outlet. He told Stephen this as he moved swiftly around his kitchen, his bare feet silent on the tiled floor. His long sleeves hid the bend of his arm and the bruise the needle made, and the track marks that Stephen couldn't quite see but must be there, all the same.

Piet was cheerful, mischievous, and Puckish, and his dark eyes sparkled with some inner glee. He cooked tandoori for them, and tender naan bread, and fragrant rice, and while he cooked, he was talking, always talking. He explained how he bought his house from an old man who had built it out of shipwrecks and the bones of ancient whaling vessels that had gone down all along this treacherous coast. The house was made of soft grey wood and natural stone, with many windows all facing toward the sea. Piet's kitchen was dark and cavelike, cool; he handled pans and pots and ladles with a steady ease. His good humor was infectious; he poured wine and still more wine and beckoned Stephen with him, into the rest of the house. His workshop was here, tacked on at the back, but hardly an afterthought. The room was circular, and the walls were buttressed with pearly whale bones, ribs and jaws and narwhal tusks. The ceiling was glass, wide open to the moonlight, and on a metal pedestal in the middle of the room, there was the figure of the crucified Christ, clinging to a wrecked and ruined tree. Christ's eyes were fixed on some unseen point in front of him, and he was staring at that hidden place with melancholy resignation. His hands and feet were pierced by shards of polished bone; his face was Piet's face. His body rose, triumphant, out of a heap of dead or dying children, their hands outstretched toward him. The thing was gruesome and compelling, Eliot's heap of broken images burned by a relentless sun.

"Will you...." Stephen wondered if he should touch it. "Will you tell me about it?"

When Piet was nine, his parents settled for a time in Russia, in a small village near the Black Sea. Piet was quick to pick up languages, and his parents felt that the presence of other children might be good for him. The school was liberal and progressive and very modern, with much emphasis on art and music, and the teacher who appraised Piet's unusual condition was serene and reasoned. Near the end of the school year, as the students were preparing for final examinations, a group of armed rebels stormed the school and took the children and their teachers hostage. They wanted recognition for their cause; they wanted the current government toppled. They wanted a great many things, or perhaps it was merely one thing with a great many pieces to it.

Piet remembered the leader of them: a tall, red-haired man with a weather-beaten face. He smelled of sweat and onions and spoke in spits and whispers. *I'll tear them up like paper,* the man said. *I'll tear their insides out.* He wore a string of hand grenades across his torso and another string around his waist. His red moustache straggled over his mouth; his hands were cruel hands, big hands. *I'll tear their guts out, all of them.* The rebels wanted the headmaster to speak on television; they wanted him to say that he agreed with them, that he would support them in their struggle, but he refused, and so—

Here Piet blinked, just once.

—and so the rebels shot the teachers and the children, lined them up against a wall in the gymnasium and sprayed them all with gunfire.

A bullet went through Piet's shoulder and he fell, was covered by the bodies of his teachers, of his friends. He awoke many hours later to the sound of sirens and of mothers crying; he alone remained alive under a pile of corpses.

Stephen's breath was whistling in his lungs. His mouth was dry. He reached for his wine glass and sipped, and sipped. He could not seem to swallow; all the air had gone out of the room. He thought about the needle, going into Piet's arm, slipping past skin and sinew, sliding into the vein. He imagined children forced to stand against a wall at gunpoint. He imagined the ricochet of bullets and the lingering smell of cordite and the dying bodies of the children.

"What are you thinking about?" Piet asked, after they had eaten and cleared away the dishes. There was music on the stereo: Erik Satie. There were candles on the coffee table, and they sat together on the floor, drinking fine Australian wine.

"You," Stephen said. This was his confession. "I am thinking about you."

"I shouldn't want to dissuade you, then." Drugs and wine had conspired to make Piet heavy-lidded and expansive, sensual. His movements were languid, as if his body were too big for him. He smiled, the simper of an odalisque. "Who are you trying to forget, Stephen? Whose name is it that you won't allow yourself to speak?"

There was a dimple in Piet's cheek that appeared and vanished as he spoke. Stephen couldn't stop looking at it. If he touched it, the tiny dent would capture the very tip of his finger, but no more. "Abelard... Simon." The admission did not come easily. "My friend. He's so far away from here." His finger moved to touch Piet's face. Piet smiled and the dimple grew, a tiny pull at Stephen's fingertip.

"Why?" Piet gently removed Stephen's finger from his face. "Why did you leave?"

"He didn't need me." The tiny rebuke was hurtful; perhaps he wouldn't touch Piet again. "He's never needed me." Not entirely true, but Stephen didn't think he could give Simon what he wanted, be the man that Simon needed him to be. *I don't want to be a poof.*

"I knew a woman once." Piet fetched out a bag of cannabis and deftly rolled a joint. "She was more beautiful than beauty could even imagine. To see her walking on the street was to see the Son of God come down. To touch her was to touch radiance. Her eyes were the sum and entirety of every sea that had ever been, and every river that men had ever dreamed upon. Sparks flew from her skin. Her name was Hedrun. She came to me because she wanted to learn sculpture. At that time I was living in Amsterdam and working out of a storefront studio, situated on a narrow street that was very dark all day except for in the late afternoon, when the sun would flood down from above, illuminating us like the floor of a hidden canyon in the desert. She came to me around five in the afternoon, when the light was pouring in. I had been working very closely all day long, hardly raising my head. I lost track of the outside world. Do you know how that is?

"Well, the bell tinkled on the door and I looked up and there she was. She had red hair, long and tumbling in curls against her alabaster skin. She was wearing a printed sarong and tights, and her body glistened with a great deal of silver jewelry. She said she had seen my work at an artisans' exhibition a day or two before, and she wanted to learn. She asked if I could teach her. She became my student.

"She was very easy to teach. No, you think I say that because of her beauty but that isn't it entirely. She had an openness about her that allowed her to not just submerge herself in the work, but to allow the work to enter into her. I began slowly, teaching her to feel the weight and textures of different materials, teaching her how to work with her hands, how to mold the clay. She had beautiful hands. She worked silently, which I appreciated, and she worked well. Within a month, no more, she was molding clay figures that we fired together in the kiln behind the studio. She liked to stoke the fire and prepare the kiln; she wasn't afraid of fire like some women are. She told me once that fire understood her, that she could speak to fire and have it do her bidding. I believed her.

"She never asked me about my body. She was always respectful. Slowly she became affectionate with me, friendly, you might say. And she learned how to turn and shape the wood, how to work with different kinds of wood, different kinds of stone and metal. I forgot about her beauty and saw instead her gifts and how adept she had become. I wanted to show off her work. I urged her to exhibit, to place some small pieces in the market, to see how they might be received, but she refused."

Stephen passed the last of the joint to Piet. "She wasn't confident?"

"She was. She knew the work was good. More than good—brilliant, wonderful." He paused to take the last drag and toss the spent ember into the fireplace. "She wasn't interested."

Stephen felt a lump in his throat. He knew how this story went. He knew how it ended. It was always the same story, over and over. "It's not your fault."

"You know this for a fact, do you?" Piet didn't bother trying to hide his bitterness. His face in the dim light was rendered fluid, wholly androgynous, and his eyes were huge. "She truly did try. She was willing to try as many different things as I could think of." He covered his face with his hands. "Finally, she could not love a body that reminded her of her own."

"Piet, you don't look like a woman." Stephen remembered it clearly, the first night they met. How could he have ever been confused? "She was mistaken. She made an error."

"Yes, an… error." Piet gazed past Stephen, out into the dark. "My dear friend, shall we walk on the beach for a little while?"

They brought a bottle of wine with them and slipped out into the balmy darkness. They walked in silence until they left the lighted house behind them, and there was only the moon, and the sound of the sea.

15: *Tea at Lyons*

THERE were sheaves of flowers waiting for him when Nestor helped him out of the car. The front of Simon's house had been transformed into an arbor; the garden was a party orchard. Nina and Gerald were there, looking relaxed and tanned after a holiday in Spain; Nina was wearing a string of Majorcan pearls. Her face and neck were a hazardous dark brown, tending toward an unflattering fleshiness. "We were ever so worried about you, love." Nina crushed Simon tight, murmuring over his bandaged hands. "What have you done to yourself? I don't know what you've gone and done."

"I'm fine, Mum. The doctor said they're only flesh wounds. There's nothing damaged." This was an outright lie. He didn't tell her about the knife-sharp shards of glass that went through each of his hands, or how his fingertips had difficulty feeling anything at all. "Only a flesh wound." Jacky wanted all the windows in the house replaced with shatterproof glass.

Bulletproof, like what the President's got in America. There'll be no one getting at you after this.

And what if she comes back? What if she's not the only one? They had been having heated conversations, he and Jacky, in the privacy of Simon's hospital room. *What if there's some other lunatic out there?* The woman's physical appearance repulsed him; Simon saw her still in dreams, hefting her giant breasts at him and grinning her demon grin. In some dreams her head was shaved and she was wearing a shapeless grey dress, like women in old prison films. Her entire body was covered in tattoos; she slid her tongue in and out of her saliva-filled mouth and leered at him. There had been other instances when fans had slipped past the tight security perimeter set up by Jacky. Once, in Norway, Simon had awakened during the night to find a young woman sitting on the end of his bed. She didn't speak a word, merely took his hands in hers and reverently stroked them. To this day, Simon still didn't know if he dreamt it. The girl was blonde and slender, with a flawless cream complexion; she was completely nude. He could have reached out for her, could have pulled her into his bed, but he didn't dare. She made a sort of spell, simply sitting there and holding his hands in hers, tracing the shape of his fingers: over and under, over and under.

He'd been at a party once, some nightclub in Berlin where he'd played three nights in a row, and at the end, the manager threw a huge affair complete with catering and booze. There were bowls of pills handed round like colored candy and people doing cocaine off the top of the bar, and gorgeous models wearing nothing except chain belts with little padlocks attached.

What's that all about? Simon had been sitting with Stephen in a private banquette near the wall. *With the locks? What's it supposed to mean?* The girls' pubic hair had been shaved, and their nude bodies glistened with oil. They wore transparent platform shoes that made them tower over everybody else, and silver wigs. *This whole thing's doing my head in.* A man in a dark jacket was standing by the bar. He turned and smiled at them, and raised his glass; he looked like Peter Lorre. *It's that movie star bloke,* Simon said, but that wasn't possible. *No, he's dead. He's been dead awhile.* The music and the booze was getting to him; he'd done a fair bit of cocaine at Jacky's urging and perceived the room around him as a series of sparkling vignettes.

One of the models came and sat between him and Stephen. She was easily six feet tall, as nude and hairless as the others. She picked up Simon's hand and looked at it: *Wo wohnt Gott?* She sucked on his index finger, tugging at his skin with painted silver lips.

I don't know, Simon said. *I don't speak German.* The Peter Lorre look-alike was smiling at him in a knowing way. His expression said this was a conspiracy, and Simon was the target. His expression said that he had planned all of this for Simon's benefit.

"Gerald and I were ever so worried, love." Nina patted Simon's hair and his face, sizing him up. "Where'd you get that shirt? Have you always had that shirt? I don't think I care for it." They'd arranged a little homecoming for him, with sandwiches and pie and fizzy lemonade out in the garden, and picnic tables set with crisp white tablecloths like this was somebody's wedding: *Guess what, man? I'm married.* A man was standing by one of the tables, wearing casual slacks and a polo shirt. He turned to speak to someone; he looked like the actor Peter Lorre, like the man Simon had seen in that Berlin bar.

"Who's that bloke?" Simon captured Jacky's sleeve as the manager went by. "That bloke by the table. Who is he?"

"There's no one there. Don't be an idiot."

Jacky had a series of concert dates already booked for Simon, six months in advance; Jacky chose to believe that Simon's hands would be ready for the task. He was assuming that Simon wanted to go. They'd had this conversation already, in Simon's hospital room, about Simon's musical career and Simon's obligations to his fans. Did Simon want to let a lot of people down? Did Simon want to cheat people? Amsterdam again, and the Oderhaus, because Simon never completed that commitment, does Simon remember?

Of course Simon remembered. *I bet you never thought you'd get a call like this from me.* The Oderhaus was in the Walletjes, the oldest red light district in Amsterdam, and Simon would be playing to a closed house, a very intimate audience of handpicked invitees. "It's gonna be real stylish," Jacky said. "That German producer, the one who did Bowie's last tour, he's doing it, and it's gonna be real posh." Perhaps they would even have naked fashion models, wearing tiny padlocks on chains around their waists. Perhaps Simon's ravaged hands might consent to work for him, although so far he'd had no luck. The problem, the doctor said, was with the severed tendons, which the surgeon had dutifully reattached but which might never recover their flexibility, their lightning-fast reaction. Jacky had received this news with an impassive face, but after the doctor had taken his little group of residents and interns and gone away, he'd rounded on Simon and cursed him. "You and your fucking hands. Why? You might as well have put your fucking head through the window. You fucking idiot."

Simon went into the bathroom and cut a couple quick lines on the lid of the toilet. He looked horrible: red-eyed and exhausted, sick at heart. His bandaged hands felt huge, like cartoon hands, and when he tried to make a fist, he fancied he could feel his bones grating against one another, deep inside his flesh. His hands were paining him, he could feel it; infection was setting in, and he couldn't say anything about it because if he did then Jacky would get angry. He didn't want a scene with Jacky, not right now, not here, with Gerald and Nina and all these people around, but there was something not right. There was something horrible going on, deep inside of him, and he had no power to stop it.

He and Stephen lay awake one chilly autumn night and swore a promise to one another: *We both go, or nobody goes.* They understood that their partnership was exactly half-and-half. Almost from the first day that they met, when Stephen produced his first song lyric for Simon *in situ*, they realized that, creative concerns aside, this endeavor was literally double or nothing. It worked with Simon and with Stephen, or it didn't work at all. They had lain side by side on Simon's narrow bed and held each other's hands: *It's both of us or no one, right?* They had whispered together just like that, the summer that Simon went to St. Margaret's Hope. The light was forever in Orkney in the summertime and the air was warm and full of dragonflies and the smell of new-mown hay. They stretched themselves in the long grass behind the house and talked while the summer stars wheeled above them in the pallid night. *We're gonna be huge with this next song, I just know it.*

Of course we are. Simon would have agreed to anything. Stephen's ratty blue shirt was missing several buttons. Stephen's chest was nearly hairless and his belly was tanned and flat. His long fingers peeled a stalk of grass. Simon's chest felt tight and there was a lump of something painful in his throat. He wanted to touch Stephen, wanted to lean close and press his nose against Stephen's naked chest and his belly, wanted to slide up and tongue the flat nipples, lave Stephen's bare shoulders and his neck. *We're gonna be huge.*

You wouldn't write with anyone else, would you? Stephen licked a piece of grass and stuck it on Simon's forehead. *You'd never write songs with anyone but me.* They were like people who had been married for ages and whose fights were often couched in language just as obtuse as this. Stephen's face was close to his; Simon could have kissed him if he'd had the nerve. *You'd never do it, would you?*

I never would. Simon's laboring heart thudded in his chest. His courage in this would always fail him. He took hold of Stephen's arm, of the sleeve of his shirt; he clenched the fabric tight in his fist. *I never would.*

When the last of the partiers had gone, when Simon was alone in the house, there was Jacky. Simon's manager had aged these past few weeks; Simon suspected the flurry of flights and late-night phone calls hadn't done Jacky any good. "You ought to rest," Jacky said. He came into the kitchen, where Simon was sitting at the table, and laid down his empty glass. "You look awful peaky."

"Can't," Simon said. "I've had too much." The room felt bright and dangerous and far too glittery and he was starting to panic. "I think something's wrong." Nestor hovered protectively near the kitchen door, pretending to collect the empties.

"What d'you mean?" Jacky crouched in front of him, holding onto Simon's arms. "What's wrong?"

"It's too bright." The light was hurting his eyes. The light was drilling into him, painful shards of broken daylight. "I think I did too much."

"Don't be silly." Jacky fetched him a bottle of mineral water. "You're just tired, that's all."

"Why doesn't he come back?" Simon gazed at his bandaged hands, was suddenly close to tears. "What's wrong with him? Why doesn't he come back?"

Promise me you'll never write with anyone else.

"TELL me about melancholy," Stephen said. He was sitting on a low stool in Piet's workroom, watching the sculptor's small, strong hands as they relentlessly kneaded a lump of clay. The clay spun on a foot-driven potter's wheel, and Piet's sleeves were rolled up past his elbows. There was a streak of clay drying on the bridge of Piet's nose and a daub of it across his cheek; he seemed expansive this morning and calmer than Stephen had yet seen him.

"Melancholy." Piet dipped one hand into a pot of water and wet the clay. "I would say that for some, melancholy is as pervasive and as necessary as air." He gazed steadily at Stephen for a moment while his busy hands squeezed the clay. "Are you one of those people?"

"I don't know." An image of Simon, his sad eyes and his gentle mouth, playing the piano at Nina's old place in Stepney. "I don't know. Sometimes, I suppose." He hadn't seen Piet for several days and now sensed a coldness in him that wasn't there before. He wondered how he could have misunderstood Piet, but realized that he must have done. He watched Piet's face, watched the dimple in his cheek deepen and relax. He remembered how his fingertip sunk into it. He wanted to touch it again but he wouldn't dare. "And you?"

Piet laughed, a harsh noise without humor in it. His hands cupped themselves around the wet clay, holding it, molding it, coaxing it into the shape that Piet held in his mind. "Ask me something else." He applied a gentle pressure with his thumbs and the wet clay flowed upward, blooming into a rudimentary spout. "Ask me anything else." The wet clay broke, dropping in an ugly lump onto the wheel. "*Fuck.*"

This was the first time he'd heard Piet curse. "I'm sorry."

Piet wiped his dirty hands on the tails of his shirt. "Not your fault. I wasn't paying attention."

"Piet, I'm really sorry."

The sculptor stripped off his shirt, stopping to sluice his hands in a large tin utility sink by the door. He offered Stephen a wry grin. "I am, as we say, 'onhandige pummel'—a clumsy oaf." His back and shoulders were burned bright red from the sun. "Come and have a drink with me." They went through to the kitchen and Piet fetched cold bottles of Amstel from the fridge.

"Have you been sitting in the sun?" Three days since Stephen last saw Piet and he wondered if the sculptor spent his weekend the same way Stephen did: sitting on the beach staring at the sky, watching jet planes puncture the fleecy clouds. Stephen could get on a jet and go back to England, go to where Simon was. He could do that if he wanted to. He could go back and pretend that everything was exactly as he'd left it, that nothing had changed between them, that he and Simon were... what, exactly? Lovers? Friends, certainly. What else?

"Yes. Yes, I spent some time in the sun." Piet moved his right arm experimentally, grimacing in pain. "I think too much time, perhaps. I did not see you these last few days."

Stephen walked to Piet's house early Saturday morning and again late Sunday night, but the windows were dark and there was no sign of Piet. "No, I didn't want to wear out my welcome." He touched Piet's shoulder: "It's very hot. You should put something on it." He was more than brazen; he realized this, but he couldn't help it. He was as hungry for this as he had ever been. He had been hungry his entire life. There was a tube of salve in Piet's medicine cabinet; Piet's sunburned shoulders were hot under Stephen's palms. Piet smelled like sand and clay and the salty tang of the ocean. If Stephen touched his tongue to Piet's skin, he would taste like stone.

"Did you come to look for me?" Piet grunted gently as Stephen smoothed the cold ointment into his ravaged skin. He seemed to sag a little, surrendering to the touch. "You can, you know."

Stephen's belly clenched. He leaned close, inhaling the scent of Piet's body, the residual smells of wood and clay and water. His hands slid around Piet's waist and Stephen pulled Piet back against him. He buried his nose in the nape of Piet's neck, breathing him in. His thighs trembled; his desire was almost painful. Piet turned in his embrace and their mouths were suddenly crushed together and Stephen groaned into the wet caress.

"No—" Piet pulled away, taking the kitchen floor and then the stairs in several quick strides, was suddenly outdoors. The midday light was bright; Piet squinted against the glare. He dropped to his knees, pressing forehead into the ground.

"You should get up. It's hot, it's too hot." Stephen reached for him, was waved away. Piet's body bent, his back impossibly arched: Piet was having a seizure. Stephen held onto him until the fit passed. He remembered being with Simon once when Simon had a seizure from too much cocaine; as soon as the seizure passed, he got up and went and did another line. There was something fundamentally self-destructive in it, but at the same time, Stephen admired Simon's perverse fortitude.

Piet lay across Stephen's knees, gazing open-eyed at the sky. "Please—this is a bad idea. My friend, this is a very bad idea."

"Piet, I'm not asking you for anything." It was loneliness; he knew this now. It was loneliness that he was feeling, the horrible sensation of being all alone at the end of the world, of having reached the end of everything, of having nowhere else to go.

Piet gazed at him, then stretched out a hand. "Come. Let's get inside out of the sun, hm?" Piet's bedroom was cool and dark, as welcome as a cave. Piet closed the door behind them, moving to stand in front of Stephen, hands on his shoulders. "There are certain... precedents I should like to follow." He leaned close, his warm breath stirring the hair at the sides of Stephen's face. "You could, if you wished—" He shrugged. "Do you understand?"

Piet's hands slid inside Stephen's shirt, caressing his sun-warmed skin, and Piet drew him closer and then Piet was kissing him. Stephen's shirt dropped to the bedroom floor and he stood back to step out of his shorts, and he was naked in the darkness and so was Piet. Stephen lay beside him, exploring him with hands and eyes and mouth. He kissed the hollow of Piet's throat and suckled at the small and tender breasts until Piet cried out. "No, you are making me want this, too. Please."

They inhabited a space of darkness, a void where nothing of the outside world existed, only they existed in the perfect silence they had made together. Stephen surrendered to exquisite sensation, hands on his skin, his body wanton and heavy and all his senses drugged. This is love, he thought. This is what it means to create love. Only this. Only this.

16: *Do It or Don't*

"...AND there's a turnaround just after that second set. You've ten, maybe fifteen minutes, but you'll be using that for a costume change, all right?" Kevin was the road manager. He was tall and skinny and bald except for a long, untidy fringe of hair around the back of his head. He came highly recommended; he answered to no one except Jacky Stride. "That all right with you?"

"Make it fifteen." Simon paused in the wings; he could hear the roar of the crowd out front, their restless shuffling. Their anticipation filled the auditorium like energetic static: fifteen thousand people packed into a tiny stadium in Holland on a sweltering September night. "Fifteen-minute turnaround. Tell Jacky, all right?" Simon was tanned and newly svelte and dressed in a sparkly silver jumpsuit with a pointy silver ruff rising from his neck like a peacock tail. His chunky fingers were adorned with a dozen silver rings. The only souvenir of his encounter with the grotesque woman was a network of fine white lines on the back of his right hand and a curious depression in his left, a shallow hole in the delicate web between his thumb and forefinger. Even in bright daylight the scars were barely visible but no one needed to tell Simon that the damage he did to his hands was permanent. His lightning-fast reflexes were gone forever, and where he would once spend two and a half hours gleefully ripping up the keyboard, he now left the fast numbers to the band. He could play piano on the slow songs, but the cold and damaged finger on his right hand would never again respond the way it used to. The two curled digits on his left had been straightened back to normal but these no longer functioned as they did. Simon sang now much more than he played, leaving the more complex arrangements to the lead guitarist and Clive, his very clever drummer. The music critics noticed this new configuration and wondered in print whether Abelard had gone for good. Simon's latest album—the one he wrote with Johnny Slaughter—was floundering badly in the charts. "How do I look?"

"Like fucking Liberace on crack." Kevin patted Simon on the arse with his clipboard and turned away. The promoter was out front, shouting something to the crowd in Dutch. A girl in the front row caught sight of Simon and started screaming hysterically, tears streaming down her face. Simon was running on adrenaline and blow: he strode out onto the stage and the lights came up with a bang and the artificial snow started cascading from the rafters and the dry ice machines were pumping out the froth like mad and Stepney Simon Duckworth turned into Abelard.

He slid onto the piano bench and smiled his familiar gap-toothed smile at the crowd. "Thank you all for coming. It's so great to be in Amsterdam again. Going to do a little number for you that we wrote a long time ago." He smiled out into the footlights, seeing nothing. This was a scripted move, something that he did at intervals; Jacky had taught him to do it and the audience always thought he was talking to them. He loved the dark anonymity of the stage, so like a protective cave, and when he played, the whole world went away. "It's called 'Love Me Like I'm Nobody'." It was a lyric that Stephen wrote when Simon told him certain truths about himself. It was Stephen's way of smoothing things over, of seeming to say something while saying nothing at all.

Screaming young women clawed at the stage apron and were carried away by security; a young man dressed like Charlie Chaplin got halfway to where Simon was before the guards caught up with him. Simon slid into the slow and gentle rhythms of "Elemental Fountain" and then gave them "My Ten-Ton Soul." A haze of tiny flames lit up the stadium when he began to sing "We Sometimes Fall." He stopped to take a drink of water and climb out from behind the piano, and then he was back at the microphone, singing a few bars *a capella* of some half-forgotten Beatles tune. He caught sight of Jacky standing in the wings and grinned at him: *See, everything is just all right.* Nobody was going to mention that Simon's selected program consisted of slow songs, the only ones that he could play. No one was going to say anything like that. Simon's forearms were aching from the strain of having to compensate for his cold and deadened fingers, and somewhere in the back of his mind, a little voice was panicking. He wasn't sure how much longer he could keep going. Something was sure to happen, sometime soon.

Jacky was standing with a slender, red-haired woman in a purple sari, a woman Simon hadn't seen before. The woman's face was somehow familiar; he might have dreamed about her some night, or met her in passing at a party.

"You're very good," she said.

Simon came offstage at a run, was busy shedding his costume, and somehow, the red-haired woman and her purple sari were in his dressing room with Jacky. "Thanks."

"You were a bit scratchy on that last chorus of "Ten-Ton Soul." I think you ought to lay off the pipe for a bit." Jacky was as sleek and predatory as ever, dressed in leather trousers and a satin shirt that looked like something Marc Bolan might have shed while he slept. "Yeah, that chorus is a problem. Maybe you're using your falsetto too much." He shouted over his shoulder to Kevin: "What d'you think, Kev? Did he nail that last chorus or was it scratchy?"

"I don't fucking know—" Kevin pushed three girls aside and shut the door. "—that's your job." He peered at his clipboard. "Eight more songs after this, right? Jesus *Christ*, you don't half make it hard on yourself, do you? Most blokes I know play maybe an hour, hour and a half."

"That's the thing about Abelard," Jacky said. "He gives them value for their money, isn't that right, my darling?" He grabbed Simon round his naked, sweating waist and kissed him resoundingly on the cheek. "Bloody winner, he is, and I knew it the first time I ever saw him." He leaned close so only Simon could hear him. "How are your hands? All right?"

"Yeah, they're all right." Eight weeks of physiotherapy and another month in the Caribbean, relaxing on a private island, daily exercises to retrain the muscles, rebuild the damaged blood vessels, heal the ravaged cartilage, and even the world-class surgeon Jacky had flown in could only do so much. Simon spent his holiday like a little boy, building sand castles on the beach and roasting wieners on an open fire. He slept on the screened-in porch of his private villa and watched the stars wheel their inevitable course along ancient galactic highways; the grotesque woman with her buzz-cut hair, her black work boots, her lurid tongue, had somehow disappeared. "That chorus, yeah, I think you're right. Why don't I get Stephen to have a look at it?"

Jacky slid an arm round Simon's shoulders. "You don't work with that wanker no more."

"Yes, but he wrote the lyrics and maybe—"

Kevin opened the door, letting in a rush of sound. The audience was chanting Simon's name. Kevin checked his watch. "Five minutes! That's five minutes, that is."

"Five fucking minutes!" Simon struggled to pull his costume up over his sweaty body. "I've not even had a piss." He was stripped to his y-fronts and standing in the middle of the room but no one seemed to either notice or to care. "Who knew the Dutch were such fucking maniacs for Abelard?" The costume change was difficult: short striped trousers with complicated suspenders that crossed over the back and a pink silk shirt with hundreds of tiny ruffles. "I can't get this on. It doesn't fucking fit me!" He yanked the trousers and the fabric split open; immediately two young women with needles and thread converged on him to quickly obliterate the damage. "Who makes these goddamn things? Was this your idea?"

"Watch your fucking mouth," Jacky said. The girls finished their work and disappeared. "Now, eight more songs... is it eight, Kevin?"

"Eight songs and no more than two encores." A joint had suddenly appeared in the road manager's hand. "Leave 'em wanting more, that's what I always say, and we've got to get this lot cleared out."

"You own them tonight." The woman in the purple sari was by his side as Simon moved back out into the dark space that stretched between him and the stage. She laid her hand on his arm for a moment; she was beautiful. "You are what they came to see."

In the profound darkness of the wings, Simon could hardly see her. "And you?"

"I came to see you, also." She smiled, the smile of a sphinx. "I've been waiting for you."

THE last eight songs on the program were nothing less than torture. The strain of trying to play was telling on him, and by the middle of the third-to-last song, the muscles of his right forearm were in spasm. Simon submitted to the ministrations of a massage therapist, who pressed and kneaded until Simon all but cried in pain. Jacky sat on one side and Kevin on the other and they sought between them to warm his ravaged hands but to no avail. Kevin shot a look at Jacky. "How much longer are we going to keep this up?"

"Let me just do 'Moses, Get Your Gun'." Simon pulled his hands away. "It's a slow one, I can manage."

"With that bloody big piano bridge in the middle?" Jacky was incredulous. "Are you mental?"

"I can do it."

Jacky shook his head. "No."

"Jacky, please. I know I can do it. Let me just do it for them. It'll be the last one." Simon grasped Jacky's arm and held on. "I hardly ever ask you for anything. You know that."

The Scotsman drew a slow breath through his nose and nodded. "All right. But that's it, just the one song and then you come off and stay off, you hear me? No fucking encores, no bows, no shaking hands with the bloody audience."

They were waiting, and as soon as Simon came back, the audience was on their feet, applauding wildly, screaming his name. He nodded to them and sat behind the piano. The stage seemed to waver and sway, and for a moment, he fancied he was back in Stepney, sitting to play his complicated Chopin nocturne for the year-end gathering of parents at his school. *I don't know how you could have made such a bollocks of it.* Nina's voice filtered through the haze of applause, and Simon felt sick. He glanced down at his hands, flexed his fingers, felt the pain in his wrists and forearms gathering itself. *I can do this.* The song was one of the more complicated ones he and Stephen had written together, with a long bridge and several difficult chord changes. *It'll be the last one.*

"We're gonna do an older song for you tonight, to finish off. This was written years ago, long before any of this—" Simon swept an arm around, indicating the stage, the lights, and the band, "—had happened. I was just a wee bit of a thing back then." He paused for the anticipated laughter, hooting, and catcalls. "No, it's true. Stephen Abednego—" A loud burst of applause at the mention of Stephen's name; the lead guitarist played a brief, resonating chord. "Stephen Abednego and I wrote this song on my mum's kitchen table back in Stepney." It was an aspect of their story the fan magazines had fastened upon, and over the years it had grown, gathering substance to itself, until it had attained the status of legend. The nascent songwriters, huddled round Simon's old piano, trying out the words and fitting them to chords; Stephen Abednego, scribbling lyrics on the backs of envelopes between sips of his morning tea. People loved the story; it had a certain working-class lucidity that they recognized. It was ultimately a fairy tale. "It's called 'Moses, Get Your Gun'." Simon nodded to the bass player and Clive, the drummer. He laid his hands down on the keys.

The moment when the faulty tendon ruptured would be seared forever in his memory. He was reaching to span an octave before changing key; the injury occurred just at the moment the thumb and little finger of his right hand were at fullest opposition from each other. Something popped in the center of his palm and a fiery pain ignited, blooming up his arm, trailing agony like acid in its wake. The stage was full of people and someone was shouting to *bring the curtain down, bring it down, goddammit* and the lights came up abruptly. Simon crouched on the floor, his hand crushed against his chest, the fingers swelling rapidly, grotesquely. "...gonna be all right." Jacky was there, talking into Simon's face. "...listening to me?"

"It's the last one," Simon murmured. "I told you, didn't I? The last one."

THERE was a certain brand of men's cologne readily available in all the shops for about five pounds. This was the same cologne that Gus had been wearing, the night it happened; Simon always kept a bottle of it close at hand. He didn't even really have to put the bottle to his nose—even the slightest whiff was sufficient to remind him. He was there again, with his underpants around his knees, binding him in place. The filthy floor was grinding dirt into his cheek and his spectacles were broken; his stomach hurt like someone punched him. The banter at the urinal replayed unbidden in his mind like a faulty record:

Watch out for the splash now, by the way.

When you get your dick out—it'll be a big one. Watch the splash, by the way!

The hospital walls were pale green tile with white grout in between and black rubber at the bottom, near the floor. The announcements on the P.A. were in Dutch, but Simon imagined they were all saying the same thing. Silent women in white passed up and down the hallways, carrying trays of medical instruments or wheeling someone in a chair. The windows in Simon's room looked out over a body of water—the Amstel, perhaps. He wasn't sure. There were buildings on the opposite side that looked like blocks of flats, or perhaps they housed important offices. The water was mirror-calm and still; it was very early in the morning, the sun barely over the horizon. Simon sat fully clothed on a hospital bed, his right hand buried to the wrist in a plastic bucket full of ice. The band, advised by Jacky that the tour was over, had flown back to England the night before. Only Clive, who had found himself a Dutch girlfriend, had stayed behind, and Jacky.

"I should like to operate as soon as possible." The doctor was a tall, thin, nervous-looking man whose grey hair had been cropped close to his head. He wore wire-rimmed spectacles and the nametag on his white lab coat identified him as Dr. van der Groet.

"What sort of operation?" Jacky hovered close to Simon, protecting him. Jacky's face looked frightened and there were dark shadows underneath his eyes. Now and then, a muscle in his cheek twitched, and he seemed to blink in an abstracted manner, as if someone had just then told him something he couldn't quite believe.

Van der Groet didn't bother with euphemism: "A complete resection of the entire hand."

It slammed into Simon like a body blow. He stared at van der Groet, his face prickling with sudden heat. "And afterwards I'll be able to play the piano again, like I always did. Right?"

Van der Groet took off his spectacles and regarded them with some degree of interest. Several moments passed before he spoke, but when he did, his voice was as careful and measured as his accent. "Mr. Duckworth, at best I may be able to restore some movement in your hand. At worst...." He shrugged. "The previous injury to the flexor tendons imparted permanent damage. I'm sorry. At this stage there's little I can do."

Simple Simon, if that's what you're calling yourself these days. She had ruined him. She had utterly destroyed him. All of this was her fault.

"Then we'll get someone else." Jacky stood in front of Simon, screening him from the doctor's view. "We'll get someone back in Britain, someone who knows what he's doing, someone who can actually tell his arse from his elbow—"

"Mr. Stride, I sympathize, I really do."

"That's bullshit." Jacky spoke in a hiss. "Are you saying this is some sort of cock-up? The surgery was no good? It didn't take?"

Van der Groet put his glasses back on. "I am saying that the human hand is a delicate instrument, Mr. Stride. We humans cannot always repair the damage we ourselves do."

Simon shifted the bucket of ice and lifted his ruined hand. "When can you operate on me?" The urge to break down crying pressed on him but he would not indulge it. "If you can help me, I should be very grateful."

The doctor flipped through a sheaf of papers on the clipboard he carried. "I can see if an operating room could be made ready."

"Thank you."

Van der Groet touched Simon's arm—just once, and very gently. "Ik wens u niks dan goed," he said. "I wish you every good thing."

Simon waited 'til Jacky left. Then he picked up the phone and dialed Stephen's London number. The call rang for a long time, the pulses going out and out into nothing, and then Stephen's answering machine clicked on.

"You have to come." Simon's mouth was pressed hard against the receiver. "You have to come. I need you."

HE WAS lying on the beach in Orkney with Stephen; they were looking at the sky. Stephen was tracing Simon's mouth with a fingertip, smiling but saying nothing. The night was warm, and it would be daylight forever because now it was midsummer, the night when lovers coupled openly in the ploughed furrows of a field, unafraid. The constellations wheeled through space, at first slowly and then frighteningly fast until they loomed over him, pressing him down into the ground with a violent whirring sound.

The air conditioner in the hospital recovery room switched on, whirring quietly, and Simon Duckworth opened his eyes. His right hand was encased in bandages to his elbow and there was a smell of antiseptic in the room. From his bed he could see a square glass enclosure with a door—probably an observation room—and hear voices over the PA system in the hallway. *I'm here again... only this time it's for good.* He wondered where Jacky was—probably pacing in the corridor and cursing everyone. The image made him smile. Jacky had been there all along, from that first frenzied night at the Picador Club 'til now, and everything in between. Jacky was forever at his side. What would Jacky do, now that all of it was over? Because it was over; Simon couldn't delude himself on that point. He would never play the piano again.

He remembered hot days in Mississippi with Stephen, sitting side by side on the piano bench and guiding Stephen's fingers on the keys. *When I was a lad, my dad's friend raped me.* He hadn't said it because he was seeking sympathy or because he wanted comfort. He'd said it because it was the truth and he wanted Stephen to know how the past and the present pulled inexorably toward each another. Those

Mississippi boys in that hotel room, beating him senseless with their fists, enraged because he was or seemed to be something they could not accurately name. *You a fag, man?* This thing he was—this thing they thought he was—appeared to give them license, spur them on to even greater violence. *Is that what you are? A dirty little faggot?*

A door opened and quietly closed and he heard footsteps. An orderly was standing by his bed, holding a paper cup of ice water. "Mr. Duckworth, how do you feel? Sometimes the anesthetic makes one thirsty." He was about Simon's age, with light brown hair cut short, and he wore glasses. When Simon attempted to take the cup with his one good hand, the man stayed him. "Let me. It's best if you sip slowly. Your stomach might not take kindly to such an assault so soon after surgery."

Simon did as he was told. The water was cold, delicious, soothing to his parched throat. The orderly allowed him to drink about half, then took the cup away. "I'm still thirsty," Simon protested.

"Enough for now, hm? Later, you can have more."

Do you know who I am? Simon wanted to ask—except he wasn't, not anymore, and before long, the hordes of screaming fans would have forgotten about him, moved on to the next big thing, the newest hot young band. He'd be merely a footnote in some musicologist's history, a passing fad.

"Heart sounds good," the orderly said, removing his stethoscope from Simon's chest. "And your blood pressure's normal. I think we can move you to your room now."

"My room?" Simon was confused. "I thought I'd be going home after this. I mean… it's just my hand. Surely I don't need to stay in hospital."

The man gave him a perfunctory smile, eminently professional and devoid of information. "I'm afraid I couldn't say. That will be a discussion for Dr. van der Groet." He patted Simon's shoulder, turned to go. "Oh, by the way." He came to stand by Simon's bed again. "I love your music."

"Thank you." Simon forced himself to smile. "That's very kind of you."

HE CAME to himself somewhere different every time. Last night he woke up in SoHo, standing by a callbox with a newspaper in his hand. He was wearing striped pajamas and a winter overcoat. Usually he would call Nestor to come and pick him up when these things happened, and Nestor always came for him, no matter how far away: *Mr. Simon, sir, what have you gone and done to yourself?* Simon sat mutely in the back seat of his car and watched the lights and landscape passing by, and felt as empty as a purged container. His mind was always filled with the same internal image: a dirty lavatory somewhere, and a high white ceiling with fluorescent lights, and the far-off sound of music. Something about the tiles was troubling to him; the tiles were a particular shade of blue that filled him with loathing and horror, although he didn't quite know why. He tried to argue himself out of this feeling and sometimes it stayed away for hours at a time, or days. He could carry on with normal life during these intervals. Eventually the blue tiles found their way back into his consciousness, however. Something would remind him of them or he might see that singular shade of blue and he was there again, his cheek pressed into the gritty floor and the high white ceiling stretching away forever.

He wanted to talk about it but had no idea what to say. He couldn't conceive of lying on some doctor's couch and talking about blue tiles on an imaginary bathroom floor, or the disconnected images that flitted across his inner vision. Small things filled him with dread: soapy water swirling down the kitchen drain was horrifying, and there were images of wet pink hands, disconnected fingers. There was a sucking noise that went along with these memories, and the yellow blanket that was on his childhood bed, and a row of dinky cars lined up on a shelf. There was a scent somewhere between tea and roses, a female scent overlaid with cigarette smoke. But he couldn't say such things to people who knew him, and so he said nothing at all. He watched a great deal of television, and wandered round his house, looking out his windows. Sometimes there was a feeling like a cold hand at his back and the sensation of being watched. There were eyes on him, he knew, whichever way he turned.

"You should have something for your tea, Mr. Simon." Nestor brought him a plate of sandwiches, an orange, and a pot of Lapsang Souchong, piping hot. "You've got to eat, sir. You'll get ill if you don't eat."

"Not hungry." He had to keep looking out the window; he had to sit so that he could always see the window. He couldn't ever turn his back on it, just in case they were looking in at him, just in case she was watching. The police had never found her, and Simon knew they never would. She had such powers; she could disappear into the ether.

Nestor made a clicking noise with his tongue against his teeth. "Are you going to eat nothing at all?" He took the things back into the kitchen, muttering to himself. "Perhaps I will leave Mr. Simon's employ and go work for someone else. Clearly Mr. Simon needs nothing I have to give him…. What Mr. Simon needs is someone to look inside his head, tighten a few screws or something." The kitchen door swung shut on Nestor's muttering, reducing his annoyance to merely a murmur of sound.

Nina and Gerald had been up to Scotland for a few days, visiting some relatives of Gerald's. They arrived at Simon's house with parcels and packages, exclaiming over Simon's pallor and his listless air. "You're not ill, love." Nina swiped his hair back from his face. "You couldn't possibly be ill." Nobody mentioned the thick bandages on his arm, his recent surgery to repair his ruined hand. Nina had tried and Simon had rebuffed her, refusing her condolences, her proffered sympathy. "Although that hair of yours needs trimming. You look like a sheepdog."

Simon wanted to make his mother happy, so he roused from his stupor, went into the kitchen, and asked Nestor to make some tea for them. Simon clumsily poured tea and handed the biscuits round and looked at photographs of Gerald's grandchildren, twins called Mark and Amy. "I'll be wanting grandchildren soon enough," Nina said. She poured more tea into Simon's cup, added milk and sugar. "It's time you were thinking about getting married, my lad. You're getting on. Can't afford to be choosy, and I'm sure there are plenty of lovely young women who'd be more than happy to be married to a pop star, eh?" Nina's fingernails were painted a brilliant, glossy red; her mouth was red as well. She rather resembled an ageing drag queen, all bouffant hair and bright, sharp edges. "Perhaps we'll get you a pram for your next birthday—something to give you a push in the right direction." Her eyes were hard, obsidian dark, devouring. Had she always been this way? Or was it only Simon's imagination that painted her in such lurid detail?

"Leave the lad alone," Gerald said, wearily. He winked at Simon across the table. "Plenty of time for that, eh? Plenty of time to think of wife and kiddies."

"No, Gerald, that's rubbish." Nina fitted a cigarette into a long black holder and lit it, waving the match out like Bette Davis. "Simon, my lad, you know I only want what's best for you. But you can't carry on this bachelor lifestyle indefinitely. There are plenty of smart, capable young women out there. You've got to put your mind to it and get one for yourself."

"I'll do that," Simon mumbled. He took a biscuit; it tasted as dry as ash or sawdust. "Do that right away, I will."

Nina's mouth contracted. "Now, don't come the old soldier with me, Simon. You know this is for your own good." She looked him up and down. "This pop star lifestyle isn't doing you a bit of good. I know the sorts of things you lads get up to. I've seen it in the *Mirror*. I think it's absolutely disgusting, I really do. And these photographs of you. Whatever were you thinking?" The tabloids had fastened onto Simon's recent convalescence in Amsterdam, had somehow taken pictures of him leaving the hospital, leaning on Jacky: ABELARD TAKES INJURY IN STRIDE. An inset showed their arms round each other, with the comment: WHO'S AFRAID OF THE BIG BAD POOF? A feature article showed photographs of Simon at various points of his career, each picture accompanied by a suitably sneering caption. The more recent ones showed a haggard and disheveled Simon, slovenly and unshaven, gazing into the middle distance and seemingly unaware of his surroundings: SIMON SAYS?

"What the devil are you talking about now?" Gerald asked. He pushed his tea cup away and got up from the table. "I'll be outside." Simon didn't have to see his face to know that Gerald was annoyed.

He'd been married to Nina since Simon was thirteen; he knew what she was like.

"Do you want to end up like your father?" Nina scooted her chair close to him. Her red lipstick was bleeding into tiny lines around her mouth; her cheeks were soft and downy, like the faces of old women. "Because that's what will happen. You'll end up like him."

"My father's dead." Simon tried to look her in the eye and couldn't. "Is that what you mean?" His hand was throbbing—a horrible, sickening pain—and all he wanted was to lie down and sleep.

"Oh, right." Nina puffed on her cigarette. "I see what this is. It's all about blaming your mother these days, isn't it? It's all Mum's fault. Everything is Mum's fault."

"I didn't say that." He couldn't seem to make his lips move; his face felt numb. He watched the tip of her cigarette, burning at the end of the long holder. "I'd never say that." He wondered why: now that everything had gone to ruin, why was he so tolerant of Nina's feelings?

"You just mind me when I'm telling you, everything I ever did was for you, right? Your father fucked off to Glasgow and left us with nothing, while he had a fine old time. Him and his fancy women."

Roger's widow Doris was anything but fancy. But Simon would never say this. "That's not what I meant."

Nina rose from the table, trembling with rage. She ripped her cigarette from the holder, stabbed it out on the tablecloth. "You little bastard." Her painted lips were quivering; she seemed unable to even breathe properly. "You little poof. You've no idea what I've been through, all these years. You've no idea. It's all 'oooh me dad, me dad' with you. Well let me tell you something…." She didn't say it. Whatever Nina had been going to say, she didn't. She stared at him for a moment, at the top of his bent head. "You're disgusting to me," she said. "Oh, I know what you've been up to, you and that other one. It's no wonder you don't want to get married, eh? You'd rather take it up the arse, wouldn't you? I always knew there was something wrong with you."

I bet you've got all kinds of girlfriends, don't you? Young lad your age. Watch out for the splash, by the way!

"No. That's not true at all. That's not true." Defensive, he sounded twelve years old again, explaining to his mother about the stains on his sheets. She'd brought the sheets to Gerald, and Simon had waited in the kitchen, sipping an endless drink of water and listening to their conversation.

It's disgusting, Gerald. I don't know how you can say...

All boys do that sort of thing, Nina. You know that. It's normal for a boy his age.

Normal! There's nothing normal about it.

"You'll be sorry someday." Nina snatched up her purse. "When I'm dead and gone. You'll be sorry." She bolted through the house; the front door slammed behind her. Simon heard their car start up and drive away. He was seized with a sudden, vicious hunger. He went to the refrigerator and stood there for a long moment, gazing at various containers. Here was a package of cold cuts, delicate thin-sliced savory meats; he took a slice of turkey and a slice of ham and a slice of something rather like salami. Here was a loaf of crusty French bread and here was mustard and real butter: he could make a sandwich, but he didn't. He tore off a piece of bread and smeared butter on it with his fingers and he ate it in enormous chunks, jaw muscles straining to force it in and chew it. Here was a tub of ice cream, sweet and brown; he clawed it into him, breaking up the cold with the fingers of his one good hand.

There was a roaring noise inside of him, and so he must go on, pressing his own guts down, managing the pictures and the sounds. The tiles were blue, gritty with dirt and the traffic of a thousand punters' footprints; the ceiling was white, soaring off into infinity. He was little, sitting in a kitchen sink and there were hands dipping in the water, hands washing him, a woman's soft pink fingers. The hands were dipping water on him, putting water in him and pushing the soap up inside of him, pulling him apart. He would come apart in pieces; he would swirl into a million fragments and disappear; he would exist only as a disconnected sucking noise, a drain. It was her. It was his mother. Long before Gus and that filthy Glasgow lavatory, she was there. She was there.

He came to himself a little after midnight. He was on Oxford Street, just outside Marks and Spencer's. He was wearing a T-shirt and a pair of shorts; his bare feet were shoved into tennis shoes. There were people in the street and there was a fire somewhere, the sound of sirens in the distance. He was holding a piece of bread in his left hand, his fingers greasy. A man was standing next to him, saying something, but he sounded strange and faraway. The man's eyes were big and sad; he was holding onto Simon's sleeve and pointing across the street. Apparently Simon crossed the street. Simon didn't remember this. Simon's throat was sore. Simon didn't know what the man expected him to say.

"I have to call Nestor." Simon's lips were cracked and bleeding; there was dried blood in the corners of his mouth. "I have to get Nestor to come and pick me up. He'll come and pick me up." He was drifting, barely tethered to his body. The city was unsubstantial underneath his feet; he was no one in particular. "I'm sorry. I'm sorry."

"WHAT are you thinking?" Piet lay on his side, smoking and watching Stephen. It was another hot afternoon in a succession of hot afternoons, the heat maddening them, unrelieved by anything except the refuge of Piet's bedroom.

"How do you know…." Stephen plucked the cigarette from Piet's lips, drew on it, and handed it back. "…when you've met 'the one'?" The cigarette was marijuana, with a dark and potent taste that made Stephen's head swim. Piet claimed to have bought it from an itinerant peddler, but Piet was prone to make up stories and Stephen wasn't sure he believed it. People sold all sorts of things on the beach, though: shells and jewelry, sunhats, candleholders made of pretty sea glass. There was even one girl—Stephen saw her every day without fail— who strolled up and down with a box of warm, freshly baked banana bread suspended from a ribbon around her neck. She sold slices for ten cents apiece, refreshing her supply as necessary from her house just up the beach. Stephen had sampled the bread, which was delicious, and turned down the proposition, which didn't interest him. He suspected his time with Leslie had broken something, had instilled in him a fear of other women like her. She had seemed so biddable, so compliant, smiling shyly from behind the counter in her Mississippi shop. He never wanted to meet her like ever again.

"The one?" Piet's smile was gentle. Piet was the gentlest person Stephen had ever met. He was sure, had he met Piet in some other time and place, that he would have stayed with Piet for always.

"The one person for you... the person you're meant to spend the rest of your life with." Stephen took the joint from Piet. "Your soul mate. You know?" He took a hit and handed it back. "Could you have already met them and not known it?"

"I am not your soul mate." Piet sucked on what remained of the cigarette, nearly burning his fingers. He offered the remains to Stephen, who shook his head. "But you know this."

"Of course." It didn't hurt his feelings, what Piet was saying. It was merely the truth. "So what if my soul mate is out there in the world somewhere and I've lost him?" His heart thudded in his chest as he realized what he'd said. "Or her." His time with Piet had proven certain subtle truths. "How do you know?"

Piet was quiet for a long time, caressing Stephen's bare shoulder with a gentle hand. When he finally spoke, his voice was subdued and thoughtful. "Sometimes I have met someone... someone I had never known before, at least in this life. It doesn't feel like meeting for the first time. It feels as if we have known each other forever and we are just picking up the threads of a conversation started long ago, in some other place. Do you understand what I mean?"

Far away in memory it was, that night at the station, but Stephen remembered everything: the long train trip down to London, the lingering unreality of it, the fear that he'd made a horrible mistake. He'd been seventeen years old, away from home for the very first time, in a huge city where he knew no one and where no one knew him.

Are you the lyricist?

And then Simon's kind face, his spectacles, and his sad brown eyes... a friend and comrade. Stephen remembered holidays away from London, visiting his family up in Orkney, and how the trip back down again seemed to take forever. He often entertained egregious thoughts about Simon not being there when he arrived, but Simon always was. Simon was waiting there for him, standing on the platform, arms wide open, smiling. He remembered being in Orkney with Simon, lying together on the sand and making silent promises with their bodies and their hands. In his entire life, who else had affected him the way that Simon did? Who knew him—and loved him—the way Simon had?

"You are thinking of someone." Piet tapped Stephen's cheek with his finger. "Is it Simon?"

Stephen was inexplicably on the verge of tears. "Yeah." He drew breath to steady himself. "I think I knew, even from the very start. I think I knew." He pressed the heels of his palms into his eyes. "I'd come down from up North." Piet knew the story of his pilgrimage to London; Stephen had already told him this, and more. "I was seventeen years old... I don't think I even knew which way was up."

"Most of us don't, when we're seventeen."

"You know, Piet, I spent the entire trip being absolutely terrified of what I was going to do in London. By the time I got there, I think I'd convinced myself that it wasn't going to work. I thought he'd see me and tell me to get back on the train and go home."

"But he didn't." Piet adjusted the pillows behind his head. "He didn't say anything like that at all."

"No." Pulling himself up out of a heavy sleep, he'd climbed down onto the platform on legs that shook. He'd had one suitcase, a dreadful cardboard thing that his father'd had since half past forever. He was wearing a green jumper with white reindeer on it, a hideous thing some relative had given him several Christmases ago, much too small, and a pair of denim trousers and the only jacket he owned. "I looked like I'd rolled off the back of a farm truck, and there he was." *Are you the lyricist?* "I think that's when it happened, when I turned round and saw him."

"When what happened? I don't follow you."

"I...." Stephen laughed at himself. "It sounds ridiculous. I know that." Suddenly shy, he lowered his gaze. "I loved him from the very first. I've always loved him. He's the one person I can't imagine my

life without, but I pushed him away. I told him I didn't want to be...."
He stopped, acutely conscious of Piet's presence. "I'm sorry."

"You didn't want to be queer. You didn't want to be a poof, as they say in England." Piet tilted his head. "Am I correct?"

Stephen couldn't speak, but merely nodded.

To Piet's credit, he didn't preach. He didn't argue with Stephen. "Are you so certain that your chance with him is gone?"

"Yeah." Simon had made that very clear. "I think it's just too late." Sadness like a hard hand squeezed his throat. "I think it's probably too late."

"TELL me about melancholy," Simon said. He was crouched under a bridge, barefoot and afraid. He'd woken up that morning in an alley, lying with his head on a stack of discarded boxes, a stray cat curled up on his feet. It might have been several days since he was home, but he couldn't be entirely sure. He knew his name; he knew his own address, but everything else about the world filled him with alternating terror and despair. He was horribly afraid but couldn't remember why, and sleep was nearly impossible. His dreams were filled with images of laughing men and urinals, and gritty lavatory floors, and somewhere high above him, a woman's hand with bright red fingernails was reaching into him and hurting him.

"Tell me what you know about it." Simon was talking to Celestina, who could only talk to him if her back was turned. Celestina was somewhere between seventeen and fifty; someone had tattooed a spiderweb on her cheek. The tattoo was done meticulously, she said, while she lay under the thrall of drugs in an abandoned fruit warehouse near Canary Wharf. Two men did it with a needle and a pocketknife. Celestina was dying of some new disease, something the doctors had never seen before and nobody knew how to treat. "I can't get no pills. They want to give me pills, but I can't take that into my body. They don't understand. I can't have that in my body." She snuffed out her cigarette, saving half for later. "Melancholy," she said. Her hair was cut short and dyed purple. "Like sadness, you mean. Like being sad."

"I can't go home." Simon sat down on the ground. There had been nothing to eat or drink for ages, but he wasn't hungry. He remembered Oxford Street and talking to a foreigner with great, sad eyes. He was asking the foreigner for directions, asking him which way to go home, but the foreigner couldn't tell him anything. He couldn't tell Simon anything he didn't already know.

"I've no home to go to," Celestina said. Her name wasn't really Celestina, but Candice. "I've never had no home, me. I've never had a holiday."

"I've had lots of holidays." Simon's left hand was sore and dirty, and the bandages on his right were soiled and torn. Jacky employed a manicurist that came with them on tour and did Simon's fingernails before he met any of the media and massaged his hands each night before a gig. Jacky always said that Simon had beautiful hands, but Simon's hands were small and sturdy, rather plain. He wasn't handsome or beautiful like pop stars ought to be. He knew that. He knew it when he was in the mental hospital. He had always known it. "I've been to America."

"Piss off!" Celestina glanced at him over one shoulder. "You have not."

"I have. Me and a mate went to Mississippi. Been to Georgia, Maryland. Even been to Florida, I have."

Simon'll come with us, won't you? Mississippi in the middle of the summer and Stephen fresh in love with Leslie. Simon on the outside, looking in like a dog at the door. *I bet Simon isn't scared.* Leslie, trying to make them go swimming. There was a little pond, and it was late at night and they'd been drinking, and it was hot as hell. The night outside was warm and full of cricket song and possibilities.

I'm for it. Simon glanced across at Stephen, still sipping on his beer. The windows were all open and the night came in. They could strip their clothes off and swim naked if they wanted to. Leslie said no one ever came near the place, not even in daylight.

Why don't they? Stephen jumped in first and floated on his back, his body gleaming in the wash of moonlight. *Why don't they come here?*

'Cause it's haunted, dumbass. Leslie pulled her T-shirt over her head and Simon looked away. *You can look all you want,* she said, *it don't bother me none.* Her breasts were large and firm, with pointed nipples. When Simon was a lad, the boys would sit outside the school at dinnertime and watch the girls go by: *Look at the tray on that one!* Leslie's buttocks were smooth and rounded, paler than the rest of her. She slipped into the water without a sound and swam out into the center of the pond. *Old man Sykes used to live around these parts. He made shine and kept a few chickens. Didn't never hurt nobody. They found him one morning with his throat cut.*

Simon stripped his shirt off, thankful for the darkness. He tucked his specs inside one of his shoes and sat for a moment on the little wooden dock, his hands in his lap.

Don't sit there like an idiot, Leslie said. *Come on! The water's great.*

She swam up to him and took his hand and towed him further out into the water. Simon had been for lessons at the Y; he was a good swimmer and not afraid of water. *I can't see too well without my specs,* he said.

Don't be frightened, darling. Leslie's hair fanned out around her. *It's just us.* She put her arms round his neck and put her face close to his and laughed. She spun in the water and dived down and surfaced suddenly, sputtering. She wrapped an arm round each of their shoulders and pulled the three of them together. *Sometimes Old Man Sykes's ghost comes out here for a swim.*

Simon was scornful. *He does not.*

He does. Leslie's mouth was against his ear. *They say he used to bugger little boys.*

The water was suddenly cold. *I should go,* Simon said. *I should leave you two alone.*

Aw, honey, I was just teasing you. You ain't mad, are you?

I'm fine. Simon dressed himself, his back to them. Leslie was giggling and whispering something to Stephen, something that Simon pretended not to hear: *When he goes home, you can fuck me.*

Simon found his way home by counting the fence posts along the road. He sat on the porch by himself for hours, waiting, but Stephen didn't come home. Simon lay in bed, wide awake and trembling at every sound. The rattle of the door latch made him bolt upright; he strained toward the noise. Stephen was whispering to Leslie.

He's asleep by now. He sleeps like the dead.

Simon padded to the bedroom door and opened it: Leslie was on her knees, her hands splayed on Stephen's thighs. Stephen's eyes were closed; his mouth was open. He panted harshly, one hand cupped round the back of her head. *Yes. Oh yes, please.*

Leslie finished him off and got up from her knees. Stephen stumbled to the bathroom but Leslie turned and stared at Simon: *You get off on looking, or something?*

I might do.

He was in the kitchen, early the next morning, before Stephen was awake. He was standing at the window, gazing out over the tobacco fields, drinking a cup of tea. It was barely seven and already hot; the heat hung in shimmering waves over the fields.

He wore me out last night. Her gaze raked over him. *Too bad you didn't get to watch.*

Simon stared at her, wordless. Then he caught her face between his palms and kissed her, and backed her up against the kitchen counter and kissed her again, and held her up against the wall with her legs around his waist and entered her. He fucked her slowly, and when she came, he felt the muscles ripple, her body clenching around him. He pressed his face into her neck and licked salt from her skin.

I'm gonna be a famous rock and roll star, he whispered. *You can tell your girlfriends that I fucked you.*

"I've been all round the States," Simon said. Celestina was picking at a scab on her arm. "I used to be a pop star."

He found Celestina the next morning, lying on the pier, her eyes staring at the sky. Simon entertained the notion that she might be alive, still, except for the gaping wound in her throat. "Wake up." He patted her cheek. The flesh was stiff and cold. "Wake up. Wake up, please." He was always polite. "Please wake up, all right? Wake up now." It's like he was doomed to sit beside the bodies of dead girls. It's like he was the one who had to see them dead or something.

He found a constable standing by a phone box just off Grime Street. The constable was very young, and blond, and not too bright, but he would have to do. "I found a girl. I mean, I know the girl. She's dead over there. There's a dead girl. Over there by the water."

"Hang on, mate, slow down." The cop looked Simon over. "Been sleeping rough, have you?" He winced as his nostrils picked up the smell. "I'll say you have. Where's the body?"

"She's over there. Her throat's been cut." *Run,* his mind was saying, *run before he thinks you did it. Run. Run away now.* His feet were moving, churning up the pavements; he could hear the cop shouting behind him but he paid no heed. He ducked down a side street and out onto a wider boulevard; his arms were pumping at his sides. It was barely daylight: how could such things happen?

He rounded a corner and stopped so suddenly that he stumbled forward and nearly fell. A man was standing in front of him. The man in front of him was saying something. The man was saying his name, very clearly and quite slowly, as if Simon were hard of hearing.

The man was Jacky Stride.

SIMON had fallen asleep on the sofa in the sitting room of Jacky's flat, a spacious loft with high ceilings and a wall of windows looking out onto the Thames from Lombard Road. Jacky sat and watched him: the gentle rise and fall of Simon's chest, the slow rolling motion of his eyes underneath the lids, the twitching of his one good hand. Simon didn't sleep quiet. He didn't fall into unconsciousness and stay there. Simon's sleep was full of tics and murmurs, subvocal exhortations that Jacky only half heard. He didn't need to hear them. He knew what Simon was saying, what Simon probably said every night of his life. He had lain beside Simon in the past, had been the one to waken him from his nightmares, to comfort and console him. There were times when Jacky was closer to Simon than he'd ever been to anyone.

It was past midnight and Jacky should have been sleeping but he couldn't bear to leave Simon. He had spent several days searching London for him, existing in the awful anticipation of being rung and told that Simon was dead—that he'd thrown himself under a lorry or that his body was floating in the Thames. One of Simon's servants had tattled to the press and news of Simon's aberrant behavior was splashed across the front of every cheap tabloid in England: ABELARD RUNS AMUCK. The damage would take every ounce of Jacky's formidable skill to undo.

Simon was dreaming: he clutched at the blankets and his breathing quickened. Jacky reached out and took hold of Simon's hand. "Shhh," he said, like someone soothing an infant. "Shhh."

Simon stirred, woke up with a start, a gasp dying in his throat. "Stephen?"

"No, it's Jack. I'm right here."

"I thought...." Simon blinked. "I thought I was still out there."

"I found you and brought you home, remember?" He smoothed the hair back from Simon's face. "You were having a bit of trouble." Jacky started to say something, stopped, then started again. "Is it... because of what happened when you were a little boy? Because you never... I mean, it didn't seem to bother you...." He wasn't sure what to say after that. Simon, despite the things that he'd endured, had always been an eager and enthusiastic lover. It had amazed Jacky that someone could suffer such insults and abuses and still manage to function normally, to have some kind of normal sexuality. Jacky wasn't a stupid man; he read a lot and always had. He knew the damage such injuries could cause.

"Where were you?" Simon asked. He'd looked horrible: haggard and filthy and stinking, red-eyed and miserable. The soles of his feet were cut and bruised; there were contusions round his mouth. Jacky had coaxed him near, the way you'd coax a sick and bleeding animal, and when Simon had gotten close enough to touch, he threw his arms round him and held him fast. *I won't let you go. I won't.*

"Out looking for you. Nestor called here, asking if you'd popped in. He said you'd gone out sometime during the night and you hadn't come home. That was three days ago."

He had burned the clothes Simon had been wearing and sent out for new ones: simple jeans and T-shirts, clean socks and underwear and white tennis shoes. He wanted to ask what had happened, wanted to understand, but Simon spent several hours sleeping, waking at intervals to sip some water, take an aspirin, and Jacky didn't feel like pushing him.

Can I come down there with you? Jacky would ask this back in the old days, when they were touring in a bus. If he was bored or lonely, and if Stephen Abednego was sleeping or otherwise engaged, he'd call down to where Simon habitually sat, at the back. *I can't sleep for the bloody racket this thing makes.*

Go on, then. Simon would squeeze up against the wall to make some room. Sitting side by side, they'd murmur for ages in the dark, and it wasn't all business talk, either.

You're going to be famous, Jacky would say. *I'm going to make sure of it.*

Right. Simon was always more realistic, and slightly scornful. *And I'm bleeding Elvis, I am.* He was reluctant when Jacky had introduced the idea of costumes, assuming—correctly—that Simon would loosen up onstage if he were dressed as someone else. Jacky'd had the costumes specially tailored to minimize Simon's bodily flaws, including hidden corsetry to hide the fact that he tended to put weight on his belly. Glam had just begun to take hold and stars like David Bowie, Gary Glitter, and Marc Bolan were at the forefront of popular consciousness. Jacky was quick to downplay any reservations Simon might have had.

You've got to be slim to wear that. I can't wear that. I'll look like fucking Billy Bunter.

All it takes to wear this is balls, my lad. Anybody says anything and I'll fucking dile 'em.

Simon had a band by then—The Livered Hearts—who were managed by Jacky; Stephen, as lyricist, tagged along with them on tour. The Livered Hearts featured Simon on keyboards and lead vocals, and three red-headed brothers on guitar, bass, and drums respectively. They had a girl singer named Jukebox Ginger, a cracking lass with a bouffant hairdo and long pink fingernails "like Dusty Springfield. I want to re-do Dusty, see. A new Dusty."

She's wearing most of Carnaby Street. Jacky didn't care for her but Stephen found her enormously amusing—more so when she screwed him in the tour van one night outside of Liverpool—and played cards with her and Simon and the rest, and lost most of his pay check to her during impromptu poker games. He wrote a song for her and called it "Ginger's Jukebox." Simon set it to a funky, syncopated rhythm and played it for her one night between sets, and she got all overcome and cried.

You're too nice to me, you lads. You're too nice.

"Whatever happened to her?" Simon was suddenly awake. "Remember Jukebox Ginger? What happened to her?"

Jacky's breath caught in his throat. "Car crash on the motorway." It was in all the newspapers, because the driver had been drinking. Ginger had been drinking, or perhaps it had been drugs. She'd been driving their old van, the one The Livered Hearts had used to haul their gear around. She'd run into a concrete bridge.

"It was a bridge," Simon said. "I remember now."

Jacky nodded, remembering it. It all seemed so long ago. "And that bouffant hairdo." Simon's face was so naked without his spectacles, he thought, utterly blind and open. "I should have listened to you. I should have helped you."

Simon reached out and Jacky came tentatively into his embrace, heart banging in his chest, the anguished rasp of his breath betraying the fact that he was trying not to cry. "You did," he said. "You did listen."

The next sentence was easier with practice: "Why were you running away?"

Simon told him. "She made me think it was all me dad." Simon shook his head. "She told me that he hated me, how she was all I had and I'd best be good to her. She was doing… that to me, and all the time…." He didn't need to explain further. Jacky understood.

"A boy's best friend is his mother." Jacky's voice was barely a whisper. His own mother had been so used up, so desiccated by a life she barely lived that she'd had nothing left for him. Like so many Gorbals lads of his generation, Jacky had mostly raised himself.

"What?"

"That movie—the one with Tony Perkins and that bird in the shower." He and Simon had seen *Psycho* at a special midnight showing the past October. Stephen was in America, visiting Leslie's parents, and Simon was predictably at loose ends. They'd gone to the cinema to escape a party Nina was throwing for some friend of Gerald's who was immigrating to Australia; Simon was afraid that if he stuck around his mother would make him play the piano. He'd had enough of that, he said, when he was a lad. The scene where Norman, dressed as his mother, came running into the basement with a knife, amused Simon to no end. *Christ, she's an ugly woman, isn't he?*

"He's in Australia." Jacky touched Simon's torn and soiled bandages. "He left the country after you threw him out."

"Where in Australia?"

"Some little place near Bingil Bay. He left me the details." Jacky was Stephen's manager as well as Simon's; it was only natural that he be the holder of such information. "Why?" Simon had just come through a terrible ordeal and Jacky knew he shouldn't push, but he couldn't help himself: "Plan on running after him, do you?" The old, familiar longing made a secret pain in his heart.

Simon sat up, stared at him. "What?"

"Going to run to Australia after him?" Jacky snarled. "Throw yourself at his feet and declare your undying love?" He got up off the couch, stalked over, and stood looking out the windows. "You really amaze me, I have to say." Anger was much safer than what he was actually feeling. He could manage anger.

"Jack, I don't understand—"

"No, you don't." He shrugged shoulders made stiff with tension. "You've never seen anything except that bloody Lincolnshire yob."

"Jacky...."

"No, fuck off!" He gestured savagely—futilely—his face twisted in anger. "I've done everything for you, right? I saw you playing in some little shithole of a pub and I put my money right where my fucking mouth is. Somebody else wouldn't have given you a second look! And here you are—" He was interrupted by the doorbell. The doctor he'd called to re-dress Simon's hand stood in the doorway, medical bag in hand. Jacky took himself into the kitchen while the doctor worked, chatting amiably to Simon as he snipped away the filthy bandages and cleaned the wound. When he'd finished, Jacky saw him to the door, shook his hand, and thanked him. He stood by the closed door for a minute, his head lowered. "Are you going to Australia?" he asked.

"Yes." Simon's voice was barely audible. "I'd like to leave as soon as possible."

Jack rubbed his hands over his face. "Why him?" He sighed. "Why him and not me? What has he got—" He stopped short. "No. You know what, I'm not going to do this. I'm not going to prostrate myself like some lust-addled fan and hope that if I scream loud enough you'll look down into the front row and see me." *You're making a fool of yourself, Jack. Best leave it.* "What time do you want to go?"

Simon's voice was very quiet. "As soon as I can."

"All right. I'll book your ticket."

Simon came to him, took Jacky into his arms and hugged him. "Thank you, Jack... for everything. Now there's only one thing I've got to do before I leave."

NINA was wearing bright pink lipstick the exact shade of her blouse. Her fingernails were polished bright pink, as well. She was wearing a double strand of Majorca pearls and a pink cardigan sweater and a grey tweed skirt. Nina had been interviewed by the *Times on Sunday* and the *Mirror*; she understood that she was the mother of a fretful pop star whose habit it was to go running round the city unaccompanied, making a spectacle of himself and igniting rumors about his dubious sanity. There were a great many things that she would have liked to say to Simon, but she wouldn't say anything with Jacky Stride sitting there beside him. Jacky was perhaps the one person in the entire world who Nina was afraid of. She sensed—correctly—that if she ever crossed him, he would retaliate in kind, and then some.

"How are you, love?" She rose from the table to kiss Simon on both cheeks and press his hands. He moved to hug her but Nina stepped away. The blouse and skirt were new, easily wrinkled; besides, she had always abhorred public display. Nina once told Gerald and Simon that an obscure uncle on her mother's side had had an illicit affair with some cousin of the Queen; this put Nina at some obscure remove from royalty. *For all I know, we're related, her and me. Oh, laugh if you like, but there's stranger things have happened.*

Simon didn't hesitate; he plunged directly in. "It wasn't only Dad," he said. "When I was little." A trembling began from somewhere deep inside him and spread and he was having trouble breathing. "I remember things you did."

Nina looked at Jacky, then back at Simon, perhaps wondering if this were a joke. "Things I did."

"When I was little… really little. When you were washing me." He spoke with his eyes fixed on some point just above the top of Nina's head, clutching Jacky's hand underneath the table. "You did things. You put—" He'd been so little, just a baby, sitting in the big sink in the kitchen, being bathed before bed. A woman's hands were dipping in and out of the water, washing him, a woman's fingers with bright red fingernails. The hands put water on him, put water in him and pushed the soap right up inside of him so that it burned like acid. He remembered crying as he was bundled into a clean diaper, put into his pajamas, put to bed.

Nina blinked at him. She blinked as if she couldn't believe what she was hearing. She blinked as if there were something in her eye. She took a tiny mirror from her purse and looked into it, freshening her lipstick. "Now then," she said. "Let's order tea. The scones here are really lovely."

Simon opened his mouth to speak but Jacky got there first. The Scotman's face sported two red patches, high up on the cheekbones, and the dark eyes were blazing with anger. "Nobody is ordering tea, you evil old bag. Let's get that straight from the get-go, right? What Simon's just told you is punishable under law, and if I were you, I'd take myself away and keep very, very quiet while Simon decides if he wants to see you behind bars." He tugged Simon to his feet. "Do I make myself clear?" And, when Nina didn't answer: "Good." Jacky took out his wallet and dropped a five pound note on the table. "Buy yourself a cup of tea and a scone, and I hope you bloody choke on it."

They'd walked perhaps half a block when Simon stopped him. He was smiling tremulously and his eyes were full of tears. "Thank you."

Jacky brushed it off. "I've always knew you were the genuine article, and I won't have some old bint giving you the works, even if she is your mother." He slung an arm round Simon's shoulders. "Right, then. Let's see about getting your stupid arse to Australia."

STEPHEN and Piet were partaking of an early breakfast on the patio of Piet's house. It was very early in the morning and the sun had only just risen, slipping silent and crimson out of the sea, banishing the Southern Cross, which sat low at the horizon. Piet was uncharacteristically quiet, giving monosyllabic answers to Stephen's polite questions until Stephen fell silent, devoting his full attention to the excellent meal Piet had set out for them. It wasn't until he'd pushed back his plate and lit a cigarette that Piet spoke.

"There is another Englishman here." Piet blew smoke in a long plume. "I've seen him."

"Another… Englishman?" Stephen was confused. "Here, in your house?"

The Dutchman smiled. "No, my friend. Not in the house. He is staying just up the beach." Piet pointed with the hand holding his cigarette. "The yellow house near where we swim. The one with the fancy screen door."

Stephen recalled it only faintly. "Have you seen him?"

Piet lifted the coffee pot and shared what was left between them. "Yes—once, walking up the beach, and once in town, at the shop. He was buying a newspaper and some razor blades."

"So he's not got a beard, then." Stephen grinned. He was genuinely fond of Piet but loved teasing him; for his part, the Dutchman took this in good faith, returning Stephen's jests with gentle quips of his own.

"Nor has he a wife." Piet's eyebrow arched wickedly.

"Is he here with anyone? Was he walking by himself?" Why was he so interested? At any given time there were millions of Englishmen, and every single one of them—or near enough—was capable of traveling to Australia if he wished it. Why had his mind fastened upon this particular Englishman? Did he hope that Simon had somehow found him, followed him to Australia?

"If you like, I can draw up a list of your questions and leave them on his doorstep." He meant it jokingly, but it stabbed Stephen to the heart. He sometimes forgot how well Piet had come to know him, and how transparent he appeared to the sculptor's keen and penetrating gaze.

"That won't be necessary." He added cream and sugar to his coffee, stirred it so vigorously that the cup wobbled in the saucer. An Englishman walking by himself on the beach was hardly unheard of in this part of Australia.

Piet reached across the table and laid a hand on his wrist, staying him. "My dear friend, I am sorry. Of course you are curious about him; it's only natural."

"I'm not curious about him in the least." Stephen raised the cup to his lips and sipped in a manner that said the Englishman on the beach was the least of his worries. "You mentioned a strange Englishman—"

"Are not all Englishmen strange?" Piet softened his interruption with a dimpled smile and Stephen laughed.

"You're a right bastard," he said.

"Not at all," Piet said. "My mother and my father were quite well acquainted, quite well acquainted indeed. Now then, another croissant?"

PIET wanted to spend some time with his current work in progress, so after breakfast, Stephen took himself for a long walk. He had no fixed destination in mind, merely a stroll along the beach; he carried a paperback book with him and his feet were bare. The sky was overcast and some low clouds had begun to form near the horizon, promising rain later in the day. There was something about the Southern Cross and its position in relation to weather but he couldn't remember what it was. It didn't really matter—not now, not today.

He walked for perhaps an hour, following the shoreline toward Tully, with the dark green bulk of Bedarra Island rising out of the water, flanked by the smaller islands, Lady Hudson and Dunk. Piet hadn't said in which direction the Englishman had been walking—and the yellow house was back the other way. *You're looking for him. Admit it. You're looking for Simon.* But that was ridiculous. He had no reason to think Simon was in Australia, and the chances of Simon being on this beach were remote to say the least. Besides, it was still early in the morning, not quite seven thirty, and most of the people who lived on the beach wouldn't be seen 'til the sun was a bit higher in the sky.

I love early in the morning. A memory flashed across his inner vision, startlingly painful: he and Simon, sitting on the beach in Orkney and watching the daylight come surging back from the almost-dark of the Highlands at Midsummer. *It's like the world's all new and nobody's had a chance to mess it up.*

He had been seventeen; Simon, twenty. He thought he knew everything, thought he'd adequately sussed the ways of the world, the reasons why people did the things they did.

I don't want to be a poof.

Is that what I am to you?

He deliberately avoided reading the English papers, not wanting to stumble across news of Simon. He'd become a favorite of the gutter press in recent years: they followed him everywhere, snapping photographs with their long lenses, crowding him at public events, and shoving notebooks in his face. Jacky had advised Stephen and Simon that they were rock stars now and such behavior was to be expected, but Stephen, habitually a very private person, hated it. Perhaps this other Englishman, whoever he was, had retreated to Australia for the same reason. Maybe he was famous and tired of being hounded around the world. Perhaps, like Stephen, he just wanted to be left alone.

He found a sheltered spot near a clump of palms and sat down, shrugging out of his shirt and spreading it on the sand as a makeshift blanket. He lay down and tried to read the book he'd brought, a ridiculous tale of sexual conquest and wealth in Manhattan's corridors of power, but it bored him, and after a while, the heat and the strong sunlight conspired to make him drowsy, so he stretched out, laying the book aside, and slept.

He dreamed he was back in Simon's house just outside London, lying in Simon's bed in the dark, gazing up through the glass ceiling at the stars, so near that he could pick out the various constellations. But instead of seeing the Plough, Ursa Major, or Orion, he saw the Southern Cross. *The stars are wrong.* He tapped Simon's naked shoulder to get his attention. *That shouldn't even be there. It shouldn't be that way.* It bothered him that even the stars were wrong and there seemed nothing he could do about it, but Simon didn't appear to be put off by it.

The stars are never wrong. Simon stroked his cheek, leaning in to kiss him. Simon's soft brown eyes were full of tiny stars. *You should know that by now, Stephen.*

Stephen woke with a start. The beach was deserted and a lid of darkness was creeping slowly forward, blotting out the sky. The trees around him began to bend, their slender fronds whipping back and forth, and tiny rooster-tails of sand scudded across the ground, racing toward the sea. The sky nearest the horizon was a deep blue tinged with streaks of violet and an ominous rumbling started somewhere to the north. The sound reminded Stephen of the minor earthquakes he'd experienced during a stay in California, some years before. He hastily slipped into his shirt and started back the way he'd come but not in time. The storm broke while he was still some distance up the beach, the rain slashing down around him and brilliant white flashes of lightning tearing electric rivers in the sky.

Up ahead he saw the figure of a man moving toward him through the rain. The lightning and the intermittent darkness confused Stephen's senses, and the figure seemed to appear and disappear at different points along the beach. "You've got to go back!" Stephen shouted, waving his arms. "The storm's too bad. Go home!"

The man gestured him closer, and Stephen thought he might be smiling. He shouted something Stephen couldn't quite make out.

"No," Stephen repeated. "You've got to *go back!*"

A jagged streak of lightning stabbed the stretch of sand between them, briefly lighting up the lenses of the other man's spectacles.

Spectacles.

Are you the lyricist?

Stephen's heart thumped hard inside the bony cavity of his chest and he was running, suddenly, his arms pumping at his sides, his feet churning up the sand, closing the distance between them. The man was wearing an orange shirt and baggy beige shorts, the sort of thing that Simon would wear; the man had spectacles and Simon wore spectacles, or used to wear spectacles and perhaps he was wearing them again. It was just like London, just like stepping off the train again in the middle of some foreign night, alone and friendless, stupefied by fear and the lingering smell of diesel, and then there was Simon.

The man got close enough so Stephen could clearly see him: midforties, dark hair thinning on top, heavy-framed spectacles, a Hawaiian shirt with a pattern of pineapples and parrots. Not Simon. Not even close.

"You're not number seventeen?" The man squinted at him through the driving rain. "Number seventeen, up the beach." He half turned, pointing back the way he came. "Looks like you've got a bit of a chimney fire, if you are." He peered up at the sky. "Rain should take care of it, though." He was an American, judging by his accent. "Are you number seventeen?"

"No." Stephen tried to smile. "No, sorry. I'm not number seventeen."

"MY FRIEND, I wish you would reconsider." Piet sat on Stephen's bed, watching as Stephen piled his belongings into two suitcases. "There is no need to go rushing away to England." It was not quite seven in the morning; Piet had come over to suggest an early swim, and was dismayed to see Stephen preparing to leave. "If he is here, we can look for him. We can find him, two of us."

Stephen shook his head. "Australia is a big country. He could be anywhere." He tossed a trio of battered notebooks into the smaller of the two suitcases. "If he wanted me to reach him, he'd have made himself easier to find." He paused. "I didn't know the houses around here had numbers. I thought they were just, you know, wherever along the beach."

Piet stubbed out his cigarette in a nearby ashtray. "The houses don't have numbers," he said. "Who told you they did?"

Stephen related how he'd met the American in the middle of the storm. "He asked if I was number seventeen."

"Number seventeen?" Piet flicked through a handful of record albums. "*Daddy Phone, Get Your Instant On, Rock Lady.*" He flipped one over to look at the back. "*Sixteen Songs About Regret*, by Abelard." Piet nodded. "Simon Duckworth."

"That's right." Stephen rolled his socks into balls and tucked them around the inside of the larger suitcase.

"So, tell me...." Piet laid aside the album. "Are you number seventeen?"

All those nights in Mississippi, lying next to a mute and battered Simon in the dark and listening to the crickets—what had he thought might happen to them both? Upon what imagined future had he insisted? "Number seventeen?"

Piet indicated the album title. "Sixteen songs."

It's both of us or no one, right? We both go, or no one goes.

"Regret."

I don't want to be a poof.

Is that what I am to you?

It stabbed him to the core. "Piet, do you think…?"

"I do." The Dutchman stood up. "If this were a stylish foreign film, the two of you would run towards each other, meeting at last in a rapturous embrace." He rolled his eyes. "But, as you say, Australia is a very large country." He checked his watch, but this was merely a perfunctory gesture: Piet always knew what time it was. "And now I am going." He put out a hand, pulling Stephen into a hug. "My friend, I will miss you. Will you come back and see me some time?"

"Yes." Stephen was on the verge of tears, and anyway, there seemed to be nothing more to say. He hefted his cases and went to the end of the lane to wait for the taxi.

CAIRNS AIRPORT was quiet, but Stephen supposed that had to do with the early hour. He could have taken a later flight, but it hardly seemed to matter what time he left; the flight was equally long either way. There was an entire world between England and Australia—an entire world in which Simon could easily lose himself, if that was what he wanted.

He bought a cup of coffee from one of the kiosks lining the main concourse and wandered around for a while, watching the other travelers, many of whom appeared to be in the same state of disengagement as him. He had only half an hour to wait before boarding, so he didn't stray too far from the gate, and anyway, there was nothing to see that he hadn't seen before in just about every airport in the world.

They'd certainly seen them all, he and Simon, back in the days when they did everything together. *I wrote something.* He remembered that day: he'd jotted down the lyrics while sitting at the breakfast table, right before he'd left to go to work. He'd gone in to Mr. Stoop's early that morning, because he and Simon had a fight and because he was afraid Simon would toss him out, make him go back to Scotland. *We Sometimes Fall,* the song was called; it had turned out to be one of their biggest hits. Simon usually sang it in the dark, his head and shoulders lit by a baby spot, and no matter where they were in the world, a hush would fall over the auditorium.

> *We sometimes fall*
> *We sometimes fly*
> *We sometimes share the sky together, you and I.*
> *When we were young how many times I told you*
> *Go, you can never live this way*
> *Oh no we sometimes fall*
> *We sometimes fly*
> *We sometimes (sometimes) slip away...*

He began to hum the tune in an absent, offhanded manner, queuing with the other passengers at the departure gate. He'd seen Simon sing it one night in Memphis, Tennessee: people were openly weeping, and at the end, he saw Simon discreetly wipe his eyes as he turned away from the piano. It was the oldest of their songs and he wondered if Simon even played it anymore, if he even remembered.

"Where are you going?" The voice came from behind him.

Stephen half turned. "Sorry?"

"Stephen, where are you going?"

He was there again, as if he'd never gone, as if they'd never been apart for longer than a moment. He was standing on the railway platform, watching the trains shuttle in and out. He was alone in the dark, and lonely, seventeen years old and seven hundred miles from home.

Are you the lyricist? That voice behind him, and there was Simon: waiting when Stephen stepped down from the train, always waiting for him, no matter where Stephen went or how long he was gone. *You can stay at mine.* The smell of chips and sausages and mushy peas lingered in Nina's kitchen, and there were socks and knickers drying on the line up near the ceiling. *I wrote something.* He saw himself at seventeen, watching Simon coax the rattling Mini into gear, Simon's strong hands on the wheel... and sitting on the beach in Orkney, waiting while the daylight flooded the early sky, or lying with Simon in the long grass behind the house and watching the summer stars wheel above them in the sleeping night. *I've something to tell you... Stephen, I love you. You do know what I mean, don't you?*

It took a moment for the penny to drop, but it fell with a deafening clang. *He doesn't look all that different. He looks the same, really.* Simon's right hand was encased in bandages. He wore shorts and a Hawaiian shirt and sandals. And then the knowledge that this was Simon, that Simon was really here, genuine and in the flesh, ripped through Stephen's body and he flung himself into Simon's arms, not caring who saw them, not caring what anybody thought. In some secret chamber of his heart there would always be that Stepney kitchen, and Simon's battered upright piano, and their bedroom with their records and their clothes...

And Simon. Always and forever Simon.

"Home," he said. "I'm going home."

J.S. COOK was born and raised on the island of Newfoundland. She holds a BA and an MA in English Language and Literature and a B.Ed in post-secondary education. She makes her home in St. John's, Newfoundland, with her husband Paul and their two spoiled rotten dog-children, Lola and Sheppie.

J.S. Cook also writes as JoAnne Soper-Cook.

Facebook: https://www.facebook.com/AuthorJSCook
Twitter: https://twitter.com/jsopercook
Livejournal: joannesopercook.livejournal.com
Website: joannesopercook.net

Writing as JoAnne Soper-Cook

JoAnne Soper-Cook

The Eye of Heaven

http://www.dreamspinnerpress.com

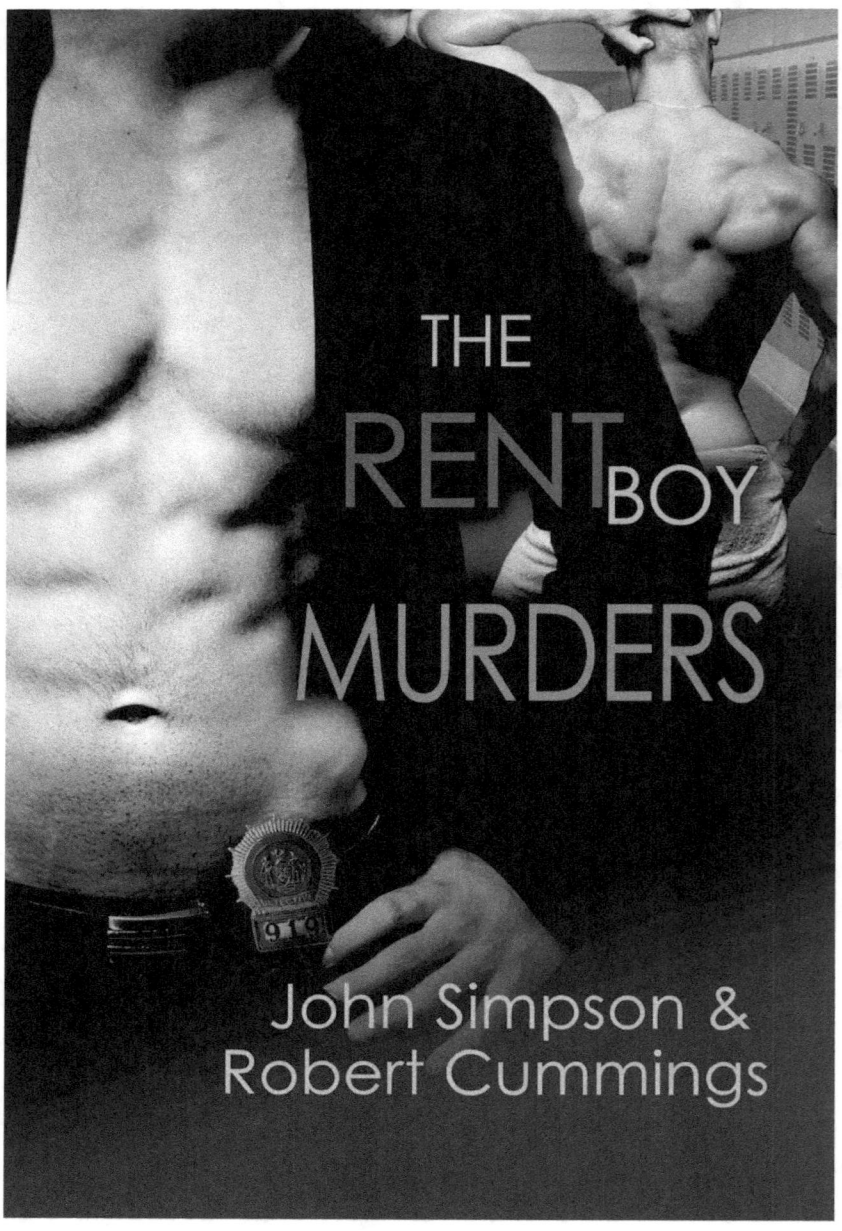

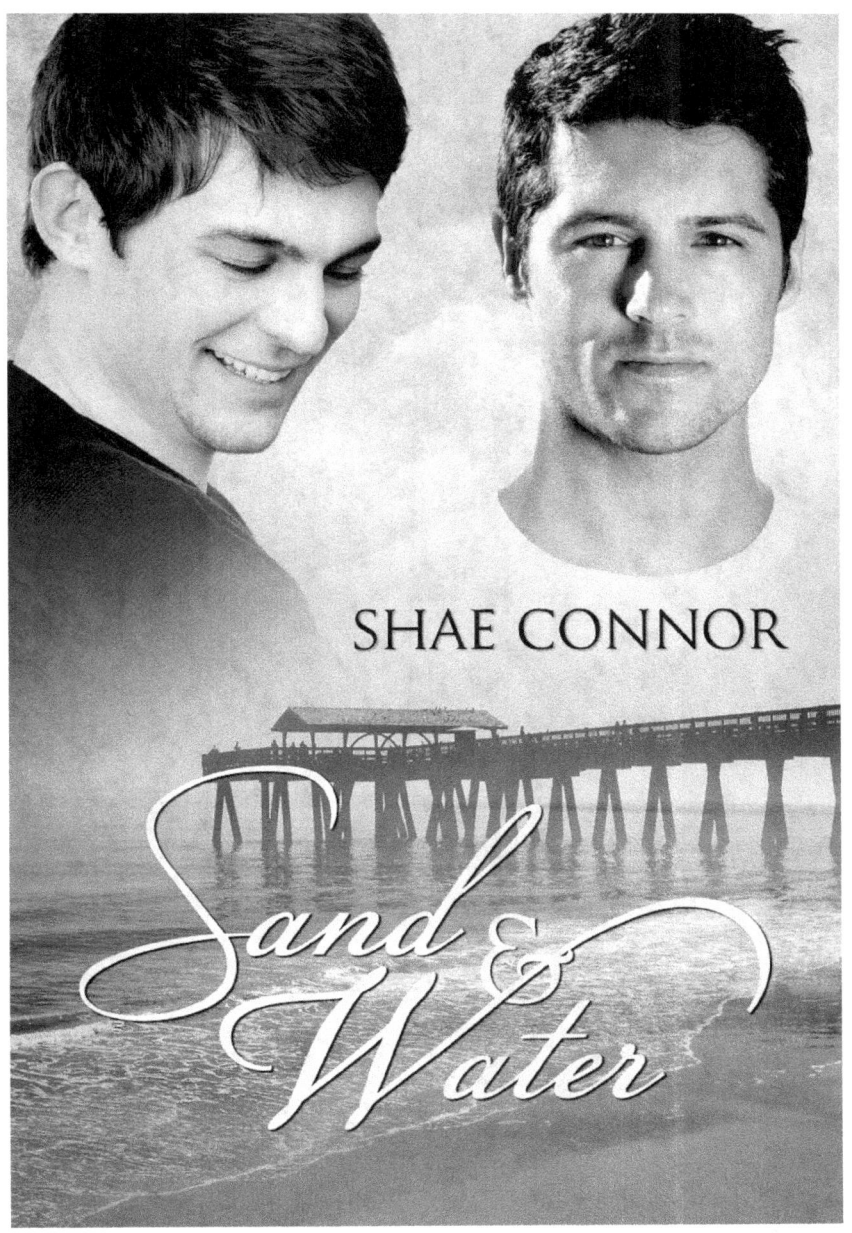

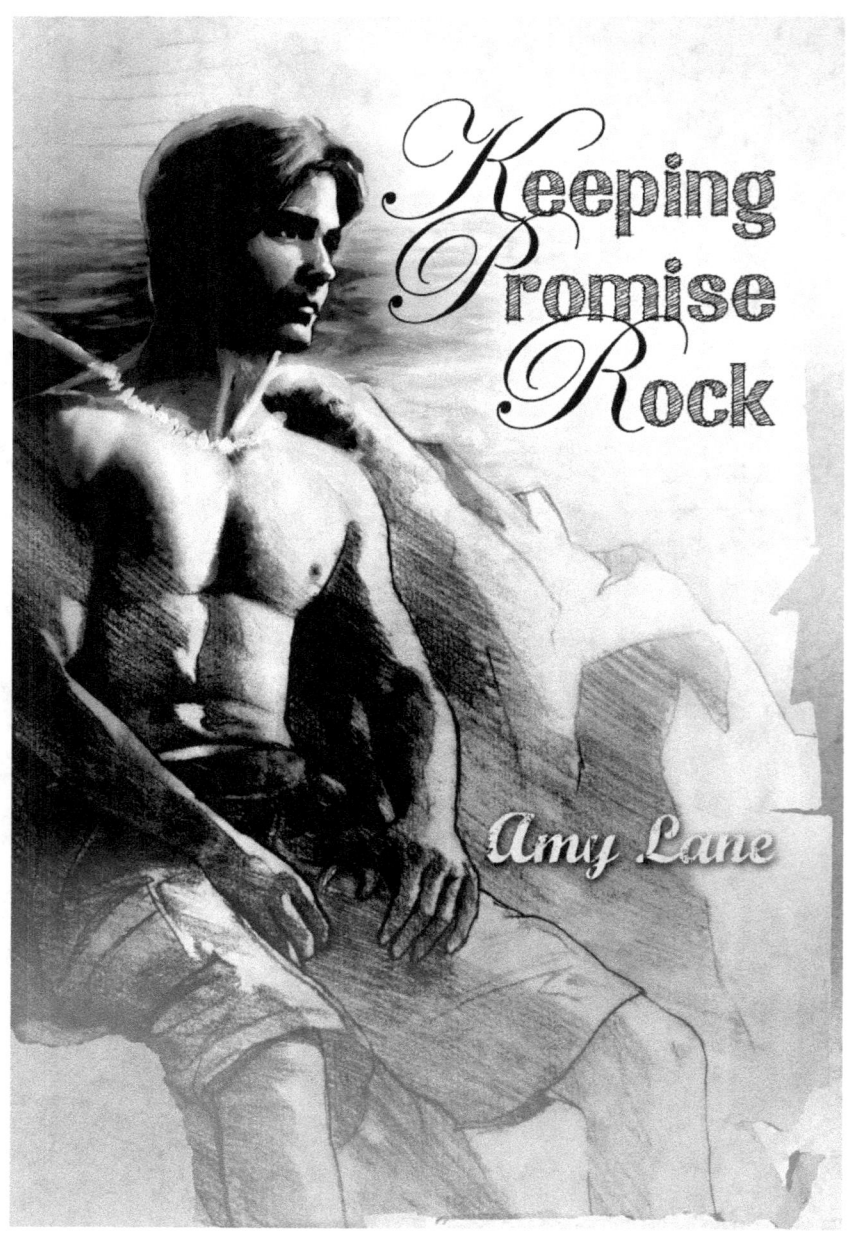

www.ingramcontent.com/pod-product-compliance
Lightning Source LLC
Chambersburg PA
CBHW070106260626
47160CB00004B/1337

* 9 7 8 1 6 2 3 8 0 4 9 2 3 *